"Susan let me read parts of *The Red Carnival*. I r[...] the end, she said to me, 'At times, I was writing this b[...] I can't write fast enough.' She wrote this book with the kind of enthusiasm and love that every writer wants to have for their own work. I kept waiting for her to sell it—she never did. I wish she had because it deserved to be read. I'm so glad it's getting an audience now. I wish I could hug Susan and tell her what a great book she wrote and what a fine, gifted, and beautiful writer she is." —Pat Cadigan (Hugo- and World Fantasy Award-winner)

"Take it from a guy who wrote a four-book series about a carnival, Susan Casper knew her stuff. *The Red Carnival* is a remarkable blend of power and sensitivity." —Mike Resnick (Nebula- and 5-time Hugo Award-winner)

"*The Red Carnival* is so intensely atmospheric that you look up from the book expecting to see the bozo, the ten-in-one, the hootchy kootchy tent. Susan Casper's harrowing novel explores the most terrifying of all ideas: that not only can any one of us be tortured by evil, any one of us can become it. Casper understands not only how fragile human beings are, but how strong. And you will never again look at a carnival the same way." —Nancy Kress (6-time Nebula and 2-time Hugo Award winner)

"*The Red Carnival* continues a great American literary tradition, dark fantasy novels about wandering carnivals. Casper's novel belongs on the same shelf as Ray Bradbury's *Something Wicked This Way Comes* and Charles G. Finney's *The Circus of Dr. Lao*." —Allen M. Steele (3-time Hugo Award winner)

"Susan Casper was a damn good short story writer. And lucky for us, in addition to the recent publication of her collected short fiction, we now have *The Red Carnival*, a previously unpublished dark fantasy novel from her fine creative mind." —Ellen Datlow (Bram Stoker and World Fantasy Lifetime Achievement Award honoree; winner of 8 Hugo Awards, 9 World Fantasy Awards, and 4 Bram Stoker Awards)

"At times dark and unsettling, this previously unpublished novel by the late Casper (who died in 2017) holds the same wonderful prose and love of the uncanny as her published short fiction. (*Up the Rainbow: the Complete Short Fiction of Susan Casper*)." —*Library Journal*

Praise for Susan Casper and *Up the Rainbow: The Complete Short Fiction of Susan Casper*, which Fantastic Books published in July 2017

"This collection… showcases both [Susan Casper's] talent and the potential…. The completed short stories are worthy reading for any fan of science fiction or darker fantasy." —*Publishers Weekly*

"The opening three stories—her first sale was in 1983—serve almost as a mini-trilogy of horror or the Weird, showing Casper's interest in eruptions of the uncanny into everyday life." —Paul Di Filippo, *Locus*

"This collection is proof that Susan remains an uncelebrated, underappreciated Tall Talent." —Andrew Andrews, *True Review*

"Whether she was writing about travel or over-protective mothers, unicorns or Pre-Raphaelite painters, Susan Casper always had something new and fascinating to say. She'll be sadly missed. Thank goodness we have this new and compelling collection to remember her by!" —Connie Willis (SFWA Grand Master, member of the Science Fiction Hall of Fame, winner of 7 Nebula Awards and 11 Hugo Awards)

"What a vivid and compelling range of stories! Terrors from childhood nightmares made disturbingly real. Wistful glimpses of a past that never was. Sly, sideways looks at venerable fictions: Oz, Middle Earth, Rumpelstiltskin, Sherlock Holmes. Casper writes with meticulous attention to detail, putting you deep into time and place. A wonderful collection." —Nancy Kress (6-time Nebula and 2-time Hugo Award winner)

"Susan Casper is one of my favorite writers. Her work is witty, well-observed, with a bite that you can never quite forget, much like John Collier. I come away from her stories thinking, 'I wish I'd written that.'" —Pat Cadigan (Hugo- and World Fantasy Award-winner)

"Susan Casper lived in the real world, and so did her characters. The fantastic impinges gently on the familiar in her fiction. We recognize the bedrooms and the kitchens, the insistent mothers and the impatient children. But wait, is that really a ghost? Is it trying to tell us something? Is that woman really a vampire? Is there a way to get to Oz? With a sly sense of humor and a profound sense of the tragic, Susan Casper crafted stories that show us the wonder and terror of our everyday lives." —James Patrick Kelly (Nebula- and Hugo Award-winner)

"I have only one problem with Susan Casper's fiction: there isn't enough of it. I have loved every story of hers that I've read, and, as it turns out, I've read quite a few of them. Personal favorites include 'The Stray' and 'Why Do You Think They Call It Middle Earth?', but to be fair, that's like picking the best chocolate from a Paris chocolate shop. They're all good. I simply prefer some to others. This long-overdue collection, edited by her husband, multiple Hugo Award- winner Gardner Dozois, is an act of love—and love this deep should be shared. If you've never read Susan's work, you're in for a treat. If you have, you'll be visiting old favorites and finding new favorites along the way." —Kristine Kathryn Rusch (Hugo- and World Fantasy Award-winner)

"An impressive collection by an even more impressive lady." —Mike Resnick (Nebula- and 5-time Hugo Award-winner)

"From the dark and disturbing to the amusing and uplifting, this collection of tales reveals the evocative depths of Susan Casper's vivid imagination." —Sheila Williams (Editor of *Asimov's Science Fiction Magazine*, 2-time Hugo Award-winner)

"Beautifully written and beautifully observed." ("The Cleaning Lady") —Samuel R. Delany (SFWA Grand Master, member of the Science Fiction Hall of Fame, winner of 4 Nebula Awards and 2 Hugo Awards)

"Finally, Susan Casper's powerful, wry, and provocative short fiction is available in one volume: a must-have collection that captures the essence of her brilliant, wild talent." —Jack Dann (Nebula- and World Fantasy Award-winner)

"Susan's stories capture you with the first word and hold on with bloody claws until the last." —Eileen Gunn (Nebula Award-winner)

The Red Carnival
by Susan Casper

Fantastic Books
1380 East 17 Street, Suite 2233
Brooklyn, New York 11230
www.FantasticBooks.biz

ISBN 10: 1-5154-1033-1
ISBN 13: 978-1-5154-1033-1

First Edition

Table of Contents

With It. 7
Teardown. 34
Pacing the Lot. 63
Setting the Gaff. 99
The Bally. 126
Turning the Tip. 152
Hey Rube.. 180
The Blowoff. 209

Part One

WITH IT

1

It was a cheap gilly of a carnival, getting ready to open for the day's business. A shrill wind whistled through the steel skeletons of the rides, rocking the seats of the Ferris Wheel and spinning the egg-beater arms of the Scrambler. It billowed the sides of the tents and made loud snapping noises with the garish posters surrounding the ten-in-one and the kootch shows, all announcing boldly, SEE… SEE… SEE… and ALIVE!, ALIVE!, ALIVE! It kicked up dust motes in the alleys between the trucks and trailers on the back lot and snatched a sign reading "office" from the side of a tan Winnebago that sat off to itself just beyond the edge of the midway.

Inside the office, Jim Dandy looked at the woman sleeping in his bed, and decided to let her sleep a little bit longer. He was a short, lean, wiry man whose dark red sideburns and solid jaw added a feeling of stubborn determination to the depression-era look of his gray slouch cap and narrow suspenders. For him, this was a crucial time, a turning point. He had made the decision that his very identity as Jim Dandy—patch and part owner of the Jim Dandy Traveling Amusement Fair—depended on what happened at the meeting tomorrow. A flip of the coin, and if it came up heads—well then, everything was hunky dory. And if it came up tails… then, by tomorrow night he'd be somewhere else—some*one* else—doing something completely different. He had been "with it" for most of his forty-six years, and he knew there was always some place to buy a proposition. Why, in his time he'd agented almost every kind of alibi and hanky pank that had ever been invented, from the shooting gallery and guess-your-weight to a gaffed flat wheel that brought in hundreds of dollars a night. There were even a few with a wrinkle all his own. There wasn't a carnival in this country he couldn't walk into tomorrow and buy a proposition. This run of bad luck wouldn't last long. Not for him.

He had dressed slowly, making sure to observe all of his superstitions, like buttoning his shirt bottom to top, and putting on his right boot before his left sock, because even lady luck had to be coddled on occasion. Then, just as an extra precaution, he slid onto his finger the diamond studded horseshoe ring he'd won in the same poker game where he'd acquired his share of the carnival, rubbed it and turned it twice.

The empty midway held a sad, sweet feel to it, like youth and beauty on a summer day. He smiled and adjusted the half a toothpick that always hung from the corner of his mouth. Off in the distance, ride boys were wiping down their equipment and agents were opening up booths that seemed to bloom like flowers in the late afternoon sun.

From where he stood, the rides seemed to have been dumped in a disorganized clump in the middle of the lot. A sorry mess they were, too. The Airplanes needed paint, and so did the Zipper and the Tilt-A-Whirl. The seats on the Ferris Wheel had been patched so many times they almost seemed to be woven out of tape, and even the horses on the Merry-Go-Round—hooves raised and teeth bared in a display of wooden ferocity—were in need of a few dabs of paint, some brass polish, new leather for the halters and stirrups. But somehow at night, with the lights on and the music playing, it didn't matter. Certainly the marks never seemed to notice. Still, it wasn't really the rides that interested him; never had and never would, as long as they were kept in working order and reasonably safe. They were the core, the flash and bright lights and music that drew people in, but it was the oddly angled array of booths that were the real carnival. Arranged so that a sucker couldn't hardly get halfway through the lot without shedding a good piece of change—hanky panks up front, nearest the entrance gates, alibis and grind stores in the back with the ten-in-one and the girly show, all sucking them in, turning them on, roiling them up and turning them away again with nothing but a bit of fluff and a great big grin. That was what the marks wanted. *Rides* they could get at an amusement park. No, they came to be gaffed. Every night, he watched them tender their dollars with sweating, anxious hands, to see a "giant" no taller than the average basketball player. Not that things were as good as they used to be. Dandy remembered a time when he could throw any old thing into a jar full of green liquid and have the marks begging him to take their two bits so they could have a glimpse of it. Those were the days.

The first lonely strains of calliope music began to drift on the air as the early comers ambled onto the lot. Dandy watched Lucinda halfheartedly aim a pitch at two chubby kids who were wandering past. They smiled cynically and kept on walking, and suddenly Dandy wanted them desperately. He wanted every cent in their greedy little pockets. And he was just the man to do it.

"Come here, boys," he said, nodding them over with a jerk of his head. He whispered to them conspiratorially, and within a minute he knew they were his. "That ain't no game for *you*," he said, hooking a thumb toward Lucinda's Ring Toss. "Now I got a *real* game here. A game where a smart young fella can win somethin' worth havin'." He led them to a booth deep in the rear of the lot. It was a game called The Swinger, Shingo-Shango's proposition, and Dandy knew that the agent wouldn't be opening up for a while. He lifted the awning, slid it into place, and hopped neatly over the counter. The prizes arranged on the back wall included several small appliances, nestled among the purple dogs and chartreuse plush snakes. "Now let me tell ya what I'm gonna do…" he started his spiel, hooking the boys with promises of Walkmen and Watchmen. The game was easily gaffed so that a mark couldn't win unless the agent wanted him to. A bowling ball tied to a string from the top of the booth and a bowling pin standing on the counter. All that the player had to do was swing the ball so that it missed the pin on the way to the back of the booth and hit it as it returned to the player. Easy enough for the agent to do during the demonstration, but a twist of the wrist when setting up the pin turned the simple trick into an impossibility. Dandy let the ball go, watched it swing to the back of the booth in an easy glide, reach the end of its tether, and turn in one smooth motion, knocking over the pin. He picked up the pin and turned to the boys. "See," he said. "Easy as fallin' off a log." He allowed the mark to try it and smiled as the pin went down. "Hah, a winnah!" he said excitedly, pulling a plastic key ring from under the counter. "Now we're gonna try for something bigger." He replaced the pin on the peg that held it in place, only this time turning it that half turn that moved it sweetly out of the path of the ball. Nobody checked to see if the hole in the bottom of the pin was centered. In fact, the bottom of the pin was painted in such a way that it would be hard to tell the hole was off center even if you looked.

The boy took the ball and released it with a jerky motion, but it steadied as it turned and glided back, missing the pin by a fraction of an inch. "Aw, gee. Looky that. You almost made it. The first time you swung it a little smoother, though. Now let me tell ya what I'm gonna do…" he said, getting ready to up the ante. By the time Shingo-Shango came to open his booth, Dandy was sporting a fat roll of bills, and the booth was surrounded by the largest crowd on the midway. He turned them over to the Swinger agent raring to go.

Dandy was a man who lived by his luck, and until recently that lady had clung tenaciously to his side. He was a roller of sevens, a recipient of aces—a winner at everything he turned his hand to. But in the three short weeks since this season had begun, all that had started to go sour. Accidents, fights, woman trouble—that was the standard bill of fare at the carnival, but somehow it seemed he was having more than his share. He'd never been one to burn the lot. In fact, he ran a fairly decent show as carnivals go. No Percentage joints with their big money gambling, and Sam's girls never worked any stronger than whatever deal he could buy from the locals. Even the ten-in-one was mostly legit. But in the last three weeks he'd been shut down by the cops four times, and if anyone ever found out that he'd been hustled for big bucks on a sucker bet, it would be all over for him. But this last thing, losing a three-day slot in Richmond, with no real time to pick up a replacement… that had been the real kicker. A sure sign that Jim Dandy's luck was gone.

But then he had found a replacement. Jeb Marcus, patch on the Lowell Bros. Carnival, had gotten in touch with him about a date that his show was offered and had to turn down. Just the right weekend, for just the right number of days. Jack Martin had gone ahead to try and swing the deal, and tomorrow Dandy would work out the details. Well, hell, he could do it. His magic was coming back. He could feel it already, coursing through his veins like whiskey on a winter afternoon. True, Somerset wasn't really that great a deal; too far north, and a hick town to boot… but it was an omen. That was the important part. Besides, being spang up against Philadelphia might be a real advantage. City marks, without the city cops. And they wanted him. Wanted him so badly that he might not get hustled for more than a couple of free passes.

"Hey, Jimbo," he called, noting his daytime security man over by the main turnstile, leaning back in his chair with a copy of *Field and Stream* open across his lap. He walked over and offered a Lucky Strike, taking one himself. "Trouble?" he asked.

"Not tonight, Mr. Dandy. Thought I saw someone acting funny over by the kootch tent, but it was just one of the posters hangin' down. Took me a while to tack it back up though. You goin' out now?"

Dandy cupped his hand around a match and lit both cigarettes, taking a deep drag and blowing out a lazy plume of smoke. "I'm headin' up to Pennsylvania. Got some business to take care of. No need to hold things up, though. Give Sam the key to the cashbox and tell him I said to take care of things while I'm gone. Any trouble, you handle it. Anything you can't handle, get Sam. He's runnin' the whole she-bang 'til I get back."

"Sure thing, Mr. Dandy. Oh… Esmerelda said to remind you that we have to pick up some supplies tonight or tomorrow. You know… the beer and stuff we collected for… for the G-top," he added, noting Dandy's quizzical look.

"Right," Dandy replied. He pulled a large wad of bills from his pocket and peeled off a pair of twenties. "Have one of the roughies take care of it, would you, Jimbo?"

Essie's battered old woody was parked across the street from the fairgrounds. It hadn't occurred to Dandy to ask if he could use it—he'd merely lifted the keys from her purse the night before. He wondered if she knew. Damn broad wouldn't say a word if she did. She'd just wait and get even later.

Even this late in the day, the Virginia sun made the inside of the car feel like a sauna. He hated to roll into Pennsylvania bathed in sweat like a backland yahoo, but a few hours on the road would cool him off. He climbed inside, punched the middle button on the radio, and sang along with Ferlin Husky as he steered the car's bulky body out toward the highway.

2

Sam Dollar stepped out of the shower and shook himself, spraying water all over the tiny cubicle. He could smell frying bacon just outside the curtain that cordoned off the sleeping area. He toweled himself lightly, careful not to jostle the small carved dragon that hung from a leather thong around his neck, tied the towel around his waist, and followed his nose toward the heavenly aroma. The Viking was standing by the propane stove wearing nothing but one of Sam's old T-shirts, which emphasized a figure that didn't need any emphasis. He patted her tenderly on her bottom and leaned over to kiss her on the neck. He was a huge man, most often compared to a grizzly bear, but she was almost as tall as he was.

"Morning, Doll," he said. "This is nice. I could get used to this." He smiled at her soulfully, looking down through thick, black lashes with eyes so dark brown that it was hard to see the pupils. There had been few mornings when he hadn't had someone there to feed him. Sam hated to sleep alone. For a long time, Katie had taken very good care of him, but she had gotten so possessive lately that he'd asked her to stay with the other girls for a while. Just once, he had gotten that close to a woman. Never again. It was better to keep your distance. And, besides, tall, good-looking Nordic types didn't often come his way. While the Viking cooked, he hurriedly threw his clothes on. A pair of jeans and a T-shirt was all he ever wore. Sneakers and his watch completed the picture. He sat down at the table to add them. "Ten o'clock... Too early for a decent human being to be awake."

"Wanna go back to bed?" she asked, turning around and throwing her arms open in an inviting pose. He put his arm around her waist and drew her toward him, gently kissing her right breast.

"Love to, Baby, but I can't. The patch is away for the day and I gotta play mother hen. You know what it's like around this joint with Dandy gone... suddenly, ain't nobody can figure out how to fart without checkin' with me."

She set the breakfast out on paper plates and squeezed into the seat across from him. "So, why do you have to do it? Is he planning to make you a partner or something?"

"Partner? Sometimes I think this's too damn much work. But I do like ownin' you girls, so I'll just go on payin' privilege to keep my little proposition, just like everybody else, and he can get someone else to do the partnerin' if he wants. I'd make a lousy owner, and an even worse patch," he added, remembering the time he'd tried to break up a simple fight in Memphis and wound up spending three weeks in the slammer. He was never sure just how he'd managed to last out two years in the Army without getting into serious trouble. Sam reached out and patted her hand. "Dandy just trusts me, I guess. Be glad I don't usually have nothin' to take care of but you girls. Gives me more time to take care of you right. Got any complaints? Didn't think so," he went on without giving her a chance to answer. She giggled. It was strangely endearing to see a woman who was almost the size of a halfback giggling like a little girl. "Listen, Baby. No need to spoil both our days. You go on back to bed and get some more sleep, and if I get the chance, I'll come back in and give you somethin' wonderful to dream about."

"Sam? Before you go, I want to ask you something." He knew what was coming. The only surprise was that it had taken her this long. He arched an eyebrow and waited for her to speak. "I figured with Mystic running off to get married, you were stuck without a lead girl. Now, I know I'm the newest one, and maybe I'm talking out of turn, but I am a real fast learner, and you can't say the *guys* don't like me. Anyway, I was wondering…? "She chewed at a thumbnail and appealed to him with her eyes for help, but he just continued to look at her as if he had no idea in the world what it was that she wanted. Eventually, she walked around to his side of the table, sat down on the edge of the seat, put her hand on his chest, and traced the carnival logo on his shirt as she spoke. "What I was wondering was… maybe you could give me a shot at the job? I could do it, Sam. I know that I could."

"Hmm?" Sam said. He kissed the top of her head and pushed her gently out of his way. "You still got some things to learn, but I'll think about it," he said as he got up to leave. Damn thing was that he had considered it, ridiculous as it was. She was first-of-May and the other girls hated her, but she had a pretty good figure, she knew how to tease, and she was willing to do almost anything. Esmerelda should have the job, damn her. Even crowding forty she could still wring a mark inside out. No one was ready to call her "grandma" yet. But the dumb broad wouldn't take it. "Sorry, Sam," she had told him, "but this is just one last tour before I retire, and I don't want to spend it fighting off a bunch of rangy teenagers." He didn't really believe her. No carny would ever ask such a personal question unless invited to, but he was sure that she must have suffered a major set-back to keep her touring at an age when most dancers had been retired for years. Her grouch bag had been pretty full the last time he'd worked with her. Probably some man. He had often thought that none of his girls had any taste in that department, although what that said about Sam Dollar had never occurred to him. Just look at Katie. Katie should have been the logical replacement for Mystic. All the girls got along with her, and she drove the marks crazy, but there were just too many things that Katie wouldn't do. "Too futzy," Essie had called her. But not too futzy to spend all of her time hanging around with Gregor these last few days. A lousy ride boy, and a foreigner to boot. He grabbed the final piece of bacon from the plate and ate it as he walked across the lot.

People had begun to stir by the time that Sam went out to check in with Jimbo. Roughies were out playing with their rides, greasing parts, testing motors, tightening bolts. Randall, the Gnarly Man—one of the last true freaks on the circuit, his ancient body covered with large hanging sacks—was enjoying a moment of sunshine in blessed anonymity. By ancient custom, freaks were the only carnies who didn't stir into town. "Hey, Sam," he called in greeting.

"How's it goin'? Seen Jimbo?" Sam asked. Randy pointed toward the gate and rolled his eyes. "I know," Sam said. "Where else would he be?"

Lucinda's daughter was playing a game of jacks in the middle of the lot. He knew that she wasn't much older than eleven or twelve, and he was startled to see how good she was starting to look at that age. He smiled at her, ashamed of what he'd been thinking. Cinda was going to have to start keeping an eye on her. She was already one of the best shills in the business. "Jen, whyn't you take that in the back lot where you won't be in anyone's way?"

"Aw, Sam, I'm not in the way," she looked up at him stubbornly. He raised an eyebrow and said nothing. She started gathering her things together, pulling her mouth to one side in a look of disgust. "Can't see anything from back there," she muttered under her breath as she stood up. Sam smiled and tousled her straight blonde hair as she went past.

Jimbo was by the gate, reading his magazine. Jimbo was always reading. It made Sam suspicious. It was something he'd learned in his Nam days—people who read were trouble. Katie always had a book shoved in her face, and it had taken Sam a long time to break her of the habit. How the hell could you trust anyone who read all the time? How could you tell what they were thinking? It was okay, Sam supposed, for one of the girls to pick up a love story once in a while... as long as they didn't take it too seriously. He leaned his hip up against the turnstile and began to clean his fingernails with his pocket knife. "Everythin' goin' okay this mornin'?" he asked.

Jimbo did not bother to look up from his magazine. "Couple of kids tried to get in. I took care of them."

"That all?"

"Just about. Some of your friends coming now, though," he added. There was a touch of venom in his voice.

Sam did not need to turn around. He could hear Katie and Gregor's voices as they approached the lot. He moved back from the turnstile just long enough to let Katie through, then leaned back again, effectively blocking Gregor's entrance. "Mornin', Doll," he greeted her. It was easy to tell where they had been. Katie's arms were loaded with grocery bags.

"Bit early for you, isn't it?" she asked. She stopped and raised her leg to shift one of the packages with her thigh.

"But not for you, huh?" he ogled her outfit—a pair of shorts and a backless halter—shook his head, and laughed. "I swear, I try to sell it, and you just give it away. Seems like no matter how hard I try, I ain't never gonna make you carny, girl."

Katie turned around and thrust the bags at Sam, forcing him to take them from her. Then she pulled the scarf from her chestnut hair, stuffed it into a pocket, and, with a voice so tightly controlled that no one but Sam could hear her, said, "My life is my own, you son-of-a-bitch. You gave it back to me, remember? So, now, what I do with it is nobody's business but my own, unless it concerns my act. Is that clear? When you are around me, you will act like a human being. So, either you let Gregor through with the beer for the G-top, or not a single one of us will work for you tonight."

Sam turned toward Gregor, an exaggerated look of surprise on his face. "Oh... Gregor... I'm sorry. I didn't see you there," he said a touch too sweetly. Gregor smiled insincerely as he passed the kootch show agent. Sam smiled back, a huge cat-and-canary smile.

"Still got a thing for her?" Jimbo asked with a chuckle.

Sam balanced one bag on his knee and reached up to finger the little carved dragon through the thin cotton of his shirt; he felt a calmness settle over his body. "It's just insulting that someone who used to belong to me could ever settle for a lousy roughie, just because I dumped her. But then, you know Katie. She's like a little kid. Trusts everybody. Dandy say what time he'd be back?"

Jimbo repeated his instructions from Dandy, and Sam nodded. Nothing to do until eight o'clock, and the Viking was waiting, but somehow he wasn't in the mood. He dropped the groceries off in the G-top and sat down to kibitz at the poker game that was a constant feature there.

3

Dandy woke up screaming. There were beads of sweat on his forehead, and he had a moment of panic before his fingers unlocked from a horrid dream paralysis. He flexed them repeatedly.

Despite the comfort of a real bed, Dandy hadn't gotten much sleep. It had been months since he had slept anywhere except the Winnebago, and he had been looking forward to a night in a motel, but there was just too much riding on the deal for him to enjoy it. That surely was what had caused the nightmare. He couldn't remember what the dream had been about. He wanted to go over the details, examine them for portents and omens, but immediately the dream had begun to fade in the sunlight like early morning fog. He lit a cigarette to steady his hands. "Scarin' yourself with booger men," he said. Well, one thing he knew. Despite the obvious, nightmares were often good omens. He took a long, leisurely shower in a tub that felt like a palace compared to his own tiny stall, then, without even the customary toast and coffee, he hit the road again.

Somerset was too small a community to show up on the road map that Dandy had picked up on the highway. He had taken the appropriate exit from 1-95, and pulled over to consult the directions he had written on the back of an envelope the other night. It wasn't much farther—just a little way up 222, over Folcroft Road to Rampo Street.

It was a vast, empty lot, fenced in by a twelve-foot, iron-spike fence that got even higher in places. It was the sort frequently used in nineteenth century school yards. Across the street was another lot, choked with weeds, which would be perfect for parking. Inside the fence was about a half acre of utterly featureless, baked-brown soil where nothing grew. He was curious about what had been there originally—an old mansion, perhaps? More likely, some kind of institution, like a church or prison, or maybe even a hospital. There remained not even a trace of the building's foundation visible above ground.

Jack Martin stood by the open gate, looking at his watch. He was wearing a suit and tie. "Hey man, do you always dress that way for a meet?" Dandy asked.

"What the hell's wrong with it?" Martin asked.

"If you're tryin' for GQ, you come closer to Woolworth's basement. Straight off-the-rack stuff. Bad fit—no class. You oughta let me take you to my tailor." Dandy tugged at the hem of his corduroy jacket.

"Oh, and who is this wizard with a needle? Cowboy Bob?" Martin asked, rolling his eyes.

"Jack, you old son-of-a-bitch. Good to see ya." Dandy thumped him on the back. "How ya been?"

"Ulcer's been bothering me, otherwise jake. You're looking pretty good yourself. How's tricks?"

"Same ol', same ol'." Dandy looked around. "Okay buddy, what's the story here? You work out a deal? I hope I don't have to throw in my new shoes." He walked into the lot and squatted down, feeling the texture of the earth with his hands.

"Usual stuff. License, rental… I don't think we're going to have to pay much squeeze: they seem pretty anxious to have us here. Seems the townies are pretty superstitious about this lot. Supposed to be haunted or something. They want us to take the onus off the place so's they can sell it at a better rate. I guess they figure if people'll come here when it's a carnival, they won't be afraid to come when it's a shopping center."

"So whaddya think, Martin? You think folks'll be afraid to come out here?" Dandy asked warily.

"That's the beauty of it all. It don't make no neverminds to us if these folks show at all. This burg has a population that wouldn't even pay your gas bill up from Virginia if they went on every ride twice. You're gonna make your nut off marks from Philly, and Norristown, and York, and Lancaster, whether *these* clowns show or not. But as far as the spook stuff goes, it's gettin' you a real good deal. Now, I checked out the codes. You shouldn't have any problem with the freaks. There are a few local statutes that may give you some trouble with the kootch show."

"What about the local talent?" Dandy asked.

"Local operator's a man named Billingsly. I don't think we'll need to set up a meet."

"Nah. He'll be around soon's we open." Dandy said, shaking his head. "Well, it all sounds pretty standard."

"I told you on the phone that I didn't need you, but since you're here, does the lot look a little short to you? They gave me the official measurements and they're fine, but it doesn't quite look right."

Dandy wrinkled up his face and looked around, measuring the lot with an expert eye. So much room for rides, so much for joints, aisles so big, the tents in the back. Plenty of room left for generators, not a whole lot of space for the trailers. The cars and the big rigs would go over in the parking area. "It's a squeeze, but I think we'll make it. Sounds pretty sweet," Dandy said with a smile. "So tell me, Jack, what's botherin' you?"

"Nothin', Dandy. What makes you think—"

"Save it for the marks. I know you a long time. *Somethin's* eatin' you."

"We've got to meet Walter Redd pretty soon." Jack Martin said as he looked around uneasily. "Listen, Patch, I'll level with you."

"What? And set a precedent?"

Martin smiled. "Didn't know you knew any words with more than four letters in it. No, there's nothing wrong here… at least nothing I can put my finger on. I just have a bad feeling about this." Martin looked away, not wanting to see Dandy's face.

"What's this… psychic time?" Dandy scoffed, "You want me to have Aunt Aggie up here to read your tea leaves?" And yet, he knew what Martin meant. He had been feeling something of the same thing himself. There were two frame houses on the far side of the lot; obviously abandoned buildings—boarded up and in total disrepair—but Dandy couldn't shake the feeling that there was somebody inside them, watching. A few people who had taken a shortcut through the weeded lot across the street stopped dead when they saw the two carnies, and stood there like statues. Not moving, not talking. They watched mutely, like a jury ready to give sentence, staring… staring… staring…

"*That's* what's gettin' to you," Dandy said, pointing them out to Martin. "Small towns," he muttered under his breath. He turned toward the group and shouted, "What the hell are you staring at?" Most of them had the good grace to look embarrassed. One woman tugged at her husband's arm and the group began to disperse. "Leazets geazo," he added to Martin, saying "let's go" in the carny idiom which was always used in front of outsiders.

"Okay," Martin said, "but let's take my car, huh? Better P.R."

Dandy didn't have to be talked into it. The burgundy Mercedes was air conditioned, and the cold air felt great on his sweat-drenched body.

"I hear Lutzy's taking all comers on the Yankees this year," Martin said as they turned onto Station Street, past the depot that gave it its name.

"If they come in over .500, he'll do okay," Dandy answered, noting with enterprising interest the used-car lot that swung past his window. Most of the cars had been large and fairly new, and a few had been very, very old. Whistling a chorus of "We're in the money," he pointed it out to Martin.

"Not bad," Martin said. "My son Jim would really like that Alpha-Romeo."

"When he gets out of law school, he might be able to afford it," Dandy said, his conversation becoming a little more animated; the next few blocks contained nothing but rows of frame houses, neither particularly big nor especially luxurious. "Seein's how he takes after his father, he'll probably do pretty good in the law. Just a different kind of conman's all."

The street widened out, pushing east-bound traffic to the right of a small center strip which housed four benches and a statue. This was the business district of Somerset: two blocks of stores, offices, meeting halls. Dandy noted that a large, modern CVS Drug Store sat right next to the dingy corner building that housed Miller's Pharmacy, with its dusty plate-glass window full of ancient trusses and hot water bottles, broken, only partially operational neon signs that offered Breyer's Ice Cream and Delicious… Refreshing… Coca Cola, and a three-inch Christmas tree that had probably been put there when Santa was a boy. "Twenty to one that place has the best malts and the worst dogs in town," Dandy offered.

"Sucker bet," Martin responded in mock seriousness. "Probably has the only malts and hot dogs in town. How can you lose?" He pulled the car into a slantwise space in front of the Jewel T Market. Dandy jumped out and tossed a couple of slugs into the meter. He hooked a thumb toward the miniature park in the middle of the street.

"I've played a few lots like that in my time," he said. He kept up a steady patter as they walked past Milly's Dress Emporium, Zei-Dee's Shoes, Doctor K. MacCourtney, D.D.S., and into a stone faced building that was a combined J.C.C. office and Knights of Columbus meeting hall. The meager collection of shops would have depressed Dandy if Jack Martin hadn't pointed out that just outside of town was the Sweetbriar Mall, which contained everything that the local heart could possibly desire including a Sears outlet and a 3—count 'em, 3—theater movie house.

Walter Redd's secretary was an unimpressive, just barely post-adolescent who wore too much makeup and chewed her nails to the quick. She announced his callers, making sure they knew they were interrupting her crossword puzzle, then pulled her Walkman earphones back into place and picked up her puzzle again. A moment later, the other door opened, and Mr. Redd ushered them into his office. It was a small but neat room, carpeted and furnished in a comfortable, business-like style, but the man inside it obviously yearned for a bigger desk. He was the polyester man of the eighties: quiet, neat, coordinated—his shiny, professionally styled brown hair just long enough to curl around the bottoms of his ears. He offered a firm handshake and directed the two men to a pair of imitation leather armchairs opposite his desk. Dandy noticed with amusement that Redd's own chair was just enough higher than the ones they were given to make visitors feel they were facing a figure of authority. Somehow, on the slender young Walter Redd, it defeated the purpose, making him look even smaller and younger.

"Actually, Mr. Dandy, Mr. Martin, it worked out very well for us that you happened to be free. This is a special weekend for us. Somerset's bicentennial. We had already planned a celebration, but it just didn't seem quite grand enough. I wanted the town to do something special. A carnival in Morgan's Field seems like just the right way to precede the ground breaking that we'll be doing there this summer. I take it that you've seen the land and that it meets your specifications?"

"Well… not quite," Martin said, playing Redd for a reaction. He got it. The young man was not able to hide his disappointment. "But perhaps if we could also use the little lot across the street for parking and storage?"

Walter looked relieved. "I think we can even have the weeds cleared out for you. Gentlemen, I understand that you run a good, clean show."

"I don't like my operators gamblin' for money on the lot," Dandy said. "What we got is a few games of skill, a few rides, and some exhibitions."

Walter Redd nodded. "Tell me about those exhibitions."

"Well, what we've got is your standard side-show—sword swallower, snake handler, tattooed man, giant and a couple of unusual people—"

"Freaks?" Redd asked.

"We don't like to call them that," Dandy answered, keeping his voice even, although he felt that "I don't like your lousy, condescending tone," would have been a better answer. "It's all in the name of good, clean fun."

"And your other exhibitions?" Redd continued.

"We have some exotic dancers," Dandy added.

Walter Redd held up his hand like a cop stopping traffic. "If we're talking about strippers, I'm afraid I'm going to have to draw some lines. I've heard about carnival strip shows. This is a small town, Mr. Dandy. This carnival will be attended mainly by children—"

Martin interrupted. "Mr. Redd, it's not that sort of thing at all! Men have certain interests. We like to think that we cater a little bit to the interests of everyone. Carnival folk have a great love for children. Why, there's not a carnival man anywhere who'd allow a child into the kind of show you're talking about. We know that you have a strong interest in keeping this town clean, and to prove our sincerity, we'd like to offer a small donation toward your campaign." He took out a thick envelope and laid it on Redd's desk. It was a small bribe by carnival standards—much smaller than the one they had paid for their current date. Ridiculously smaller than the one they would have to offer the local crime boss to keep from being rousted. Redd looked warily from the envelope to Dandy and back. Had the young pup never been offered a bribe before? For a moment, both the experienced pitchsters were afraid that they had run into that legendary contradiction in terms, the honest politician.

"Now look, Mr. Redd," Dandy started in, using the same tone he used in spieling marks, "we're all businessmen here. We're not out to corrupt young kids or shock old ladies. What we offer is no worse than what can be found in those joints out on the highway. No different than what can be had from almost any video tape place. The only real difference is that we're very careful about who we admit."

Redd nodded, and put the envelope into his pocket. "A campaign contribution, that's all, but if you run the kind of show you say that you run, there won't be any trouble," he said.

Dandy smiled. "Now why don't you come around on Friday night, and I'll show you around the place. I think you'll be pleased with the operation I run. I think you'll find that even the dancers are well within the standards. They're actually very nice girls, Mr. Redd."

"There's one more thing I think I ought to tell you before you leave," Redd added as they started from their seats. "There's a bit of local superstition about the lot where you're setting up. There's a local rumor that the lot is haunted. I guess every town has a place like that, only it's bad for business. We're hoping that having your carnival out there will break down the superstition, so we can get a good price for the land.

We've already had one offer, but I think we can do much better. I don't think it will affect your business too much, because even if the locals don't go, and I think they will, you'll still get all of the surrounding communities." He stood to shake their hands. Dandy was amused by Redd's crestfallen expression. If he stayed in politics, he would learn. Greed got them all in the end. Old P.T. was right: You can't cheat an honest man… or buy one off, either.

There was always a coffee urn and an ice chest full of beer in the G-top, as well as the ubiquitous card game. When Katie came in, two games were going in different corners of the tent, but they were so noisy that it was almost as good as being alone. She poured herself a cup of coffee, and found a quiet corner where she could set up folding chairs for herself and Esmerelda. Essie was her confidant for all her problems with Sam, and Katie was still as hot as a smoking pistol over her run-in with Sam at the gate. "Where the hell does he come off talking to me like that? Who the hell does he think he is?" She turned to look at Essie, and suddenly started to laugh. "You know, I think he actually does believe I'm having an affair with Gregor."

"Well, good. Let him. The son-of-a-bitch. I hope it's drivin' him crazy. Sam's a nice guy, an' the best boss I ever worked for, but he's got a real problem when it comes to you, Katie. All I can say is, you must be either a fool or a saint to wait around for him like this. Maybe someday he'll appreciate it." The older woman snapped the tab on a can of beer and began to drink.

"Definitely a fool, Es. I just can't help it. I know I ought to pack my bags and run for the nearest exit, but every time I make up my mind to go ahead and do it, I catch him looking all lost and lonely, and I just can't do it."

"That, kid, is because he's playin' you like a mark. He knows exactly how long the show should be, and he's got just the right timin' on the intermission. Every time it looks like you're not gonna put up with it any more, that's when he comes around and tells you that he just can't live without ya, so's you'll never be able to leave him without tellin' yourself if you'da just stuck it out for a little longer, it woulda worked out." She took a long pull from the can and reached for Katie's hand. "I've known Sam a long time. He was just a snot-nosed punk didn't know which end of a woman was up, when I went to work for his father. Was a time when he was the most considerate guy any woman could get her hands on. Then he went into the army. Now I don't know that he met anyone while he was in Nam—maybe it was just the war—but he ain't been the same since.

And you, Katie. It's worse with you. You want to know if Sam loves ya. I'll tell you, yes, he loves ya. He loves you and it's killin' him, because the more he wants you, the more he has to prove that he can do without ya. And I don't think that's ever gonna change."

Katie looked over her shoulder. Essie had been talking softly against the loud conversation of the poker tables, but Katie felt uncomfortable knowing they were not alone. "You know," Katie whispered, "I never minded much with any of the other girls, but Christ, this Scandinavian bitch is an insult."

Esmerelda smiled. "You think *you* hate her? Don't even mention the Viking in front of Maggie. Imagine—that big slob practically knocking Maggie over to grab center stage!"

"Maggie would have killed her too, if you hadn't stopped her," Katie giggled. "Maybe you shouldn't have."

"I've got better ways to take care of... Oh, hi, Pritt," Essie said as Peter Carger walked over to say hello, his bare chest displaying a full set of tattoos.

"Private conversation, or can anybody join?" Pritt asked.

"Sorry, Pritt. Private," Katie answered. He winked and backed away. Katie watched from the corner of her eye as he grabbed a beer from the ice chest and went over to join the card players.

"I just wish that Sam and I could be a little more like Pritt and Cinda."

"Yeah. I can see it all now. A cozy little ski lodge to winter in, and a restaurant with a back room so he could get a little action whenever he wanted. It wouldn't be any different, Katie. Women come to ski lodges, too. Men! They just ain't worth it. Now me, I've given up on men. End of this season, Grandma here's gonna retire so pretty it'll shock the neighbors when one of ya comes to visit. I'm gonna buy a little shop somewhere where the carnival doesn't go, and I'm gonna sell flowers and seashells to the tourists, and I ain't ever gonna raise my skirts to no man again."

"*No* man?" Katie asked with a laugh. "That doesn't sound like a whole lot of fun. And besides, what will we do without you?"

"Just the same as you're doin' now, only not as good. Come on back to the trailer. I picked up some material in town that'll look real good on you."

The lot was a going concern when Dandy showed up, a bottle of Johnny Walker red in his fist. The rides were running about half full and some of the flats hadn't opened yet, but both of the grab joints were crowded and the Bozo was doing a booming business. He had one poor man—balding early and more than a little bit paunchy, an easy target—riled up to the point where his face was red and he would have given his last penny to get even, but the rest of the crowd was laughing. Dandy clapped the Bozo agent on the back as he went past. "Everything runnin' smooth?" he asked in the carny idiom, adding a z in the middle of every syllable.

"Dry as a bone," Maxie said, nodding his head in the direction of the young man who sat perched inside the Bozo cage. Was that Larry or Jeff? It was hard to tell what face was under all the greasepaint.

"Hey, Patch!" Shingo-Shango called to him from the Swinger booth next door. "When we pull outa this dump, don't put me next to any microphones. My voice ain't what it used to be, and I can't win a cent if'n no one can hear me."

"I'll see what I can do," Dandy said. "How's the new snake workin' out?"

"The wife ain't had no problem with her. Pritt says she looks so mean that marks won't even come up after and try to pet her like they used to do to Lulu."

There was a fight over near the Mitt Camp. Two marks trying to kill each other over some broad. Dandy had them both off the midway quickly, without even having to pull his knife. Everything seemed to be running normally, and he felt a pang of jealousy at not finding the place in a shambles after his absence. He played the stick at Cinda's ring toss, winning a lighter and a stuffed elephant which he tucked conspicuously under his arm as he continued his tour of the grounds. Once around the lot, stopping to shill whenever necessary. He broke up a shouting match between a mark and a roughie who ran the Sky Diver, sloughed the High Striker because Fred was too drunk to work the gaff properly, and paused to admire Stoney's spiel at the ten-in-one before going off to look for Sam.

"She can bump and she can grind, she can make you lose your mind. This gal's got the bounciest bottom in four counties…" Mick was ready to turn the tip at the kootch tent. Dandy didn't interfere. He mouthed the word "Sam" silently. Mickey Kelly pointed with his eyes without ever breaking stride. "Tell ya what I'm gonna do. Just for this performance only…"

"Sounds pretty good," Sam said when Dandy finished describing the days deal.

"Good? Man, I think he would have paid us to play through there if I had pushed it any further," Dandy said. He added another three fingers of scotch to his glass, and a somewhat smaller bonus to Sam's. The Viking had already been dispatched to work her show.

"Why didn't you?" Sam asked dryly. There was a mocking edge to his voice, but Dandy didn't seem to notice. A bad sign.

"You think you coulda done better?" Dandy asked. Sam slid out of the booth and walked back into the bedroom area. He sat on the edge of his bed and ran his fingers through his straight, black hair.

"What about the sheets?" Sam asked, referring to the advertising posters which usually saturated a town well in advance of the carnival's arrival.

"Man, I knew this was going to be a piece of cake. I didn't see no reason to wait. They were printed up two days ago, and if they aren't already on every telephone pole and lamppost within a hundred miles of Somerset, they will be by mornin'. Don't I always take good care of you?"

"Yeah," Sam said. "Real good."

"Dealin's *my* job, just like fuckin's yours. I deal and you fuck. Neither of us can help it. It's in our nature. Now, that don't mean that you couldn't handle a po-litico any more'n it means that I can't take care of a sweet young thing… but the other way around it's more a way of life than a recreation."

Dandy was drunk. Sam had never seen him this drunk before. Not this early anyway; never heard him rattle on like a mark being fairbanked, either. One lousy five-day stand in some jerk-water town, too far north, where there'd probably be a rube the minute Magda went into her act—and Dandy was making it sound like he'd just taken New York by storm. Sam didn't like it. He didn't like the whole deal. It didn't smell right, didn't feel good.

"Hey, Patch. Come on now. Take it easy," Sam said, watching Dandy gulp his drink and pour himself another.

"Man, it's a celebration. I've got my magic back."

"Huh?" Sam asked. "What magic back?"

Dandy sobered instantly, an angry scowl playing across his face. He pushed the glass away and sat up a little straighter in the booth. "Never mind," he said softly. "I can handle it." He slid out of the booth and walked over to where Sam was sitting. "You just take care of the girls," he said angrily. "I can handle everything else." And with that he stalked down the aisle and let himself out of the trailer.

Dandy never weaved. He never slurred his words. Never showed in any normal way that he was drunk, but Sam knew. Something was clearly wrong. He would have liked to talk it over with Katie. There was a naive innocence about that girl. She had none of the true carny instincts, couldn't palm a buck or tell a marked card, but she was very smart, and she had a way of putting things into perspective. But even when they were still together, he couldn't bring himself to give her the upper hand like that. For now, just have to play his cards the way Patch dealt them, and hope for the best.

In the little tent next to the Dark Ride, Abigail Miriam Goldbloom, known to the carnies as Aunt Aggie, and to the marks as Madam Auden, sees all, knows all, was taking a local teenager for a ride. "I see a man," she said. "Dark," and watching for the minute, tell-tale signs of disappointment, quickly added, "in mood as he is fair of countenance." Usually, she could read a mark as easily as a grocery list, but not tonight. She'd been doing a lot of hunting. Fortunately, most marks were so eager to believe, so frantically anxious to have it be real, that their faces told Aggie all she needed to know. Aggie examined the girls's hand, spieling off yards of mumbo-jumbo about what each line and bump and valley really meant and how they told her things. Actually, the girl's every-hair-in-place manner told her a lot more. "You have a tendency to be very exact and very cautious and this is very good, but you must be careful. There is a wild tendency which causes you to do things you sometimes regret, and you have a tendency to talk yourself out of following your impulses. This man is a free spirit, steady him, but do not become a weight. Together, you complement each other, but you must not go too far. Be free. Let your inner core direct you. Your instincts are sound, you must follow them." She was coasting now. The rest was easy; promises of a rosy future, money yet to come, a distant tragedy that would steady and mature her; the usual promises with enough blots to make it sound plausible. After this she could go and have a nice pot of tea, put her feet up and try to figure out what the hell her problem was.

It had been bothering her all night, that odd feeling in the marrow of her bones, an itching at the base of her spine, a strange, niggling feeling inside as if something were just a little bit off center. The mark crossed her palm with silver—a Susan B. Anthony, she'd have to remember to change that before she accidentally stuck it into a pop machine or something. She stood up and placed the "BE BACK IN TEN MINUTES" sign on the front of the tent and tied the flaps off. The lot had emptied out fairly quickly, but a couple of stragglers had headed in her direction as she started to leave. "I'm sorry. The spirits have deserted me," she told them as they begged her to stay open just a little bit longer.

Once she'd crossed the boundaries that marked off the public areas, she started doffing as much of her costume as she could. Scarf, shawl, bangles; it was too hot to be dressed in all that garbage. Inside her trailer, a little soap and water would turn her back into the plain North Jersey housewife she'd been until her husband, David, God rest his soul, had his fatal heart attack. It had been at his funeral, with the kids trying to mother her and all the neighborhood widows waiting to welcome her with open arms as if they had been looking to this moment for a long time, that she realized that sewing circles and Haddassah were not for her. Susan was married and Joey away in college; there was nothing to keep her from returning to the only profession that she had ever really liked. A profession that had taken her from a very repressive, orthodox Jewish home in Springfield, Illinois, when she was sixteen, and had supported her until her marriage to David. Once the funeral was over, she hadn't even waited for the house to be sold. She'd told Joey to make arrangements to stay in the dorm, picked up a copy of *Amusement Business*, and answered the first ad for a Mitt Camp that she saw.

As soon as she entered the trailer, she put the water on to boil and went into the bathroom to wash. By the time the kettle started whistling, she had already changed into her nightgown and was finally reading the *Good Housekeeping* she'd bought last March. But she wasn't quite as ready to relax as she had thought. She picked up the cup and saucer she'd set out on the table and discovered that her hands were trembling.

Something's wrong with the kids—the thought flashed into her mind. She walked over to the shelf by her bed where she kept their picture, but the moment she touched it, she knew with a rush of relief that it wasn't them. It was someone else—and a very long time ago....

Somebody knocked on her door. The sound startled her like unexpected thunder in a silent room. "Hang on a minute," she called as she threw on her velour robe, and then, "Who is it?" She felt silly. Who the hell would it be? Pritt and Cinda, or maybe Katie.

"Aunt Aggie, it's me, Jennie. I can come back if you're busy," the voice came soft and muffled through the door.

"Sweetheart, I'm never too busy for you," Aggie said, throwing the door open.

"I got something here I wanted to show you. I wanted you to be the first to see." She held a small box in her arms as she stood on the step of the trailer, wagging her body back and forth in a semi-circle, cheeks flushed, eyes wide with excitement. With exaggerated care, she carried the box over and set it down on the table as if it contained something fragile and very precious. Then, as theatrically as only a young child could be without self-consciousness, she peeled back the sections of the box top one at a time until all four were standing straight in the air. Then she moved between Aggie and the box, hiding her actions with her body. Aggie could see her lean over and pull something out, then straighten up and arrange herself perfectly before turning around. "Ta-da," she sang as she turned around to face the older woman, pushing her hands out in front of her.

Nestled in the palms of Jennie's cupped hands was a tiny kitten, barely old enough to leave its mother, ragged fur flying in all directions and wide blue eyes that would have been at home in a Keene painting. His face and his tail were gray, as were the tips of his two front paws, the rest of his body was white and it was obvious that he was, at least in part, a Persian.

"I've decided to name him Diablo," Jennie said, proudly.

"Oh, he's adorable," Aggie forced herself to say, even forced herself to stroke the animal for a minute before she patted the child on the cheek. Already, she could feel her eyes beginning to water. She placed a hand on the child's head. "Jennie," she said, her voice sounding suddenly distant and mechanical, "Don't go in the house. Don't... go... in the *house*."

"What house? What are you talking about, Aunt Aggie?" Jennie asked.

Aggie grabbed the child's arm and looked down at her; looked, in fact, right through her, and in the same blank and distracted voice said, "No, it wasn't you."

"Who wasn't me?" Jennie wrenched her arm free and backed up several steps.

The woman's body shuddered, and then, as though the last few moments had never happened, she smiled once again at the kitten. "He's a real beauty," she said. "How did you ever manage to get Pritt and Cinda to let you have him?"

Jennie stared at the palm reader for a few frightened moments, then shrugged it off. "It was easy. No other kids my age this season. Now tell me what you meant about the house."

"What house?" Aggie asked.

"You said that I shouldn't go in the house. What house?" Jennie asked, putting the kitten back into his box.

"When did I say that?" Aggie tried to remember her last conversation with Jennie. What on Earth could the child possibly be referring to.

"Just now you said… oh, never mind. I guess I'd better take him home now." Aggie walked her to the door. Did her own children act so strangely when they were this age. It was hard to remember. She watched the child retreat to her family's Winnebago, taking a deep breath of the warm summer air. It was a beautiful night, even if it was a little too hot. She gazed up at the sky.

Flames battled against the starry night. Flames blackened by thick smoke like a moving hole in the sky, and someone running past the window of a house about to be engulfed by the fire.

Aggie shook herself. The night sky was a smooth black velvet laced with stars. She went back into the trailer and shut the door.

Part Two

TEARDOWN

1

Strands of light washed across the tattered rug in pale stripes as the moonlight seeped through the shuttered windows. Occasionally the old boards of the house would shudder and groan like a giant tossing in sleep, and the night breezes would sneak through the ancient window frames to stir the velvet curtains. It was an old man's sickroom, with trays of bottles neatly arranged on the table next to the unruffled bed. Over in the darkest corner, Eli Jefferson sat in his wheelchair, watching the dust motes swirling in the strips of light and trying his best not to go to sleep.

He was not entirely alone in the house. His nurse, Mrs. Duffy, was asleep in the upstairs bedroom that had been Eli's and his brother's when they were boys. She was an old biddy... old despite being a good many years younger than her charge, and he enjoyed being difficult with her. What a fuss she had made when he finally refused to allow her to stuff him into that bed. It was something he'd wanted to do for weeks. Didn't she have any idea what it was like? Hour after endless hour, awake and helpless in that bed, unable to do anything but lie there and wait for her to come in the morning. Did she think that he could sleep? But then, he hadn't told her about the dream.

How he dreaded the dream. A horrible dream the likes of which he hadn't known since his boyhood... not since those long agonizing months in the hospital when no one was sure if he would live, or even if he should. A dream that made the sleepless nights a pleasure. It was more than just a replay of the night of his accident, with the smoke and flames, the terror of Werner Morgan, the fall, and the pain—there were other things; things that he had never revealed to anyone. Not even Jake. For even his brother might think he was going mad.

It wasn't too bad, staying awake like this. He was an old man, sedentary, without much need for sleep. He rolled across to the window and pulled the shutters open. All of the lights were off in the houses across the street, except for one way down the block. Were the lights off now in Jake's house? Was Jake soundly sleeping in his bed? And Joella in hers? Eli was fairly sure that they were. Joella was worse than Mrs. Duffy. Smothering, overprotective, just like her mother had been. Yet, even now Eli could remember how much he had wanted Trish, though he knew she was revulsed by the sight of him. It was as if she were seeing her beloved Jake when she looked at him, but a Jake somehow maimed and distorted and ruined—for even now, in their eighties, the resemblance between the twins was remarkable.

It wasn't fair… they had always done everything together, until Werner Morgan came along. Their mother used to say that they had been born holding hands, and he had always chosen to believe it. But that was a very long time ago. Eli knew that Jake had always gone out of his way since the accident to include him in everything, but it had never been the same. They had chosen their paths in boyhood, and had gone different ways.

"Do you have nightmares too?" he whispered to his brother across the night air. He slammed the shutters so forcefully that they banged back open. He left them that way and wheeled himself into the middle of the room. Jake would not have nightmares. Jake remembered nothing of that awful night when Eli had laid his own soul on the line and gone out to commit murder so that he might save his brother's.

It wasn't long before he heard the sharp groan of floorboards in the upstairs hall, the soft sloosh of slippered feet on the carpeted stairs. Damn, he'd woken the ogre. He backed into the corner behind the door and waited. The bang of the door and the blinding flash of the ceiling light announced her arrival.

"Are you all right, Mr. Jefferson?" Mrs. Duffy asked, stepping into the room and looking around in a puzzled way for a moment before she spotted him.

"Yes, Mrs. Duffy. I'm fine, Mrs. Duffy," he snapped. "I'm always fine. Life has been very kind to me."

"Oh, feeling sorry for yourself tonight, are you? What was that noise? Scared me half to death." The nurse began fussing over Eli, straightening his blanket and changing the position of the foot rests on his chair. He shrugged her away.

He said, "You know I've been in this chair over fifty years, Mrs. Duffy. There are a few things I've learned to do for myself."

"Then why don't you do them?" she asked sharply.

"Is that how you got rid of Mr. Duffy? Killed him with kindness?"

"What you should be worried about is what I'm going to do to you if you don't let me help you into that bed right this minute."

"I don't want to get into bed. I don't want to go to sleep. I'm practically asleep all day as it is."

"Well then, how about if I make us a pot of cocoa and get the cards. I'm not feeling sleepy myself, and with what you pay I could stand to win an extra week's salary at cribbage."

"Mrs. Duffy, please," the old man shouted.

"Look, Mr. Jefferson, I'm sorry to be fussing over you so. Truth to tell, I just can't stand to see you bothered like this. I want to do something to help, that's all."

"I know that you just want to help, Mrs. Duffy, but there's nothing you can do except leave a poor old man alo… actually, there is one thing you can do," he said. "Tell me the truth. Do people ever talk about my accident? What do they say?"

The nurse looked at him curiously as she eased herself onto a corner of the bed. "They don't talk much anymore, but boy, did they ever warn me about you when I took this job! I know that you were injured in a fire at the old Morgan place, and that some folks think you set the fire. I don't believe it, though. Some folks use to believe that Morgan was the Devil, silly as it sounds now. I remember Miss Roseville saying once a long time ago that she never could understand why this happened to you, when it was your brother who was the wild one. I don't think I ever heard anything else."

Eli wheeled the chair over to where she was sitting and patted the back of her hand. "You've helped, Mrs. Duffy. Believe me, you have. Now go to bed and get a good night's rest. Tomorrow, I'll have Jake come over for a while, and you can have part of the afternoon off."

He watched her walk out the door, carefully blinking back the tears that sprang so easily to his eyes these days. Mrs. Duffy was not usually so kind and sympathetic, and he wondered if it was because she too knew that he was dying. He was aware that he didn't have much longer. He had been convinced of that when the nightmares returned. Why, he hadn't given the accident much thought at all for most of his adult life, and suddenly, it wouldn't go away. He was glad of the warning. There was something that he had to take care of before the end, and his brother was going to have to help. He and Jake would have a nice, leisurely dinner, and Eli would work up to things slowly.

2

The inevitable poker game was going on in the G-top. Pritt grabbed a cold bottle of beer from the ice chest and walked around to look at everyone's hand, then turned the only empty chair around and sat on it backwards, leaning his arms on the back rest. Lutzy had a full house, but he was low on cash, and Pritt could see that Sam had him psyched. Dollar had the perfect poker face. No one could ever tell what he was thinking—until it came to Katie, and then Pritt suspected that everyone knew what Sam thought, except maybe Sam. Shingo-Shango laid a twenty dollar bill on the table, then added an extra ten. He was holding two pair, aces and nines; Sam's trip ladies had him beat.

Jeff Petticola, one of Maxie's bozos, leaned over the chat. He had already folded his hand and was waiting for the next to be dealt. "Hey, Pretty Pictures, what's happening," he asked.

"I should be askin' you that," Pritt said, pointing to the stack of bills in front of Jeff. "Folded?"

"Too rich for my blood," Jeff said. He was a good kid, college student bumming for the summer. It was his third season working bozo, and Larry Michael's second. Maxie, who was nearing sixty and planning to retire to Florida any season now, said he liked using college kids in the cage because they knew how to get the digs in real good, they never caught cold, and they mostly stayed out of trouble. Pritt motioned Jeff closer with his index finger.

"You holdin'?" he whispered. A moment later Jeff pressed two pills into the palm of Pritt's hand. "Thanks, man. Catch me later," Pritt said.

"Nah, it's a present," Jeff whispered. Pritt nodded. He tossed the pills into the air one at a time, catching them on his tongue like popcorn and washing them down with the brew.

"You know, I think I've had enough action for one day. Wanna sit in?" Jeff asked.

"You shittin'? After the wad I dropped yestiday? Cinda would feed me my ass." He took a longer pull from the bottle.

"Did you notice if they had any Heineken over there?" Jeff swept his money off the table, folded it into a neat stack, and shoved it into his pocket as he walked toward the cooler. Pritt followed.

"Hey, where the hell are you goin'?" Lutzy called after them. Jeff raised both hands in surrender. Pritt thought the old man looked like he was in bad shape. There was sweat dripping from his upper lip and his hands were shaking. From the way some of the older guys talked, Lutzy must have been some great carny in his day, but the grab joint was about all he could handle now.

The tent flap breezed open and a head popped through, in and out so fast that Pritt wouldn't have recognized Dandy if he hadn't heard his voice. "All operators on the midway. Fifteen minutes," Dandy called, departing with a crisp snap of the canvas.

"Nothin' important," Sam Dollar said to the nervous Lutzy, who was still debating whether to throw another twenty into the pot. Pritt smiled. Sam was very good, but not quite good enough. Lutzy folded the bill and put it back into his pocket.

"Gotta go," the carny said, pushing his cards across the table, face down. Sam looked at Shingo-Shango.

"All right, let's see them," the swinger agent said, tossing two tens into the pot. Sam laid his cards face up on the table. "Didn't think you'd work so hard if you really had somethin'," Shingo-Shango said in surprise as Sam raked in the pot. He carefully folded the rest of his money and put it back in his belt clip. "Let's hear what the boss-man has to say. You comin' Sam?" he asked, as he replaced the battered derby that usually covered his iron-gray curls.

"Be along in a minute, but I think I know what it's about," Sam said, scraping his winnings off the table.

"Wanna fill me in?" Pritt asked, rising slowly from his chair.

"He's picked up a date for this weekend, so your three days of freedom just went down the drain. But he'll fill you in on the details," Dollar said as he headed toward the back lot exit. "I'd better get the bed jockeys. Tell Patch be along in a minute."

Pritt looked at his watch and wondered who Sam thought would still be asleep at quarter to three. He tilted the bottle back and let the last of the cool liquid flow down his throat, then placed the empty in a plastic can. Outside, in the sunshine, the rapidly growing group of carnies was milling around, speaking softly to each other. Pritt found Cinda talking to Aunt Aggie. He snuck up behind and began to massage her shoulders.

"Where's Jennie?" he asked, as soon as there was a break in the conversation.

"Still playing with that damn cat. I think she's gonna wear the damn thing out. I know you can't refuse that child anything, but I really don't think this was a good idea."

"Time'll tell," Pritt said, "If she's got the patience to teach it to walk on a leash, then it's gonna be fine. If she gets tired of it in three or four weeks, we'll give it away. She knows. She's a good kid."

"I know," Cinda responded, sounding like she wasn't quite sure. "Oh, guess what her new thing is. I think she's got a crush on Larry. Told me this morning that she wants to be a bozo next summer."

"What did you tell her?" Pritt asked, laughing.

"Whaddya think? I told her she was *already* a bozo. She gave me that look and said, 'Oh Mom! You think you're so smart,'" Cinda did an imitation of her daughter. "Aggie, did you ever…" Cinda turned back and noticed Aggie's retreating back. "Well now, where on Earth is she goin'?" she asked Pritt. Her husband shrugged, and the flowers on his neck did a little dance. "She's been actin' funny all mornin'," Cinda continued.

"Jennie said somethin' funny about her last night when she came back from showin' off the critter. I'm not sure exactly what, 'cause I wasn't payin' a whole lot of attention, but I think she asked me if Aggie was a real fortune teller, and when I told her there wasn't any such thing, she just looked kind of puzzled, like she didn't quite believe me. You don't suppose Aggie's been fillin' her head with stories, do ya?"

"Aggie? Oh, come on, Pritt. Aggie's the sanest person I know. She'd be the last one. Remember that time Magda leant Jennie that book of ghost stories?"

"Yeah. I almost killed her. The kid had nightmares for a week."

"Yup. And wasn't it Aggie who convinced her that there's no such thing as ghosts and that she didn't have nothin' to be afraid of? And that…" she paused and turned at the sound of Dandy's voice.

"Okay, folks," Dandy said, motioning for silence. "Okay, folks. Quiet down. I ain't gonna shout," he shouted. "I know I told you all that we were sloughed in Richmond this weekend. Some of you probably made some plans. Well, the rest of you will be glad to hear that we picked up a slot. Now, it's a little farther than we usually travel, and I know some of you have certain feelin's about workin' in the terrible North. Anyone who can't make it, see me today and we can meet up in Waycross, but I'd like you all to be there, and I'm gonna guarantee for any of you that thinks there's gonna be trouble, that it ain't gonna be no different from what we got right here." There was a lot of muttering and grumbling along with a scattered sound of applause, but Dandy motioned for silence once again, and they gave it to him. "The town we're going to is called Somerset, and it's just a little bit outside of Philadelphia. For anyone who'd prefer to stay at a motel, there's a pretty good one just down the highway. You got a problem, Shingo-Shango?"

"Damn straight I got a problem! Last time I played Philadelphia was with Nick Bazoukis in '67 and I vowed I'd never go back. Wanna know why? 'Cause the bars wouldn't serve us, and I wound up sittin' in jail for two weeks on some lousy, trumped-up charge I never even heard of. Lost my proposition, too, and couldn't find another one 'til the summer was almost over. I don't like Philly."

"You weren't with *my* show then. Don't I take care of you all? First of all, we won't be *in* Philly, we'll be just outside, which means Philly audiences without Philly cops, and second, I don't think there'll be any problems, because they asked us to come, but like I said, no one has to show up. All I ask is that you let me know if you're not coming. As for the rest of you, it's a long drive, so I'd appreciate all of you hittin' the road as soon as possible after teardown. That's all, and thank you."

3

The news that Dandy had called a meeting hit Aggie like an ice cube on the spine. Bad news. She was certain of it. Not that she believed in premonitions or the rest of that supernatural stuff—that was for the marks —but it wasn't like her to have anxiety attacks either. She was glad to find Cinda milling about with the crowd, latching on to her like a salve for an open wound, only to find that her nervousness was made worse by trying to hide it. She was glad when Pritt found them, giving her a chance to slip away. She watched them together for a polite moment. What a strange couple they made, with Cinda a pert and rounded five-foot-nothing next to Pritt's tall and skinny frame. She had the look of a down home country girl, while he was obviously an ex-hippy, right down to the stringy, shoulder-length hair. Even some of his face was illustrated, unusual for a tattooed man, and his pictures ranged from mediocre cartoons to virtuosities worthy of a master painter.

When, after a moment, they still hadn't given her a chance to make a polite excuse, she left anyway. It had been a rough night. Not that she'd had any bad dreams, exactly—at least, none that she could remember— but she had awakened this morning feeling as if she had never shut her eyes, and there had been a faint burning smell in the trailer for which she could find no source.

When Dandy arrived and began to quiet the crowd, Aggie backed away without knowing why she did so, stepping on toes, bumping into people, almost knocking over Shingo-Shango's proposition before she realized that she couldn't go any farther. And, as he began to speak, it almost seemed that a cloud had floated over the sun and it became very dark, just like that moment before the rains came in a hurricane. Very dark, and very, very cold. She saw the people spread out in front of her through a veil of gauze, each surrounded by a halo of light that was somehow so close to their very natures that she almost felt she could recognize them by their auras alone. Some were very bright, some almost non-existant, some a smoldering red while one or two had a fiery blue-white brilliance. They moved and played around the bodies they encircled almost as if they had a life entirely their own; and like the corona around the eclipsed sun, they shot long trailing streamers whenever one person neared another. And, as she watched, some grew to almost blinding brightness, while others slowly dimmed and faded to a dull green—an image on the eyelid after a photo has been taken—and then they winked out entirely.

Alone in the unbroken darkness, the cold intensified. So cold that her teeth began to chatter and she was forced to rub her arms with her hands for warmth. "Aggie?" The sound came from very far away, floating toward her in the darkness. "Aggie?" She followed the sound, moving through the darkness toward the light and warmth until there it was before her. Like going from a tunnel into the blazing summer sun, there burned before her a light so bright that she was forced to throw up her arm like a shield and turn away. The light broke and kaleidescoped into a riotous jumble of color, solidifying slowly into the frozen mass of the Ferris Wheel, standing in solemn stillness in the bright warmth of the Virginia sun.

"Aggie, are you all right?" Katie was saying, hovering over her nervously.

"Yeah," she answered vaguely, "I'm fine. I've just got this real splitter of a headache." She rubbed her eyes with thumb and finger. What was *wrong* with her lately? Something physical, she hoped. Oh, God, how she hoped it was something simple and physical, like overwork, or a vitamin deficiency. *Take this shot and stay in bed three days and you'll be fine.* She looked at Katie and forced a smile. There was no way she could explain what had happened even to herself, much less to Katie; a bright young girl like that, college educated, with none of the silly superstitions that the other girls had. *Katie, do you believe… can people really… is it possible?* Stupid old biddy. Next thing you know, you're really going to believe that you see things in tea leaves. More than likely it's just a case of *say something long enough and sooner or later you'll start to believe it.* It was time to quit the fortune telling business, is all. "I think I'll just go take some aspirins and lie down, Katie, angel," she said.

"Okay, Aunt Aggie. And if it's still bothering you later, I'll come help you tear down after closing. Meanwhile, just think about how close the family is to Philly. You'll probably be seeing them pretty soon."

So they were going to Philly? That was Dandy's news. Well, then it hadn't been bad news after all. She could breeze over to Jersey in the early afternoon and see the kids. And maybe, if this problem hadn't gone away by then, Susan would know what to do. That was… should she tell Susan? "That'll be nice," Aggie said as she started back to her trailer. "Really nice."

4

The dining room of the Cafe Vietnam restaurant was one tiny room with ten tables, flocked wallpaper that had seen better days, and a few oriental decorations that had been bought at auction when the *Sezuan Flower* closed. The lunch crowd was gone and the dinner trade would not start for several hours. It was the time that Mei Chou Phan liked best.

She carried a bowl of crab and asparagus soup to her only customer, waiting patiently while he rearranged his newspaper to make room for it, refilled his water glass, and then sat down again on a chair in the back of the room to wait until something else was required of her. It was not a bad life for a sixteen-year-old—much better than the life she had had before she came to Philadelphia—but lately, she was restless. In the last two or three days she'd had the strangest urge to just pick up and leave. It made her feel disrespectful and very guilty. What would Mother Chem say? True, it had been to both their advantages to claim kinship, as women with children were given first preference by immigration. Still, she had been a nobody, living on the streets when Mother Chem had taken her in. She owed Mother Chem quite a bit.

The customer seemed to be finished with his soup, and she went to collect the bowl. "Carnival's coming," he said, pointing to his newspaper. She nodded and smiled, looking at the paper, just to be polite. A carnival! Suddenly, she was filled with excitement. She had been to lots of carnivals. They played the local church benefits all the time, but this was a real big carnival with lots of rides and a side show. She had never been to one of those. Probably most of the kids from school would be going. Maybe if she talked to Shari, or Tanya? But that was silly. Mother Chem would never give her time off to do anything as frivolous as going to a carnival.

She cleared away the dirty dishes and brought the man a steaming plate of banh cúon, taking another look over his shoulder. Somerset. She had never heard of the place, but it couldn't be too far if they were advertising in the Philly paper. She could sometimes get away on Friday night, if Mother Chem was in a good mood. She didn't have to tell her exactly where she was going. She had never lied to the woman before, but somehow, this seemed important. She wasn't quite sure why, but she knew that she had to go. And if she had to go, there would be a way for her to get there. Maybe Tanya could get her father's car.

She took another quick look to memorize the time and dates. "You like carnivals, huh?" the customer asked. She smiled and nodded again.

"I'll see what's keeping your food," she said, and went in the back room to use the phone.

5

The door closed with a jangle of bells behind the last of the customers, and the neons over the bar winked into darkness. A few moments later, a slender redhead peeked around the door to Arthur Billingsly's office. "That's the last for tonight, except for the sleep-ins," she said.

"Okay, Mary, you can send the rest of the girls home now." He arched an eyebrow at his companions. "Unless, of course, Ron, you'd like some company?"

"You'd love that, Dad, wouldn't you? Look, all I want is to get this whole thing over with so that I can get home and get some sleep. Besides, Darcy's beginning to forget what I look like, and my children are starting to call me Mr. Billingsly." Ron took a sip of his scotch-rocks and noted the amused look on his father's face. The fat man sent Mary off with a nod of his head, and turned the cat and mouse look on his son.

"Ah yes, the little woman," he said in a fairly good impression of W.C. Fields. "I almost forgot you were married," he added in his normal deadpan.

"Just so Darcy doesn't forget. Anyway, it's your own fault that she doesn't speak to you. You had to go and try everything you could to break us up. Hell, you're still trying. You'll be the one to lose in the end. Hate to tell you this, but she means more to me than you do." Ron finished off his drink and slammed the glass down on the counter.

"I'm not still trying to break you up. You're a grown man. I didn't want to see you throw over an heiress for the town dolt's granddaughter. Too late now. I just don't want to watch my only son being pussy-whipped."

"Cut it out, Dad, or I'm leaving right now," Ron said. "I've told you before, if you want me to work with you, my marriage is a forbidden topic."

"I'm only looking out for your best interests. Darcy's a nice girl but... okay, sit down. I won't talk about it. How'd our little business deal go this afternoon?" Billingsly pulled a cigar from the box on his desk and went through the whole ceremony, rolling the cigar between his thumb and finger, smelling it, and finally snipping the end of it with a small, gold guillotine that he took from his vest pocket. He puffed it into a brilliant ember.

Ron coughed. "I didn't think it was possible, but those smell even worse than the last brand you smoked. I checked out the area. It's just right for the operation, both size and layout. Right off the highway, and just the right kind of neighborhood. But you know the council is never going to sell you Morgan Field. Redd would rather die than let you have it. He's already said so."

"If only it wasn't inside the county line," Billingsly said through a blue cloud of smoke.

"I don't think Veransky and Chipps would be too much of a problem, but you've got to get it past Redd. 'I'll keep the land for a parade ground before I'll let him build a brothel there,' was his picturesque way of putting it. The rest will go along with him. How could they not? Even if they could push the zoning proposal through without him, imagine what he could do to them at a town meeting if they did. Neither one of them could get re-elected. Everyone knows what kind of 'nightclub' you intend to build," Ron said.

"I never did like that little snot-nosed prick. You know he issued a permit to let some damn circus play through town this weekend?"

"It's a carnival, Dad, and so fuckin' what?" Ron stood up and paced across the empty bar. He didn't like his father's half-coughed laugh, nor the smile on his face. There were certain aspects of the old man's business that Ron would rather not become involved in.

"The problem with you is that your mother had too much of a hand in your rearing. How much do you know about what goes on at a carnival?" He picked up his glass and Ron's and took them both behind the bar for a refill. "I'm serious. Tell me. What do you know?"

"Boy, this is just like third grade. Okay, I'll play. A carnival has rides, it has some game booths, concessionaires, and a fun house or two. The one that comes with the circus has a side-show, but I don't know if that belongs to the carnival or the circus."

"You're mistaking a carnival for a cross between an amusement park and a church bazaar. I'm not sure you've ever been to a real carnival. They don't come around this way much, anymore. You're right about the game booths, only they're usually fixed and there's often some heavy gambling going on there. They'll also have a tent full of hootchy-kootchy girls."

"I thought they went out with kewpie dolls," Ron said, wondering why his father thought this was so important.

"Don't just sit there with your thumb up your ass. Show me that you inherited at least some of your genes from me. If Walter Redd issued a permit for that carnival to bring in a tent full of over-aged, pot-bellied strippers, doesn't that give you any idea how we can get some advantage out of the situation?"

"Dad, I hate to sound like a small-town hick, but I'm not even sure what it is that hootchy-kootchy girls do," Ron said, though he felt rather stupid. It was obviously something he was supposed to know, and he suspected it was something a little raunchier than a simple strip. "If this is something so important to my education, why the hell didn't you ever take me to a carnival when I needed to go? You certainly knew that Mother wouldn't."

"Sorry, son. Sometimes I forget what a blue-nose your mother was. Now, don't go getting defensive. I loved her more than you ever did, but it wasn't the kind of place she would have wanted me to take you." He handed Ron a fresh drink. "Exactly what a carnival dancer does depends on the carnival, I guess, but often you'll find them doing things that make the acts at my place look tame. Well, maybe not tame, but certainly middle class. I remember seeing one broad who could pick up a pop bottle, drink it dry, and then spit it across the tent without once using her hands or mouth." He sighed reverently. "Get the picture?"

"I think so. So just how are you going to use this against the great Mr. Redd? He could always claim he didn't know what they were going to do. After all, I didn't."

"Not when I get through with him he won't. Don't worry, I'll arrange the details while you keep your hands clean. All I want from you is to fix it so Gaylen Schuster is at the carnival Friday night. Redd doesn't know Schuster, so it should be okay. I want him playing the tourist right down to the camera and I want lots of pictures taken of Redd, particularly if anything interesting should happen. If I can work things out the way I'm planning to, Mr. Walter Redd will be begging me to move into that building. If not… Well, I'll see to it that there isn't any 'if not'." He gripped his son's shoulder affectionately. "I also want a meeting set up with whoever's in charge at the carnival as soon as he blows into town. I'd better go out there, though. It'll go better on his own turf."

"You're planning on setting Redd up so that you can blackmail him. Dad, I won't do it," Ron said. "I have to draw the line somewhere. I don't mind helping you out with the hookers and the strip and gambling joints, because nobody gets hurt there that didn't ask for it. But this is different. I won't help you blackmail. Not even Walter Redd. Hell, I went to school with Walt. I don't think you can blackmail that prig if you try, but if you do, you'll be hurting an awful lot of people, and Walt is the least of them."

Billingsly shook his head sadly. "Don't worry. You won't have to be a party to anything. I can do it without you. You just go on home to your angel wife and your cherub children, and by all means, keep your hands clean."

"You've gone too far, Dad. I told you to lay off my wife and kids." Ron stood up and gathered his cigarettes and lighter together.

"Now, Ron, I meant that sincerely. Darcy reminds me a lot of your mother. Tell her I really would like us to get along better. Tell her that maybe it's time we made peace. In fact, I'd like to do something nice for the two of you so that maybe she won't think so hard of a corrupt old man. How would she like to go on a cruise this summer? Talk it over with her, will you?"

"All she wants from you is to be accepted into the family," Ron lied. Darcy would be polite to the old man, but she would never forgive him or accept the way he made his money, and she certainly wouldn't accept his gifts. Ron watched as the fat man put his hat on and turned out the last few lights in the bar. The sun was coming up over the tops of the trees on the other side of the highway as they got into their respective cars and headed in opposite directions.

6

"That you, Walt?" Alma Redd called from the kitchen, as if it could be anyone else. She could tell by the squeals of the kids that it had to be her husband. He was home early for a change. A pleasant change. She checked the sauce that was simmering slowly on the burner. It was a long time until dinner, but then she hadn't expected Walt home this early. They had gotten used to eating quite late.

"Hey, honey, come on out here. I have something for you," he called in a coy and teasing voice that was something else Alma wasn't used to from him any more. Curious, she came into the living room to find him sitting on the sofa, a child on each knee; Santa Claus in his youth. Beside him, a small box, all wrapped up as if it were her birthday. At first she eyed it suspiciously. For a long time after Walt decided that someday he'd be a senator and started keeping late hours, coming home distracted and exhausted, ignoring her and the kids, getting strange phone calls and running out in the middle of parties, dinners, in the middle of the night, for heaven's sake—Alma wondered if he was cheating on her. Then, after she had become involved—to a limited extent—in his work, she had discovered just how time-consuming it was. Especially if you wanted to make it B-I-G. Now the old idea began to resurface. Home early, and with a present. "What's the occasion?" she asked.

"Nothing special. I just made some extra money in a deal today, and I thought I'd do something nice for the family I've been neglecting." She noticed now, the tell-tale scraps of paper, the two new toys the kids had been playing with, the impish, mischievous expression on her husband's face. He was really enjoying this.

"Well, aren't you going to open it?" he asked, impatiently.

"I don't know. It's too small for a fur," she said, staring at the package without touching it, teasing him. "Too big for a diamond. Not the right shape for a trip to Florida."

"I'll bet it doesn't rattle either," he hinted.

"Oh, all right, I give up," she said at last, and, playing up to his mood, she ripped the paper like a child on Christmas. "Oh… Walt…!" was all she said when she finally got it open. It was the blouse she'd been staring at in Milly's window for the last month. How had he ever known? It was a beautiful, bright-blue silk, with lace insets at the shoulder. It would go perfectly with her gray suit, but it was so expensive. "Oh, honey, thank you," she said, throwing her arms around his neck and squeezing really tight.

"Alma, I know I haven't had the time for you that you need. I really would like to be able to keep hours like a normal person, maybe take a vacation."

"I know you would, honey," she interrupted.

"Listen, I have two really important things going on right now. If I can keep that louse Billingsly from moving his operation into Somerset, then I will have done a real public service. And if I can pull this ground-breaking off at Morgan's Field, then I can write my own ticket. We'll be out of small town politics and into the real game. Honey, you'll see. Winters in the islands. Private schools for the kids."

Pipe dreams, Alma thought, but she patted his hand and smiled. "Walt, I'd be happy, we'd all be happy, just to see a little more of you. All I really want is for you to spend some time with the kids before they're all grown up. We don't need to be rich, Walt, we only need to be together." There, she'd spoiled it for him. Now why had she gone and done that? A minute ago, he'd been like a happy, carefree kid, and now his usual scowl was back in place.

"Alma, can't you see I'm doing all this for you? How it grinds me to listen to Lizzie MacCourtney brag to you about how Kevin is taking her to St. Croix for New Year's. Wally needs braces and Jessie will too, soon, and then it'll be party clothes, and believe me, if you knew what I know about the funding for the school board, you wouldn't be pooh-poohing private school, either." He was shouting now.

"Yes, Walt, you're right, of course. Money comes in very handy. I'm only saying that it doesn't take the place of having a father to do things with. If only you'd take a weekend off once in a while. Take them fishing, take them to the circus, take them for a ride down to Lancaster to see the Amish farms. Just *once* in a while, come home in time to read them to sleep. And for God's sake, Walt, don't back out of promises! Some-times… oh damn!" Jessie began to cry and came to her mother for attention. "Oh, baby," Alma said, clutching her child and smoothing down her hair. "Mommies and Daddies sometimes have loud discussions, but that doesn't mean they don't love each other. Mommy still loves Daddy, and they both love you," she said, looking at Walter as if to say *Now look what you've done.*

Walter Jr. looked at his mother cynically. "That's not why she's crying. She's crying because I won't let her play with my new Zorch. She wants to help me put it together. But Mom, she doesn't know how. She'll break it!"

7

The costume looked terrific. A brilliant, electric blue to bring out Katie's eyes, and cream colored spangles to highlight the peach tones of her skin, with a black lace heart in the middle that was guaranteed to drive any mark into a frenzy, especially when it came off. Esmerelda bit off the thread and held it up to admire. "Well, whaddya think?"

Magda backed up about a foot and cocked her head to one side. "I keep tellin' ya, Es, my color's red," she said as she circled her thumb and forefinger together and winked.

"'N I keep tellin' you, so's your personality," Essie laughed. "Hey, Glory, how'dya like it?"

Glory was back in the corner of the tent, razor in hand, with one foot up on a wooden crate, shaving her orangey-yellow pubic hair into a heart. All of Glory's hair had been dyed that same stop-light yellow. As was often the case with Glory, she hadn't heard a word that was said.

"Shit, Glory. I don't know how you can do that with a razor. I'd itch for days," Maggie said.

"No sense, no feelin'," Essie said with a sigh, and put the question a little louder.

"Huh, Es? Was you talkin' to me?"

"You know anyone else with the poor taste to call themselves Glory?" Essie asked. The woman blinked at her vacantly, then put down the razor and came over for a look. "Katie?" she asked.

"Well, it's certainly not for you. Couldn't get the whole thing over your tits." Essie said.

Glory smiled and pushed at her breasts. "*Sure* you could," she said, and smiled. "Got any more dexies?" she asked Magda, as she walked back to her crate and picked up the razor. Essie held the costume up to her body, wishing that there was a full length mirror that she could see herself in. She envied Katie that gorgeous complexion, and she envied her youth, but she didn't have to envy her figure. They were exactly the same size, except that Essie's middle was beginning to show the slightest tendency towards a roll. Well, after this season she could get as fat as a house and not have to worry about it.

"Uh-oh, here comes Miss Piggy," she heard Magda say. She looked up in time to see the Viking sweep into the room without a word for anybody. She was already in costume—a gaudy affair in banana yellow—a color which was considered the worst sort of bad luck—and then managed to compound the injury by sitting down in front of the makeup mirror to primp in spite of the fact that scattered paint, bits of costume and a robe clearly marked the spot as Magda's for the moment.

Essie could see trouble brewing. The Viking sat before the mirror, totally absorbed, putting on eye shadow, combing her hair, admiring herself, without a glance at anyone else in the room, and all the while, Magda, and Glory too, were staring at her, open-mouthed. It was Glory who moved first, calmly, deliberately, muscles rippling under the burnt toast of her skin. "'Scuse me," she said, pulling the Viking's chair back away from the mirror while the Viking was still sitting in it. Glory leaned over and stared at herself in the mirror. The Viking was out of the seat in a flash, ready to fight.

"You bitch," the Viking screamed, arms raised, bright purple nails flashing in the distant light, ready to strike but hesitating just a bit at the last moment. She was a tall woman, but not nearly as big or as muscular as Glory who was calmly staring at her. Essie decided that it was time to interfere. Besides, she had something better in mind for the Scandinavian.

"Glory!" she said in a soft, but commanding voice, "you too, Goldilocks! We've got a show to do in just a few minutes, and I'll be damned if I'll pick up the slack for anyone covered in band-aids." She checked to make sure that the Viking wasn't looking at her, and signaled silently for Magda and Glory to leave. When they were gone, she turned back to the Viking. "I don't know," she said, then paused until she was sure she had the blonde's attention. "Sam used to keep them under better control for Katie." The Viking gave her a dagger glance, which pleased Essie. There was no way of knowing if things would work out the way she thought they would, but if not, the fun of baiting this creature was its own excuse. "Of course, Katie always did have Sam wrapped around her little finger."

"Not any more, she doesn't," the Viking said, petulantly. Essie was finding it hard to hide the smile that tugged at her lips.

"Yeah? Well if that's so, how come he *still* won't let her work strong?" Essie asked.

"She doesn't want to. He told me so," the blonde replied—the tone of her voice reminding Essie just how young she was. Essie raised an eyebrow and smiled unbelievingly. The Viking sputtered. "He doesn't give a shit about her any more! And as far as those two cows go… he's gonna take care of *them*, and you, too! Just wait and see!" She stormed out of the dressing room.

Essie picked up Katie's new costume and put it away. It was strange that the set-to had not made her feel as good as she thought it would. Too much like swatting a fly with a sledgehammer; she'd forgotten just how young the girl was. Still, it had to be done. There is a minimum level of politeness without which a person deserves no consideration. The Viking had opted herself out of the human race.

As Essie sat down to do her own makeup, she caught sight of the Viking in the mirror, standing edgily by the entrance of the tent, waiting for the music to start. She would grab the center spot today, of that Essie was certain.

8

"I'm high and I'm dry and I'm lookin' me for a ballplayer. Hey you, over there, with the carrot thatch. Your hair embarrassed for ya?" It was the same thing night after night. Jeff called them in, egged them on, and always, he hoped, with just enough humor so that they didn't stay angry. At least not after they saw everyone else laughing. Just angry enough so that when Maxie offered them three chances to get even for only a buck, they would eagerly jump at the opportunity. Three baseballs, and a target so big it looked impossible to miss, though a surprising number of them did in fact miss it. Jeff didn't care. He loved the water. And on the chillier days, a wet-suit kept him dry.

Guys with dates always seemed to be the easiest targets, and the least likely to really take it seriously. Guys in groups were also fairly easy, as were fathers with their children. It was a remarkable act between getting them to laugh at themselves and embarrassing them past the point of no return. That was the difference between a good bozo and a riot act.

Right now, though, he wasn't really all that interested in winning money, and his calls to the marks were only half-hearted. Earning summer money had been only part of the reason he worked with Maxie every summer—though off-hand he couldn't think of any work that would have paid him more. Still, it was the girls that really lured him to the carnival every year. It was the girls. Young and sweet and ready for adventure with someone who wasn't going to be mouthing off in the locker room the next day. There were always plenty of them. There had been one last night, cute as could be with big blue eyes. She hadn't quite promised to return, but he had seen her a few minutes ago by the grab joint, staring at him. Usually, Jeff hated repeat performances, but it did beat hours of searching, and she had been quite a treat. Besides, they'd be miles away in the morning with no chance for entanglements. He wanted to catch her before she decided to leave, but Larry was late, as usual. He appealed to Maxie with silent signals, but Maxie was winning money hand over fist on this, his last night in the south. He was a little worried about playing up near Philly, and so he chose not to see.

An alarm went off, and Jeff found himself in the water. No sooner did he climb back onto the perch when it happened again. The fellow had a good arm. "Hey, hey, hey, you must have played the bigs. Yes sir, a Yankee from Virginia." Again he took a bath. It was a warm night and the water felt good against his face. He climbed back onto the perch. He could see Larry now, leaning up against the grab joint right where his little townie had been. "Hey you over there, with the fat head. You look like you'd float. Whyn't you come over and try this for a while?" Jeff shouted into the microphone. Maxie laughed. Larry pointed at the man who was throwing with uncommon accuracy and shook his head, laughing. Again the man threw. Again, Jeff went into the water. Enough was enough. He leaned his face against the bars of the cage and spoke to Maxie in carny. "I'm leaving right now whether that chump gets in here or not. I've got plans."

"All right, kid, just give me a minute. I'll take care of it," Maxie said. Jeff climbed back on the perch once again. Maxie sold three balls to someone new and went over to talk to Larry. Larry disappeared and Maxie walked back to his pitch holding up two fingers to indicate how many minutes it would be before Jeff was relieved. He didn't quite believe it, but at least it wouldn't be too much longer.

It was, in fact, ten minutes before Larry knocked at the back of the cage for admittance. Jeff skinned out of his wet clothes and blew his hair dry in record time. He felt a little silly. This was a big lot and he had no idea where to find her. Of course, he was fairly certain that he could find somebody, if she wasn't around.

She found him, calling out to him from the Ferris Wheel as he went past. He waited for the ride to finish, surprised to find that she had two girlfriends with her. "Hi," she said, walking up to him. "I was hoping I'd get to see you tonight. You promised to show me around if you weren't too busy. You're not, are you?"

"Too busy for you? Of course not," he said, fumbling around for her name. He seemed to think that it started with an R. Rose... Rita... he couldn't quite put his finger on it.

"I'd like you to meet my friends, Joyce and Linda."

"Listen Ruth, we're going to the side-show. I promised Chuck we'd meet him there after the ride. You coming?" Linda asked.

Ruth looked at Jeff. "I'd rather you let me show you around," he said, picking up his cue.

"If you two can get a ride with Chuck, I'll find my own way home. Okay?" Ruth asked.

"No prob," Joyce said. The two girls left.

"I'm glad you're here. I didn't think I was going to see you tonight. Or maybe you'd be with someone when I came," she said when they were finally alone.

"I'm glad *you're* here. You saw me working?"

"Yeah. You were amazing. How do you think of what to say?"

"A lot of it's shtick. Just stuff you use over and over. Of course, you do have to think pretty fast sometimes."

"I wish I could do that. I don't think I could stand it when it got cold, though," she said.

"We wear wet-suits under the outfit when it's cold. Say, why don't we go back to the 'bago and have a drink," he asked, painfully aware that teardown was in just a few hours. He put his arm around her shoulders and pulled her close.

"Okay, but there's something I'd like to do first. I hope you don't think I'm too much of a—what do you call people who come to the carnival—a mark, right? But I'd really like to go there first." She pointed at a sign that read, MADAM AUDEN, SEES ALL, KNOWS ALL.

"You want to go in the Mitt Camp?" Jeff asked with a sigh. Aggie would think he was crazy, but getting laid was cheap at twice the price. "Don't tell me you believe in fortune tellers?" he asked.

"No, not really. I just thought it would be fun."

"Well, maybe it will be. Come on," he said.

9

Aggie spotted Jeff and quickly spilled the mark she was working on, promising him large sums of money and the woman of his dreams. It had been a good night, in spite of the lousy start she'd had on the day, and the vague headache and stiff neck that still plagued her. She had finally decided that it was the damn circus jump coming up that had her in a snit. It was the only thing she truly didn't like about being with it, and this was a five-hour drive in the middle of the night with that damn trailer in tow. That was why she was so glad to see Jeff. Pritt had offered to let her ride with them in the Winnebago—sleep the whole ride away in the extra bed. All she had to do was find someone else to drive the trailer for her. Jeff was perfect, young and strong, with no car of his own to drive. Maxie and Larry could certainly handle the drive without him.

"How's tricks, kid? What can I do you for?" she asked.

"Tonight we're strictly a pair of marks," he said, winking at Aggie from behind Ruth's head. "I want you to meet someone," he said, making introductions.

"Pleased to make your acquaintance," Aggie said, offering her hand. Ruth was a cute kid, nice, firm handshake. It didn't take a mindreader to know what Jeff's plans were for the evening. She looked the girl over carefully without appearing to. High school ring told her the girl had graduated. It was not brand new, and too feminine to belong to a boyfriend. Something about the cut of the clothes, the mannerisms, the hair style said college. A dozen subliminal things told her that the girl was raised in an upperclass home but was anxious not to appear wealthy. Aggie took a stab. "University of Richmond?" she asked.

"That's right! How did you know?"

"But I'm supposed to know. That's why you came in here," Aggie said. "Jeff, before we start I'd like to ask you something."

"Sure, Aunt Aggie, what is it?"

"I was just hoping if you didn't have other plans that maybe you'd drive my rig tonight? I don't think I could handle a five-hour drive."

"Okay," he said, "If you're not planning on leaving too soon."

"Oh, I'll be riding with Pritt, so you can leave any time you want to, s'long's you get there before morning." She watched his face split into a wide grin.

"Sure thing, Madam Auden. Happy to do it!" he said. She passed him the key to her car, then thought better of it and added the key to the trailer. What harm could it do? If he was going to seduce the girl, or vice-versa, then better they should use the trailer than to hide in the bushes somewhere.

"Now, young lady, sit right down here." Aggie gave the girl the whole treatment, noting that Jeff was taking it all in as if it was a physics lesson. Smart as a whip, that one. She would have been willing to bet that before too long he'd be owning a carnival. After a few minutes the whole affair got rather silly, and they all enjoyed giggling at some of the ridiculous promises that Aggie made. They were having so much fun that Ruth insisted Jeff have his future told before they left. Jeff protested, but offered his palm.

It was happening again. Aggie felt a shock the moment she touched his hand, much stronger than the usual static electricity. His hand was hot, and flames surrounded him. The merry-go-round was burning, and in the flames she saw someone, flailing, crying for help. She saw the Bozo cage; a twisted wreckage, glowing like bright orange neon against the night sky. Spiders! Spiders as large as cats, spinning and turning on the horizon. The water in the cage bubbled like a pool of acid. Someone was screaming.

She dropped his hand. "Oh, God!" she said. "Oh, God, what's wrong with me?" Jeff flew around the table and put his hands on her shoulders to steady her.

"Are you all right, Aunt Aggie? My God, you're white as chalk. Why don't you go back to Pritt and lie down. I can tear down for you."

Aggie waved him away. "It's all right. Whatever it is that's bothering me, it comes and goes. I'm okay now. Besides, it's early yet. There's money to be had. Why don't you buy this young lady some cotton candy and take her on a couple rides, and if you want to be helpful, you can tear down for me later. After all, you're not in any hurry to get to Philly. Nothing for you to do for hours yet."

Jeff smiled. "You're absolutely right. As usual, Madam Auden sees all, knows all. I'm going to show Ruth a side of the carnival that most people don't get to see. Then I'll come back and take care of your proposition, and I don't want to find that any of the work's been done when I do. You just leave it all to Jeff," he said. Aggie nodded. She was badly frightened; not by the images of flame and destruction, she discounted those as the workings of a troubled imagination—it was the episodes *themselves* that frightened her, and the very real symptoms of headache and weakness that seemed to follow them.

She put on a cheerful act as she let Jeff and his friend out of the tent, then immediately turned away the waiting customers and closed down. If Cinda would let her, she was going to lay down. Maybe she would even be asleep before they pulled out.

Jennie let her into the trailer. The child was playing with the cat as if it was a doll at a tea party, but the animal didn't seem to mind. It put up with Jennie's ministrations with a patience that astounded Aggie. Or maybe the cat just liked it. It was more than the palm reader could stand, however, on a night that had held enough tension to suit anyone. She had Jennie direct her to her bed, and before either Pritt or Cinda had gotten back to the trailer, she was sound asleep.

The road bumped by. It was raining. The sound of tires on the wet macadam mingled with Cinda's snoring and Jennie's sleep-drugged moans to create a not-unpleasant symphony. It should have lulled her right to sleep. Instead, it just gave her something to focus her attention on. The first bump woke her up, though she had been feigning sleep for the past three hours. Suddenly she just couldn't stand to lay there for another moment. Perhaps talking to Pritt for a while would take her mind off things, she decided, and pulled her tired form to the front of the vehicle. The storm was worse to the north. Lightning split the sky in front of them and she jumped in her seat.

"Nasty weather ahead," Pritt said. The phrase struck her as particularly appropriate. That was the feeling she'd had all day and all the night before. That she was heading into a terrible storm and she was not sure that she'd be returning.

Yes, there was *nasty* weather ahead.

Part Three

PACING THE LOT

1

The parade of trucks, vans, campers, trailers, and motor homes began rolling into Somerset on a cloud of dust before the sun had even lightened the sky to purple. By the time that Arthur Billingsly had turned off the lights in the back room of the Blue Light Bar, Dandy had pulled his Winnebago onto the midway and had already begun to determine positions for the tents and rides. Outside, a milling crowd of early-birds waited expectantly for word from within so that they could begin their set-up chores and maybe get an extra hour's sleep for the day. By the time Carole McCluskey wiped down the counter at Miller's Pharmacy and started pre-cooking bacon for the morning rush, numbers were being chalked on the ground in yellow while Dandy fielded arguments from everyone who didn't think their proposition had been given the best territory, and Gregor had all of his rides unshipped and was already supervising the gang of roughies who would assemble them. And by the time that Alma Redd reached over Walter to turn off the alarm clock and started the tedious business of trying to wake him, grifters were pushing their booths into shape and stuffing them full of slum and those few *actual* prizes necessary to lure the marks. Tents were being erected at the back of the lot to house the Kootch Show, the G-top and the long garish posters were being strung from the tents with extreme delicacy, as they were expensive and difficult to replace. Roughies laid out thick black ropes of heavy cable, connecting rides, lights, microphones, and music systems each to their various generators. The soft, damp ground bubbled and squished under the busy mass of booted and sneakered feet. And by the time that Mrs. Duffy stirred a secret dose of sleep medication into Eli

Jefferson's farina, all of the carnies, from the ride boys to the dancers, from the grifters to the freaks, had all gone off to whatever accommodations they favored, trying to catch what sleep they could before showtime. All except for Jimbo and his crew, who would guard the grounds until it was time to open—and Gregor.

Gregor had a problem. The Spider was broken. He'd examined the motor, checked the power lines again and again for a break, and checked the generator's output. There was nothing wrong with the equipment as far as he could see; it simply wouldn't work. Cursing in Hungarian, he tossed a wrench into the dust, wiped his hands on a grease-stained rag, and, using the time-proven method of all mechanics, administered a sharp kick to the cover plate. Once again he turned on the motor and pulled the gear stick forward. Nothing.

"Hey mister, what time do you open?" Gregor turned to see a young boy, tow haired, baby-fat, his head poking through the wrought-iron fence as far as his rounded cheeks would permit. He reminded Gregor of his son. When Gregor had first come to America he had thought of his son all the time—of how much he loved the child; perhaps he shouldn't have left Hungary, but he had felt smothered in his homeland, and Marti, either out of fear or patriotism, had refused to follow him to America. Now, he realized to his shame that neither of them had crossed his mind for quite a long time. Without stopping to count, he wasn't even sure how old the child was. Perhaps he was not even a child any longer. He smiled at the boy.

"You come back, maybe four tirty," he said.

"How much are the rides, mister?" the child asked.

"You come back. I give you a free ride," Gregor said. The child looked to be full of questions, but before he could ask another, someone shouted, "Keith!" and the boy looked nervously over his shoulder and hurried off.

Gregor laughed and shook his head. He would look for the child later, see to it that he got his free ride. Maybe too, he would write to Marti. Would she be glad to hear from him, he wondered, after all these years?

The interlude had taken his mind off of the broken ride. Now he sneered at it, too tired and too distracted to give it any further time. He locked the gear stick back in place and went off to get some sleep.

2

Billingsly parked the silver Mercedes right in front of the main gates, making as ostentatious an entrance as he could. He knew that the guard on the front gate would have little clout, but such things were never wasted. He eyed the set-up with interest, ignoring the watchful gaze of the day man. When he had spotted what was sure to be the main office, he walked up to Jimbo and announced his business.

"Arthur Billingsly. I'd like to speak to the head honcho around here," he said.

"Sorry, Mr. Billingsly, the carnival won't be open until three or so. You can see Mr. Dandy then if you'd like," Jimbo said.

"Correction," Billingsly said in a very soft voice, "the carnival won't be opening at all unless I speak to Mr. Dandy *right now*."

Jimbo yawned and scratched his chest. "Wanna show me some credentials to back that up?" he asked. The fat man nodded toward the car, and two large men emerged from the back seat. Neither said a word. Their presence was all Billingsly usually required. Jimbo seemed unimpressed, but, the basic reason for the visit having been made clear, he pulled his walkie-talkie from his belt and depressed the button. "Yew Rog. See if Patch is awake. If he is, tell him there's a Mr. Billingsly here to see him. I think he's expected." Jimbo placed the radio across his knees and leaned his chair back against the fence, staring silently at the visitors until his machine called out to send them back. Jimbo unlatched the turnstile. "My man'll be here in a minute to show you the way."

Billingsly pushed through without waiting. "I know the way," he said.

Billingsly smiled. He had been fairly certain that Dandy would want to see him. True, he had never done business with the carnival before, but he knew that it wouldn't be terribly different from any of the other slightly shady operations that had moved onto his turf in the past. In fact, this one was going to be much, much easier, because this time it wasn't money he was after.

The motor home's door opened just as he got to it, and he found himself confronting a man dressed in nothing but jeans. He allowed Billingsly to pass, then shut the door before the bodyguards could enter.

"Not a good idea," Billingsly said. He opened the door and told his men to wait outside. Then he turned his attention back to Dandy. Actually, it quite suited him to have the men wait outside. This was a little chat that he wanted to have in private. "Mr. Dandy, I'm Arthur Billingsly." The fat man offered a manicured hand. Dandy held up both hands to show a can of beer in one and a lit cigarette in the other.

"Have a brew?" he asked. Billingsly declined.

"I don't know how things are done among you people, but it seems, sir, that you are invading my turf," Billingsly said, then he waited.

Dandy looked him up and down. "Well, the way things work among *us* people, Mr. Bullinzy, is that we don't invade anyone's turf. No, sir. What we do is kinda like rentin' a piece of the action. I think you'll find that we're very good tenants." He picked up an envelope from the desk and slapped it against his palm.

"In this case, Mr. Dandy, it's not money I'm interested in. In fact, you are in a position to do something for me that's worth quite a bit more to me than whatever is in that envelope." Even though Dandy remained poker-faced, the fat man could tell he'd surprised him. He outlined his idea to Dandy, suggesting that perhaps some suitably sweet looking young thing could be persuaded to show Mr. Redd around when he came to look over the carnival. "You get the job done right, and I guarantee you won't be sorry, but if it isn't done by midnight, you won't open tomorrow."

"'Scuse me, Mr. Billingsly, but it seems that you'd be in a better position to provide a girl for the job than we would. Our girls aren't hookers, they're dancers," Dandy said.

"In the first place, I'm not looking for a hooker. A little hand holding is all. But in the second place, there's a pretty good chance that he knows all of my girls. Somerset is a very small town. Besides, a hooker would be the last thing I'd want for this job. Now I know a man in your position knows quite a bit about the human condition. Psychology. A prig like our Mr. Redd would be a real sucker for someone sweet and innocent who may be on the verge of falling into the pit. It's the rescuer's syndrome." Billingsly smiled and walked over to the bar. "May I?" he asked, lifting a half-empty bottle of Johnny Walker. Dandy reached into the cabinet and pulled out a pair of glasses.

"Now let me get this straight. You want me to find a girl, a, uh… sweet young thing, as you put it, to show Mr. Redd around the carnival tonight, and you don't want me to have her seduce him? Just a little hand-holding, right? While some guy takes pictures without being seen." Dandy scratched his head.

"Oh, don't get me wrong. I would love to have photographs of the clean-living Mr. Redd in a compromising position, but I don't think you can do it. If you try, you'll lose him. However, I don't want to ruin the man. I simply want to shake the confidence certain of my associates have in his discretion and honesty. Remember, it has to be one of the dancers. Do you have someone who can fill the bill? Oh, and it's probably better if she doesn't know that they're being photographed either."

"Well, if all you want is what you said, I got someone who might do. Whether she can get him to hold hands, or even look romantic, is another kettle of fish. Suppose it don't work?" Dandy swilled his liquor and refilled his glass.

"You provide a girl who fits the description I gave you. Tell her whatever you want, but make sure she looks at him like she's going to melt. You do that, and you're off the hook whether it works or not. And now, Mr. Dandy, I've got to say it's been a pleasure doing business with you." Billingsly let himself out of the motor home before Dandy could ask him any more questions. The whole plan was a long shot, but it was the only plan he could come up with on such short notice. He had to make it seem like Redd had been bribed with some young pussy to let the carnival into Somerset. Now to find Gaylen Schuster. It was almost ten o'clock. He would have to hurry or he'd be late.

The Viking reached for Sam as she slept. He felt her hand on his thigh and gently removed it. She was not the woman he had been thinking of in the heat of the early morning. He reached up and grasped the tiny carved dragon that he always wore under his shirt. It seemed to comfort him. She had woken him from a very pleasant dream and he wanted, more than anything, to fall back into sleep, for in his dream, Thot had been alive.

He looked at the woman sleeping next to him, her chest rising and falling in the shallow breath of sleep, her long blonde hair splayed around her head like a corona. She was beautiful, but she wasn't Thot. Her sounds and scents, her shape and textures were all wrong. Thot had been a sweet and delicate flower; the Viking was a tall and stalwart tree. He had loved Thot.

The essence of sleep began to overtake him once again, and his dream took him back to the oppressive heat of the jungle, made bearable only by the woman by his side. Even in his sleep he clutched the carving. She had given him the dragon and told him that it would keep him safe. Why hadn't she kept it? Tears welled up behind his closed lids, and he blinked them back. He let go of the carving and pulled his hand away roughly. This was ridiculous. He had vowed that he would not live in the past. He reached for the Viking and began to make love to her with a hard and selfish passion. She responded with a pleasure that disgusted him. The worst of it was that he kept seeing her as Katie, but why would it be Katie he wanted to punish?

Finally, exhausted, he lay down by her side and wished that she would go away. He was too tired, too upset to deal with the kind of idle chit-chat that the Viking all too often brought to the morning.

"Oh, Sam, that was wonderful," she said rather automatically, as she brushed the curls back from his forehead. He grabbed her hand and pushed it away once again.

"Go make breakfast," he said.

Katie sat on the bumper of her '72 Chevy wagon—legs splayed, hair pulled back and hooked behind her ears—fanning herself with a piece of cardboard. Her thin cotton dress was soaked with sweat that ran like tears down the back of her neck and behind her knees. She had thought somehow that it would be better this far north. Instead, it was a swamp. Too hot to sleep, she was too tired to really be awake. Desultory was the word. Desultory. She ran it around her tongue, tasted it, tried it out loud. It reminded her of books read in high school. Books about antebellum life; about southern belles, their hair pulled up in dripping ringlets, their bodies cased in delicate gowns of beautiful pastel lace. Then she remembered that the word she wanted was sultry. Damn carnival. A bunch of ignorant hicks and she was becoming one of them. She hadn't read a book in over six months. And why? Just because Sam didn't like her to? *Katie, are you reading again? Jeezus, woman, every time I want you, you're off in some corner with a book shoved in your face.* or *You think you're so much smarter than everybody else just cause you read all the time.* What makes him so high and mighty? Lousy bastard! So busy pumping his new blonde bimbo that he wouldn't even notice if she spent her whole three days in Somerset in the public library. And the Viking thinking that screwing Sam made her so holy, as if she were the only one. Now this new thing. Giving Katie heat just because she wouldn't work the show as strong as the others. Since when was it any of the Viking's business how Katie worked? Who knew what kind of bug she was putting in Sam's ear about it? Bad enough he wouldn't be faithful—though she'd never minded much with Magda and Glory and most of the others—but now he was being a traitor, too.

Cinda walked past with Jennie on their way to the G-top. They waved and called a greeting. Katie waved back, then remembered that a moment before she had cursed all these people. She was so ashamed that tears sprang to her eyes. These were the people she loved. Cinda and Pritt, Essie and the rest; they were her family. It didn't matter whether they read or not or that their teeth were bad and their grammar worse. Who the hell was *she* to judge?

Lucinda was back and heading right toward her. Katie quickly brushed the tears away with the back of her hand, then covered the motion by running her fingers through her hair. She knew that the woman had seen her cry, knew too that she wouldn't ask about it unless invited to do so. She was a true carny, born into the business, bright, pretty—in a puffed up, country-singer sort of way—and as close-mouthed a woman as Katie had ever met.

"Honey, I brought you a present," Cinda said, holding up a small bit of bright blue plastic. "Just a piece of slum, but I thought you could use it. Look." She pressed the button, and two white arms flew out and began to rotate.

"Oh, it's a fan!" Katie said. She patted a space next to herself on the car hood, and Cinda bounced up beside her.

"You'll just make yourself hotter using that old thing," Cinda said. She picked up the square of cardboard and tossed it frisbee style across the lot. It just missed hitting the Viking, who had picked that moment to step out of Sam's trailer dressed in a brightly colored Japanese kimono. "Bitch!" Lucinda said softly.

"Morning, *ladies*," the Viking said as she passed the car.

"Don't worry," Cinda said to Katie. "Sheazeel be geazone seazoon." It was carny talk, a language all their own, and Cinda's way of saying that the Viking really wasn't one of them. Wouldn't ever be. "Too talkative and too damn snotty," Essie had said of her when she first joined up.

"Yeah, but when?" Katie asked as the Viking disappeared into the girls' trailer. Katie hopped down from the fender and did an imitation of the Viking's exaggerated gait, throwing her hips from side to side as she took each step. Lucinda laughed, and Katie laughed with her.

Sam stumbled out of his trailer, yawning, and scratched his side with a big hairy paw. "Big ape," Cinda said, making Katie laugh again.

"Donniker's all stuffed up," Sam excused himself as he rushed past the pair of them. Katie and Lucinda stared at each other, each with the same thought, barely able to restrain themselves until Sam was safely out of earshot.

"Been tellin' you for months that he's full of shit," Cinda giggled at last.

5

An uneaten egg sat congealing on the edge of Dandy's plate. No amount of staring at it could manage to make him hungry. Damn! This was the screwiest thing that he'd ever gotten himself involved in. Not that it would be a good idea to cross Billingsly. Carnies who crossed the local mob didn't stay in business very long. It might have been okay to refuse the deal in the first place, but Dandy was painfully aware that he hadn't done that. Why the hell hadn't he been content to hijack the show for money like everyone else? And how the hell was Dandy going to get Katie to go along with what he wanted her to do? He had talked it over with Essie, and she had given him an idea which she said would help both him and Katie. Dandy had his doubts, but he had to try something, and at least Essie promised to help if he did it her way.

Dandy spotted Sam Dollar running across the lot and rushed to the door of his office. "Hey, Sam, come here!" he called. "I need to talk to ya!"

Sam stopped and turned, a pained expression on his face. "Have a heart, Patch. I'm tryin' to get to the donniker," he said.

For the first time that morning, Dandy smiled. He shook his head, clicking his tongue against his teeth. "Use mine," he said at last.

"Okay, where's the fire," Sam called through the accordion pleated door of the office bathroom a few moments later.

"I need Katie for tonight," Dandy said. There was a silence. Dandy took two cans of beer from the mini-refrigerator, opened one and left the other ready on his desk. A moment later Sam burst out through the sliding door almost as eagerly as he had rushed in.

"Katie?" Sam asked. "What the hell for?" Dandy pushed the extra can of beer into Sam's hand.

"I need her to play hostess. Doin' some entertainin' tonight and I need her to show one of the bigwigs around." The patch found it amusing to watch his kootch show agent trying hard not to be jealous about a woman he claimed to have no interest in. Composure won. It was a studied and measured voice that came from Dollar's blankest poker face.

"It's not Katie you want. She's not good at that sort of thing, and besides, I can't spare her. She's too important to the show."

"It *is* Katie I want, and she's the only one you *can* spare. You let me worry about how to get her to do what I want. You just send her over." Dandy was enjoying Sam's discomfort.

"Tell ya what I'm gonna do," Sam said. He was smiling now. "I'm gonna let you have Magda for the evening! Maggie'll have your man smilin' in no time flat."

"Katie!" Dandy said emphatically. He was beginning to laugh.

"She won't do it," Sam warned.

"You let me worry about that. Just send her over, and I do mean now. Got me? Oh, and send Esmerelda over too, while you're at it." Sam nodded reluctantly. He chugged the remains of the beer and left. When he was gone, Dandy turned his ring three times and rubbed the stone for luck. This was going to be one of the trickiest con jobs that he had ever tried to pull off. He ran the patter through again in his head, trying to outguess any problems that might arise. He was going through it all for the third time when Katie and Essie knocked on the door.

"What's up, Doc?" Essie asked, sliding herself into the nook that served as Dandy's kitchen table. Katie squeezed in across from her.

"Katie, I got a job for you to do tonight. There's a fella comin' around, and I want you to show him around the lot. Sam's already said he can do without you for this show, so…"

Katie looked at him warily, but before she could answer, Essie stepped in. "Hey, Patch, what the hell are you gettin' her into? You ain't never asked any of us to do any… entertainin'."

"That's not the kind of entertainin' I had in mind. In fact, that's exactly why I picked Katie here. I don't even want her comin' on to the man. This guy, his name's Walter Redd, by the way, is king of the prigs. If I set Magda on him he'd slap a warrant on us in fifteen minutes for runnin' an indecent show."

Katie smiled. "Just show him around? That's all?"

"Yeah. Introduce him to people, let him win a stuffed teddy bear for his kids, give him a little inside dope on how the fire-eater and the magician do their act. That's it." He held his hand up in the air as if he were taking an oath.

"But ain't that askin' for trouble?" Essie said. Dandy looked daggers at her. She wasn't supposed to be fighting him… but no, she was on his side after all. "You know how Sam gets if she even looks at another man," she added.

"Yes, I know how Sam gets, and frankly I'm sick of it!" Katie broke in. "I can talk to whoever I want. It ain't none of Sam Dollar's business anyway. I'm a free agent!"

Essie leaned across the table and laid her hands on Katie's arm. Her voice was conspiratorial. "You know, I have a good idea how you can get back at that lousy so and so. Remember that talk we had the other day. Well, Sam makes a big fuss about you spendin' time with Gregor, but that's all. He ain't gonna do nothin' about it. That's because Sam thinks of Gregor as beneath him—you know, not worth the notice. But *this* guy is a politician, an educated man. An *important* man. If Sam thought there was anything between you and this Redd person... well, I bet he'd do something *then*."

"Hey, what are you two plannin' here? Didn't I say I didn't want no funny stuff goin' on?" Dandy said.

"Oh, stuff it. She don't have to sleep with the guy. All she has to do is look cow-eyes at him, and maybe take his arm when she walks him across the midway. Nothin' any lady wouldn't do. Sam's so jealous of Katie, his mind'll do the rest. Whaddya think, honey?"

"I don't know, Essie. I'm not sure I want Sam anymore," Katie said, then looked at her friend and smiled. "All right, so I do want him. But this is rather dangerous, don't you think. I mean, suppose Sam punches this poor guy out or something. He wouldn't even know what was goin' on."

Dandy smiled and said, "I ain't worried about Sam punchin' anybody out. Even Sam knows better than that. No matter how sore he might get, Redd is still one of the powers that be."

"And that's what makes it all the sweeter, Katie, cause no matter how mad he gets, he can't do diddlysquat about it!" Essie grinned smugly.

"But I still don't like it," Dandy sputtered. "This guy is a real prig, and I'm supposed to be showin' him what a clean, wholesome show I run, and now you want her to make a pass at him?"

"Slick as Katie is, he won't even notice anything. If there's anyone around here who knows how to be a lady, it's Katie. Why, I'd be willin' to bet that she could have everyone around here convinced she was marrying this Redd guy tomorrow, while at the same time this poor chump would be walkin' away thinkin' what a nice sweet girl she was."

Essie smiled and pointed at Katie. "Whaddya say, Katie? Take the advice of grandma Essie. You wait too long to reel Sam in, you're gonna lose him for good."

Katie sat back and bit her lip, and for a moment, Dandy was convinced that they had overplayed their hand. "Okay..." she said at last, "I'll try it."

"Just be careful," Dandy added, barely able to hide his smile until the women were out the door. Sonofabitch, if he hadn't gone and *done* it! His luck really *was* back in, for sure.

In a badly lit corner of Miller's Pharmacy—wedged in between the bottles of alcohol, rolls of bandage, a rack of Dr. Scholl's foot care products and various other medicinal potions—an old man opened a magazine and stared at the centerfold. She wasn't as good as the one they had last month. Her hair was blonde and short and her tits were too small. He liked the last one. She was a redhead. He had always liked redheads. He riffled through the pages, looking for some of the other beauties.

"Mr. Jefferson, you put that down. This isn't the public library," Carole McCluskey called to him from behind the fountain. He held up the picture, and cackled when she blushed. Now Carole had nice tits. He wondered how she would look laying across a tiger skin rug. She wasn't a redhead, though.

"Why don't you sit down and have your malted? I'm going to be leaving early today, and you know Joey doesn't make them thick enough for you.

"Leaving early? Why? Got a date?" His eyes twinkled.

"You're so bad, Mr. Jefferson. I sometimes wonder why Joella doesn't put you into a home!" Her voice was stern, but she smiled to let him know it was only a joke.

"Is that what you're planning for your father? Don't worry, you'll scare him to death with one of those boys you go out with long before he gets a chance to be this old. Now, where would you be going on a date this early in the day?"

Carole dished ice cream into the metal glass, added some milk, and put it on the mixer. "I don't have a date, not that it's any of your business. I'm having my hair done. I'm going to the carnival tonight with some of the girls."

"Carnival, huh? I didn't know there was a carnival. Know if they've got any hootchy-kootchy dancers?" he asked, only half teasing. She blushed again.

"I don't know what they have. I haven't been there yet. It's only just opening today," she said stiffly. She wiped down the chrome lid to the freezers, wrote out Mr. Jefferson's check, and placed it in front of him.

"It's only out at Morgan Field, if Darcy wants to take the kids." She felt the old man stiffen, and looked up. His face was white.

"The old Morgan place?" he whispered. "Your Mama lets you go out there?"

"Oh, Mr. Jefferson, that's just some old superstition. Just because someone died there once. Gosh, it was long before my *mother* was born. It's just a plain old empty field now, except for this weekend it's full of rides and cotton candy." She pulled the malted down from the mixer, pausing it under the blades to catch the last few drips, speared a cone-shaped paper cup in a silver holder, and poured the viscous liquid into it. She placed both the cup and container in front of the old man. "That'll be one and a half," she said. He picked up the check, pretending to study it for a moment, then pressed it into her hand along with three ones.

"That's for the rides. You have a good time, but be careful in the haunted house. Remember that fire they had in Jersey a little while ago," he said.

"Thanks, Mr. Jefferson," she said. She looked for a second as if she were going to kiss him, or maybe it was just wish-thinking, cause she took her apron off, threw it behind the counter, and shouted into the back room, "Mavis, I have to leave now and Joey's not here yet, so listen out for the customers, will you?" Jake wished that just this once Mavis would come out from the back room and wipe down the counter. He hadn't talked to her in quite a while. What a wonderful woman, and how scandalized the town had been when she decided to follow in her father's footsteps and become a pharmacist. Nowadays so many young women were taking up professions that everyone had forgotten how hard it had been in Mavis Miller's day. He watched Carole leave and wondered what sort of profession she would be studying for when she started college in the fall. Unusual nowadays for a girl that young to have the time to swap barbs with a man of his age.

So there was a carnival out at the old Morgan place... all life and lights and music. He wondered why he still felt uncomfortable about going there. Carol was right, it was just a—how had she put it—*just a place where someone had died in a fire a long time ago.* The kids would love a carnival, and so would Darcy. Besides, it was about time for him to bury that memory of Morgan's burning. It wasn't an easy one to live with. Strange that a sense of menace should persist around that place when there were only a few old codgers left like himself and Eli who had ever even seen the old bastard. He wished that Eli could put the whole thing behind him, but then, his brother had his own special reasons for remembering. And did this carnival have anything to do with the urgent summons from his brother to come have dinner tonight? Morgan's name was certain to come up. It would be good if he could finally get Eli to talk about it. Then, if Eli let him go early enough, he would take the family to the carnival.

Suddenly, his head ached. He took two aspirins with a long last rattling pull on the straw, and slid off the stool. The more he thought about it, the better the carnival sounded. Imagine himself and Joella and Darcy and the kids, four generations of Jeffersons all spinning around on the same Ferris Wheel… and on the lot where Werner Morgan's house had stood! The idea appealed to him. There was a certain cosmic justice to it. He waved to the back room just in case Mavis was looking, and tottered up the street to the dress shop.

"Hi, Milly," he said to the dark, heavy-set woman behind the register. "How's Reba?"

"Ma hasn't been doing too well lately, Jake, but I'll tell her you asked after her. She'll like that. She's very fond of you." She sighed and pulled her glasses off, tilting her head back to rub the bridge of her nose. Jake shook his head. Many years ago, his contemporaries had started dropping like flies, each death ushering in a major depression in his life, but now it was the kids who were starting to go, or the people he'd thought of as kids—though he realized that mid-sixties was hardly young by anyone's standards but his own. Reba had not even started school yet when Jake and Trish got married. He had known her since she was a baby. It was hard *not* to think of her as a kid; hard to think of her being old. Age was such a relative thing.

"Darcy's in the back. You go ahead back there if you want to talk to her," Milly said.

The old man pushed his way through a pair of heavy curtains to a back room littered with boxes and slips of paper where a woman in her early thirties was leaning over a desk. Her Claireled hair was cut mannishly short, and she was taking a quick series of short puffs on a cigarette, as if she were making an effort to get it all smoked in a very short time. He crept up behind her and threw his arms around her waist. "How's my Darcy?" he said.

"Granddad!" she shouted, turning to give him a hug, as if she hadn't seen him in months, instead of the night before. "Well, what on Earth brings you here?"

"Carnival's in town! What do you say you and Ron and Jo and the kids all go out there this evening? I can buy Noah and the twins some hot dogs and cotton candy and take them for a ride on the carousel and—"

"And watch them puke their guts out over everything," she finished for him. "Oh, Gran, I think we must both be getting a little senile, but it sounds like heaven. The trick is going to be convincing Mom." She gave him a gentle squeeze, and then her face darkened momentarily. So quickly was she all smiles again that Jacob wasn't completely sure he'd really seen anything. It was her next words that convinced him. "Oh, I don't think Ron's going to be able to make it. Some kind of meeting tonight or something," she said. "Tell you what. You go home and convince Mom, and I'll pick you up about seven thirty. Okay?"

"Well, I did promise your Uncle Eli that I'd have dinner with him tonight, but I should be ready by then. And if we're not done, I'll be very anxious to have an excuse to leave. Say, maybe if Ron's not going to be home, you could have Joella to your place for dinner, and we could simply kidnap her."

"That sounds even better. And if Mom refuses to go, we'll go without her. A date, like when I was little and you used to take me out."

Jake smiled. "You always made me take you down to the Big Boy's on Route 222 and buy you a hamburger, onion rings, and a chocolate malt. Do you remember, you made me sit through *Bambi* three times while you cried your eyes out?" She laughed, and Jake wagged a finger at her. "Don't laugh too hard, Darcy. You were the only date I was ever sure to get a goodnight kiss from."

"My handsome grandfather? I don't believe it for a minute."

"Well, I'll let you get back to work now. If I don't get home for my nap soon, Joella won't let me go anywhere. Thinks she's *my* parent." He waved good-bye, and let himself out of the store, pausing only a moment to chat with Milly. He didn't like the lines Darcy was getting around her mouth, the blue circles under her eyes, or these *meetings* that Ron had to go to all the time. He knew his granddaughter's husband pretty well. Knew her father-in-law, too. He had tried his best to keep her from marrying into that family, and probably only succeeded in making it twice as important to her. Well, he'd been forced to accept Ron, and so far the father-in-law hadn't been a problem, but Darcy wasn't hiding anything from his ancient eyes. At least for tonight, he could take her out and show her a good time. Take her mind off of things for a little bit. It was the least he could do.

7

Aggie stared stupidly at the wall across from her. Her mind refused to focus on anything. She became aware of this, pulled her mind into sharp focus, and suddenly found that she had been daydreaming again. It was the way she often woke after a night short on sleep. The banging of the trailer door echoed through her fog-bound brain like the kettle drum cannons of the *1812 Overture*. She had been meaning to do something about that door for quite a while.

Suddenly, her mind cleared, and she realized that someone had knocked on the door. "Just a minute," she called, and threw the top sheet on the floor. She was almost sound asleep again when she heard the second knock.

"Okay. Okay, I'm coming," she said, this time waking just enough to sit up in bed and throw a robe around her shoulders. The third knock was the charm, pulling her fully into wakefulness. She slid her feet into furry slippers, and walked to the door.

"Morning, Aunt Aggie," Jeff's cheerful face beamed up at her. She motioned him in with a wave of her arm. "Not doing too well this morning?" he asked. His smile was at once mocking and sympathetic, and she wondered how he managed that trick. It was one she would love to master herself.

"Feel like death warmed over," she croaked. She turned on the gas, lit the flame under her kettle, and reached her Mellita down from the shelf. "What brings you around so bright and early this morning?" she asked.

"Bright and early? It's half an hour to opening."

"Really? That late already? Christ. I shouldn't feel like this, then. I got almost a full night's sleep," Aggie said.

"I just wanted to see if you were doing all right. You didn't look so good last night." Jeff sat in the booth that surrounded her table. "I didn't think you'd still be asleep. Not this late."

"Well, you're right. I shouldn't be. I've got to earn a living, after all. I guess I should thank you." The kettle started to whistle, and Aggie made a pot of coffee. "Want some?" she asked, already having poured a cup for him.

"Cream and lots of sugar," the bozo said. "It's chilly today, and I have to be in the tank. In fact, the luck I've been having lately, Satchel Paige will be out there today." Aggie laughed at the mournful tone in his voice.

"You love to go into the tank and you know it. Gets the girls to feeling *very* sympathetic." She poured a cup for herself, and sat down opposite him. "I must have looked pretty bad last night for you to trouble yourself," she added, noting with relief that at least the terror of the day before seemed to be gone, and with it the violent headache. Somehow, it all seemed unreal in the clear morning air. She had made much too much of it. "Just a case of nerves," she said out of nowhere, but Jeff knew what she meant.

"It's okay. We all have them," Jeff said gently, patting her arm. He tasted the coffee, made a face, and added several spoonfuls of sugar on top of the three she'd already put in. "But you take care of yourself," he added, smiling. "We can't lose you. After all, I'd have to get married," he shuddered to emphasize what a dreadful fate that would be, "to get my morning coffee if you weren't here."

"Well, don't get used to it. I rarely even make it for myself." It was a lie. She knew that she would be glad to make coffee for this charming young man any time he wanted it. It was almost like having her Joey back home again. At least for the season. She smiled to let him know this, and he smiled back.

The mood obviously embarrassed him slightly, for he colored and looked away. He grabbed her cup and his own, and walked back to the propane stove. "Another?" he asked, turning the flame on under the kettle.

Aggie heard him scream. She saw a spark leap up from the burner like lightning; saw him shake and blacken, his eyes popping out of their sockets, his lips strained back from his teeth. She saw him fall. Fall dead into the water that bubbled and hissed and boiled around him. "No!" she shouted, thrusting herself out of the booth.

"All right, Aunt Aggie, I won't make you any. You don't have to get so excited," Jeff said calmly. There was nothing wrong. There was no lightning, no boiling water. His eyes and skin and smile were calm and normal. Still, her heart was pounding in her chest, and the air seemed ripe with the smell of burning flesh. "Is something wrong?" Jeff asked, looking at her anxiously.

She laughed. It was the awkward sound of forced laughter. "I guess not," she answered.

"Another attack of nerves?" Jeff asked.

"No, really, I'm all right. I just thought you burned yourself," she said, waving him back to his seat.

"Well, but it's just a little burn. Nothing serious, honestly. The kettle was hotter than I thought. Got any vitamin E? That should fix it right up." She gave him the bottle of capsules.

Her heart was beginning to slow down, and she could breathe more easily. Maybe it was just her nerves. Maybe she should skip the next town and go visit her kids for a few days. Dandy wouldn't mind. She could leave on Sunday, right after teardown. She smiled at Jeff, and saw the worried look leave his face. "So, tell me all about your plans for the winter," she said.

8

Mei ran up the narrow stairs, tears blurring her vision, still shouting at the woman below. "This is not the old country. I am an American. Here girls do not stay home on Friday nights to be slave labor at their parents' restaurants. Don't treat me like a baby. I'm sixteen years old! In this country, girls my age *do* go to carnivals. They meet people. They have a good time." She was shouting in English, and she knew that the woman she called Mother Chem would only understand one word in ten, but she couldn't bring herself to speak Vietnamese. She was an American. She spoke the American. Most of her friends had been born here. She had tried to make friends among the other refugee children, but most of them had made fun of her mixed breeding. Her father was an American. It didn't matter what her green card said, if her father was American, then she was American. She ran into the tiny room that she shared with her "sisters" and threw herself onto the bed.

She could not stop crying. Mother Chem had always been good to her, but there was no love there. Conflicting thoughts tore at her mind. True, the woman had adopted her when she was all alone, but that had simply made it easier for them both to relocate. True, she was given a place to stay and food to eat, but she was also forced to work long hours at the restaurant. Three other women in the house had children, and none of them worked as long or as hard as she did. No, Mother Chem did not love her. Nobody loved her. She began to cry again.

When she woke a little while later, the house was silent. Mother Chem must have taken the other children to the restaurant with her. Mei felt empty, as if someone had drained all the blood from her body; her mind was shrouded in fog. She knew that she should dress and hurry down to the Cafe before the evening rush, but she couldn't bring herself to do it. She slid off the bed and felt underneath it for the floorboard that was loose. Her own secret hiding place. Under the floor, in a velvet ring box, was something that was truly hers. It had been hers in the days before she met Mother Chem, the only thing she had brought with her to America on the long trip from the old country.

She opened the box and curled her fingers around the tiny carving. Her dragon. She did not have any idea where or how she had gotten it, she'd had it for as long as she could remember, but she had woven a legend around it in her mind. It had belonged to her mother. It was a talisman of protection, and her mother had given it to her, had given up her own protection for her child's sake, sacrificing her own life so that Mei Chou would be safe. And the child knew that so long as she carried it, she *would* be safe.

Mei Chou stole into Mother Chem's room and took a golden chain from the woman's drawer. She knew that this was stealing, that it was wrong, but she had stolen before for her own protection. Stealing didn't bother her if there was a good reason for it. Now she needed all the protection she could get, for she didn't think she would be returning.

Into her purse she put her green card, her social security card, her library card, and the twenty dollars she had managed to save out of her tips. She threaded the chain through the carving and hung it around her neck. Then she was ready.

It was too late to get a ride from Tanya, but perhaps she would meet her friend there. All she knew was that she had to go, and because she had to go, there would be a way to get there. Quietly, like the thief that she was, she stole out of the house, even though no one was home to see her go.

It was a five minute walk to Broad Street. Another five minutes until the cop car drove away from the newspaper stand across the street, then she stuck out her thumb. She had never hitchhiked before, but it didn't seem very hard. Almost immediately, a battered red Pinto pulled up, and the driver leaned out and asked her where she was headed.

"I'm going to the carnival in Somerset," she said nervously.

"That's quite a ways, little lady. Are you sure that's where you want to go?" he asked. She nodded. "I can get you as far as the expressway. After that, you're on your own."

9

The air in the G-top was a blue haze of smoke, and the pot on the table had grown to fairly large proportions. Dandy sighed in disgust as Pritt threw a full house on the table and swept the money away with a flashy gesture. "S'all for me, gentlemen," Dandy said. "Time to go to work." He had been the big winner for most of the afternoon, but part of the game was knowing when to quit. He pushed his chair away from the table, and smiled and nodded in response to the groans from some of the bigger losers.

Outside the tent, he was surprised to see that it was still daylight. Though he knew that it was still afternoon, it seemed as though he'd been sitting in there half the evening, leaving him with the feeling that it should be dark. He strolled the midway, noting that the crowd was fairly thin... but then it was only a little past opening. Most folks were getting ready for dinner. Yet even with this small a crowd on the lot, there was trouble brewing. He couldn't hear it, couldn't see it... he just *knew*. The same instinct made him reverse his direction, taking him back past the G-top and over toward the ten-in-one. "See the man so ugly that he dare not show his face in public! See Reptilia, the woman who can charm the spots right off the snake! Our sword swallower..." The pitch was going down as usual. He almost walked past, but some vague sound changed the direction he was headed, again before he even knew what he was doing.

Without hesitation, he pushed his way through the milling crowd, past the platform where Lord Donovan was holding up two nasty-looking swords for public view. He strode purposefully through the main area, which was divided with sheets of canvas so that the acts could appear one by one before a strolling audience, each booth equipped with its own little stage. He squeezed through the back flap and out into the screened-off area in the back where the performers were getting ready to put on a show.

Among the carnies, only the freaks do not venture into town. Not alone because of the hostility they might meet, but because to do so would be to give away free the only thing they had to sell. True freaks were a real rarity in the carnival circuit these days. You were much more likely to find a van with a geek inside, labeled "LSD baby", or "The Drug Generation".

Dandy was proud that Pritt had a real ten-in-one, instead of the poor substitutes found on so many lots today.

Randall the Gnarly Man could usually be found here catching a bit of fresh air, but even without him, right before a performance, the yard should be full of people getting their equipment together. It was empty. He followed the noise around to a small area on the side where Emma Mae's trailer was parked. Alone, of all the performers, Emma Mae could not leave her home. "Eight hundred pounds of feminine pulchritude" the brochure said, though five hundred would in truth be closer. She lived in an oversized truck that had been converted for her comfort. The ten-in-one was arranged around this so that the side opened up, creating a stage on which the fat lady could be viewed.

"Over here!" Pritt shouted as Dandy rounded the corner. "Emma's down and we can't get her back up again!" he said.

"Damn!" Dandy swore. "Get Sam!" he called to no one in particular, then pushed into the center of the throng to see what the situation was. Emma was laying by the bottom step of the ladder leading down from her truck. He couldn't tell if she had been going in or out when she fell, but she must have grabbed at the side of the tent, because she lay half in, half under a strip of canvas that was still partially attached to the tent.

"You hurt, Emma?" he asked.

"I don't know," she choked, trying to hold back the sobs. "I don't think so, but I can't get up!"

"We been tryin' to pull her to her feet," Pritt said, with a motion that included himself and Leroy. We need someone to get behind and push."

"Well, let me see what I can do," Dandy said. He knelt by the fat lady's shoulders. "You ready for us to try again, Emma Mae?" he asked.

"Let 'er rip," she said with slightly more control. Dandy was here now. Everything was going to be all right.

"Happened to the fat lady when I was with the Morgan Circus. We had to get a derrick to fix 'er up again," Pritt said.

"Okay, when I count three…" Dandy said. He had gotten to "two" when Sam ran into the enclosure. "Get over here, Dollar!" Dandy shouted. "Women are your department," he added with a wink.

"Not *all* the women," Pritt countered.

It took three tries before they had her on her feet. She was almost there the second time, but Pritt dropped the arm he was tugging, and Sam barely got out of the way in time to keep from being buried underneath her. They rested for a moment, then helped her back into the truck.

"Emma Mae, what in the world were you doing down here right before a show?" Dandy asked.

"Sorry, Mr. Dandy. I usually don't go out without someone to help me—but, I don't know. I just felt kinda… antsy. You know."

Dandy waved his hand, and began a quick fix-up on the tent.

"Mr. Dandy, can I talk to you a moment." This was Nancy, Shingo-Shango's bride of less than a year, who was breaking in a new act as Reptilia the Snake Handler.

She pointed at the snakes. "I been havin' a real problem with 'em all night. Last show I thought they was gonna kill me. I don't know what's got 'em so spooked, but… Shingo-Shango don't want me to go on to-night. Will it be okay to slough my act, Mr. Dandy? It's just for tonight."

"Darlin', you see Mr. Pretty Pictures over there. This here is his proposition. I don't run it for him. You go ask Pritt if it's okay. Got me?" Dandy shook his head and walked off, pushing his way through the crowd that was just being let into the tent.

Dandy made the rounds of the joints, collecting the privilege from each agent and shilling at the booths when it was called for.

"Nancy get a chance to talk with you?" Shingo-Shango whispered to him as he handed over the money.

"Damn it, Shingo-Shango, she's first of May, but *you* been around. You know I'm not the one she's suppose to talk to. I think Pritt's goin' to slough her for tonight, though. She couldn't get them snakes to settle down. She said 'somethin' spooked 'em."

Jim Dandy walked slowly down the midway, whistling. He bought a corn dog from Lutzy's grab joint, and stopped to watch Jennie win an armload of slum from her mother's store. Cinda played her perfectly, allowing her to win just enough to draw in a crowd, then sending her off to play the stick at somebody else's joint. Jennie was safe with the booty, which would be returned that night before she went to bed. Cinda then sold a set of rings to two of the marks waiting in line—rings just a trifle smaller than the ones that Jennie had been using—and walked outside the booth to talk with Dandy while they played.

"Take a look at that, Patch," she said, pointing to the rides across from her booth. She spoke in the carny lingo to keep it private from the marks.

"Damn thing's been goin' like that for twenty minutes. Ain't no one there. Gate's shut, too. Prob'ly the only reason some mark ain't been over there yellin' 'lawsuit' yet."

Dandy looked at the place where she pointed. One ride sat between the Bozo joint and the ten-in-one, lights off, busily spinning its black and empty cars with no one in attendance. He nodded to the Ring Toss agent, crossed the midway, and vaulted the waist-high fence that blocked the ride off from the public. He pulled the brake lever up and watched as the cars slowed, shook themselves, and finally came to a stop. That done, he reached down to shut off the main motor. It was already off. He took a closer look, pulling his hand back as if he were afraid of being bitten. It was off. What the hell had Gregor done to this machine? Dandy had never liked the damn thing anyway. Especially when it was folded up and looking like some giant insect with its legs curled up, dead and disgusting against the lighter black of the night sky.

"Tell Gregor I said, *in my office, now!*" he shouted to the ride boy who worked the nearby Zipper. He stalked off across the lot with his fists clenched and a tic working feverishly in his jaw.

A few moments later, Gregor was standing across from Dandy's desk, staring uneasily down at the carpet while Dandy read him the riot act. "I can't allow this sort of thing. You got a ride with a short in it and you just leave it sittin' there, unwatched, with the brake off, waitin' for someone to get hurt?"

"But I don't," Gregor said softly.

Dandy continued, ignoring the interruption. "One accident already this season. Lawsuits are bad enough, you want the Feds on our tail, checkin' me out? Oh, they'd love an excuse to come nosin' into my business. Word gets out that my rides ain't safe and we'll all be sloughed for the season. No work, no dough. You gonna carry us, Gregor?"

"Mr. Patch, listen, please. I check that ride out this morning. It don't work. I strip the motor. I check the wiring, the cables, everyting. She don't work. I can't find out what's wrong, she just don't work, so I turn the motor off and I clamp the brake back. How long do you know me? It's not possible that she starts by herself."

"Oh, it was runnin' alright. You saying somebody started it? I don't see how they could when the motor wasn't switched on. It had to be a short, and that means that you left the brake unclamped."

"I never leave the brake unclamped," Gregor said.

"Don't matter. I want it off the lot until you got it runnin' right, and I want it double-checked before you put it back on." Dandy watched him leave, and slammed his fist down on the desk. Damn son-of-a-bitchin' foreigner. He should have known better than to give him the concession, no matter what kind of reputation he had. Then the grifter laughed at himself. He was beginning to think just like Sam. Boy, what a bunch of shit he was going to have to listen to when Dollar got wind of this one. He looked at his watch and wondered where Katie was. Almost time for Redd to show up.

Eli scraped the dirty dishes and put them into his lap. With the ease of years of practice, he wheeled around until he was sideways to the sink and gently laid the stack of dishes inside.

"I'll do them if you like," Jake offered.

"Mrs. Duffy'll do them when she gets back. That's what I pay her for. You pour the coffee though, if you don't mind." He had put off the discussion all through dinner, and now there wasn't much time left until Darcy came to pick Jake up. "Let's take our coffee into the parlor. There's something I want to talk to you about," Eli said.

Jake put his coffee down on the table and snuggled himself into their mother's old overstuffed sofa. "You should see the pretty little girl that was handing out free samples on Station Street today. Cigarettes. I got four packs."

"When did you start to smoke again, Jake? I thought you gave that up years ago," Eli asked, absently.

"I don't," Jake said, and winked at his brother. "Got them for Darcy."

"Jake, I didn't invite you over just for company. There's something I need to talk to you about."

"Well, you'd better do it fast. Darcy'll be here before you know it," Jake said.

"Can't you call her? Tell her to come a little later? This is important."

"Hell, Eli, I wish you'd told me. I promised her I'd take her and the kids to the carnival tonight."

"A carnival? Now what kind of a place is that for a man your age? Where the hell is this carnival, anyway? And how come I never heard about it?" A carnival. Eli shook his head. Jake always had to rub it in... always had to let Eli know how spry he was. And the worst part was that Jake really *was* in remarkable shape for a man his age, but that thought didn't please Eli the way that it should. It was like that story about the man with the magic portrait in his attic, only Eli felt like *he* was the portrait. It wasn't fair. Yet sometimes he was certain that it was his own infirmity that allowed his brother to remain young. Eli sometimes wondered if, when his own death came, his brother would also crumble into ashes.

"It just opened tonight. I'll bet the whole town goes, even if it is at the old Mor…" Jake stopped talking, and looked down at the floor sheepishly. Eli jumped on his unspoken words.

"It's on the grounds of the old Morgan place, isn't it? The damn fools."

"Eli, don't get so wrought up." Jake said. "It's just an old empty lot. Nobody's lived there for over fifty years. You can't expect the whole world to stop cranking just because you got injured there."

Eli shook his head. Strange, those dreams coming just when people were about to start using the old place again. Maybe it wasn't just the bad nerves of an ancient and sickly man. Things were beginning to fall into place—and something was terribly wrong.

"It's not just that, you know. I went out there once. Just once. It was a long time ago, back when I had that nurse from Allentown—what was her name… Eva, Eva something-or-other. I made her take me there. Mostly because, like you, I couldn't believe what people were saying about the place. It was strange. It wasn't just the memories, I'm sure of that. There was a trace, just a trace of… something. The hairs stood up on the back of my neck. It was almost as if I could turn around and see *him* standing there. The lousy bastard." Eli sighed, and touched his brother's hand. "Jake, do you remember anything about the night I had my injury?"

"How the hell could I forget? Finding you like that, and the fire?"

"But before that, Jake. Do you remember what was happening before that?" Eli pushed.

"I remember visiting Morgan. I remember that you tried to kill us. I never did understand why. Still, you paid the price. You never would have fallen out the window if you hadn't set that fire, and you'd have died if I hadn't been there to help you." He sounded smug and incredibly self-righteous.

Eli banged his fist against the arm of his wheelchair. "But you must remember," he shouted, redfaced. "It didn't happen quite like that, Jake. It wasn't just jealousy. I had a reason for what I did. Don't you remember, Jake?" Jake looked at him as though he thought Eli had finally lost his mind. The old man took a deep breath and sipped his coffee. "Listen Jake," he went on in a calmer tone, "Please try to remember the way it was. He had some sort of control over you. Sometimes I think he still does."

"Werner Morgan's been dead over seventy years!" Jake shouted, "and I don't want to talk about him any more. Eli, I forgive you, if that's what you want to hear. I never understood why you tried to kill us, but I really do forgive you."

Eli shook his head sadly. "So, Morgan's been dead seventy years, has he? Oh hell, I know it sounds stupid, but I've been having these dreams. Nightmares really."

"Still? After all this time?" Jake asked.

"No. Actually, I used to have bad dreams right after the accident. Dreams where I could see the flames and feel the heat. I don't know if you remember me telling you, but one thing I know I never said to you is that you were in them. You were there in the room, surrounded by flames, and you were calling for me to help, but I couldn't stop running. Morgan was chasing me, his body engulfed in flames, but he wouldn't stop and he wouldn't die. They didn't even slow him down. He just kept coming and coming no matter how fast I ran. Oh, God, Jake, sometimes I used to dream that you had this smile on your face and you were calling to make me stop so that he could catch me."

"My God, Eli!" Jake reached out for his brother, and Eli took his hand.

"It's all right. That was a long time ago. I was jealous. I didn't think it was fair that I was the one who got hurt when it was you who... Anyway, I haven't had that dream in a long time. But just the last week, I started having a new dream, and it's worse than the dream I had before.

"It's a very surrealistic dream, and it starts out very nicely. I'm floating in a warm, dark place, and at first it's very pleasant, all solitary and restful. It's more like floating in a black sea. I can see myself quite plainly. Then suddenly, I hear a voice. It's his voice. Even after all these years, I still recognize it. He says, 'They're coming. I can feel them.', and I know that someone answers him, because I can feel the vibrations pass right through my body, but no sound comes to my ears. Then, there's a moan. 'But they're dancing on my very bones,' he cries. Another response from the unheard one, like lightning surrounding me, and my skeleton trembles. 'Yes, I understand. But I am prepared. I left my seed behind. Once I locate it, I can return. They will pay for this desecration.' Then, suddenly there's a scream. I feel hands, touching me, mauling me, and it's very cold. So cold that I can feel my skin get hard and waxy, as if I'm already dead. Then the hands leave me, but another vibration trembles through me, another unheard voice, and I'm floating again, though it isn't any warmer. 'You are right. That is not the one.' And I know that it's you that he seeks. I look for you, but you aren't there in the blackness. There's a scream, and suddenly I realize that it's me who is screaming. That's when I wake up." Eli swivelled the chair in a tight semi-circle until he was facing the window. "That's why it's to important for you to remember." A horn sounded outside, and Jake stood up.

"That's Darcy. Eli, I have to go. Please promise you'll have Mrs. Duffy call Dr. Grant."

"Jake, I know that you think I'm just a sick, crazy old man, but humor me, please. Don't go to that carnival. Don't go out to the Morgan place for any reason."

11

Katie showed up at Dandy's office at seven. Since the afternoon, she had waffled back and forth over whether she should go through with this silly idea to make Sam jealous, and had finally decided to play it by ear. She wasn't stupid. She knew that Patch and Essie had an ulterior motive in suggesting this scheme, but she trusted Essie not to manipulate her into doing anything that would hurt her. She suspected that Patch thought Sam would be more controllable if they were back together. That might be why he was doing this. Maybe he was right. Well, she would show this Redd person around, no matter what. She owed that much to all of them, and to herself, to show him that a hootchy-kootchy girl could also be a lady. Her hair was pulled back at the sides and pinned there with two silver barrettes that had belonged to her grandmother, so that the shiny, chestnut mass hung straight down her back. The dress she wore was a thin, sedate cotton in muted pastel plaid that revealed nothing while emphasizing a figure she was very proud of. She had just enough makeup on to enhance her own natural good looks. She was ready.

Dandy gave her the once-over at the door, then nodded and let her in. "Well, Katie, don't you look nice tonight. This here is Mr. Redd. I promised him a tour around the lot, and I've got so much to do that I'll be tied up here for hours. I was wonderin' if you would mind givin' him the tour, darlin'?"

She looked at Walter Redd, and knew him instantly with an accuracy that only the course in human nature that was the carnival could give her. He was married, with children, more than one, driving a small foreign car, a BMW or a Volvo, dying to get laid and disgusted by any woman who was easy enough to go to bed with him. Exactly the sort of man she had joined the carnival to get away from. And Dandy was right. He was just the sort that would make Sam wild with jealousy. She hoped the old bastard was watching. This was going to be the most fun she'd had all year.

"Why, I'd be delighted to show Mr. Redd around the midway... that is, if he doesn't mind," she said, offering her hand, then choosing a moment when he wasn't looking to shoot Dandy an okay sign. Walt took her hand like a pimply boy on his first date. Was he afraid that she'd lead him off into the depths of the midway and force him to commit some unnatural act? She disentangled her hand from his stranglehold, then took his hand again with a lighter grip, and led him out to the infield.

Sam was coming to the office just as Katie and Walt were going out. She paused to introduce them. "Mr. Redd—may I call you Walt?—this is Sam Dollar. I'm not sure exactly what it is that he does around here, but I'm sure that Mr. Dandy can fill you in if it's important," she said. Without giving Sam a chance to respond, she led her charge over to Lutzy's. "Give us a couple of pops, Lutzy," she said.

"That'll be one twenty," Lutzy said when he returned with the drinks. Katie looked up at Walter Redd expectantly. With a look of surprise on his face, he belatedly reached into his pocket for some change. Katie sat down on the long bench, almost empty in spite of the crowd, and stared off dreamily into space. Within seconds, Walt was sitting next to her.

"You're not at all what I expected," he said.

"What *did* you expect?" she asked, smiling.

"Not you. You're so... so... I don't know... different, I guess." He took a sip from his drink, looking very uncomfortable. "Whew! This stuff is really terrible. What *is* it?" Katie suppressed a giggle. Lutzy was quite a character. He had given her an orange pop. She looked at the carrot colored liquid that Walt was drinking.

"We call that stuff flookum," she said.

"For obvious reasons," he laughed. "Does anybody actually drink this stuff?" He set the still-full cup on the counter, and, standing up, offered Katie his hand. Then he turned slowly, as if taking it all in for the first time. "Gosh, I can't wait to bring Wally and Jessie here," he said.

"Your children?" she asked. There was a look of such tenderness in his eyes. It hadn't occurred to her that a man like Walter Redd would feel that way. She warmed toward him a little bit. "How old are they?"

"Walter Junior's ten. Jessica will be... let me see... eight next month. You know, it's funny, they're the most important things in my life, and yet it seems like I never get to spend any time with them. Alma's had them up to Dorney Park and the Allentown Fair and Great Adventure, but I've always had to work. In fact, I've never even gotten to ride a carousel with them. Makes you really stop and wonder what's important in life. Tomorrow, I think I'm going to play hooky for once. I'm going to bring those kids here myself. Carpe that old diem. I'll take them on all the rides and let them play any games they want, and they can eat cotton candy until they get sick." He turned to Katie, grinning, and looked suddenly much younger. She wondered why he hadn't brought them along tonight, but then this was official business, at least in his eyes. "You know, I love carnivals. Always have. There's something about a few rides and some calliope music that has the power of healing. Makes me feel like a kid again. Not you, I suppose. I guess you must get very tired of the place. It almost seems criminal."

"No, actually, it's kind of fun being out here like this," Katie said, amazed to find that she really meant it. "When you're around something all the time, you rarely ever stop to look at it. Besides, I don't get out here much while everything is going on. I usually have to work." There was an unwritten law in the carnival that showgirls didn't walk the midway, but she didn't see any reason to mention that. "In fact, I think it would be fun to take a couple of rides. That is, if *you* want to."

"You don't have to twist my arm," Walt said, staring off down the midway. "Race you to the Ferris Wheel."

12

Aggie ushered the mark out of the tent. Damn, there was a line waiting to get in. She had been hoping to take a break, but obviously it wouldn't be any time soon. She bowed the next sucker in, sat across the table from him, and took his proffered palm.

"Oh, a good, strong love line," she said with a smile. "You do well with the ladies." His embarrassed grin told her that she was right. "Though I do see several breaks. Not a one-woman man, eh?" She watched him for further clues, and told him of future conquests so various and manifold that Don Juan would have envied them. It didn't take a psychic to foretell that this one would give her an enormous tip when the reading was through.

"Now," she said, noting his time was almost up, "Let's take a look at your life line." She bent over his palm again. The light glared on his skin, making his lifeline appear to crawl and move over his hand. She turned the hand back and forth to get a clearer view, but the hand seemed to be wrapped in haze.

It was happening again. She wanted to scream, wanted to drop his hand, but found that she was unable to move. All at once she was seeing him, his hand curled into a fist. She could see the rock come down hard on his head, the explosion of blood that seeped down over his face, running along the sides of his nose and in the folds of his cheeks. Dazed and stunned, he stumbled across the carnival grounds, still reaching out to strike at anyone he passed. Again, someone hit him. He went down like a stone, landing in a heap on the carnival grounds, and lay there in a pool of his own blood, while people walked around or stepped over his bloody form. And all the while flames danced about in the background, reflected in his unseeing eyes, as he lay under the dead black sky. Flames! Here on the carnival grounds. And soon. Very soon.

The image faded as quickly as it had come, and she looked away, knowing the shock and confusion that showed on her face. "Go home—now!" she said. "Don't wait for your friends, don't wait for *anything*. Just leave!"

The mark laughed. "Good show you put on," he said. He reached in his pocket, took out several bills, and offered them to her. She pushed his hand away.

"No! I can't explain. Keep your money, but *please*, if you value your life, leave *now*!"

The mark winked at her. "Sure, Grandma," he said. "Anything you say." He was amused rather than scared. Obviously, he thought she was crazy. She wondered if he was right.

After he was gone, Aggie stayed in her seat, not yet ready to put on another show. Death was all around her. She could feel it... taste it in the very air. Death, and not just his death. Oh no.

Maybe she *was* going crazy. Maybe so, but still it frightened her. Something was coming. It was coming quickly, and it was close. Death, or maybe something worse than death.

It was almost here.

Part Four

SETTING THE GAFF

1

The battered blue station wagon pulled slowly onto the weed-choked lot and squeezed into a space that left little room to open the doors on the driver's side. "Pop-Pop, I want to go on the tilt-a-whirl," Alex shrieked as he slammed the rear door into the side of a well-polished, two-year-old Ford. He squeezed out of the car. Darcy, too, had to squeeze to get out. She had left much more room on the passenger side.

"Pop-Pop's gonna take us in the Haunted House first, aren't you, Pop-Pop?" Keith nudged. Joella laughed at the twins as she got out of the car and held the door for her father.

"All right you two, calm down," Jake Jefferson said with mock severity, sliding out of the car with the agility of a much younger man. "When we get over there, we'll see what they have, and then your mother and Grandma and I will help you decide what you want to do most. We can't do everything."

"But we'll sure try," Darcy said under her breath.

"I swear, Darcy, your grandfather thinks he's still in his twenties. Look at him," Joella said. "I'm afraid he's going to overdo."

"Oh, Mom, leave him alone. He's having a good time. I'm sure Pop's smart enough to know when he's tired." Darcy said.

"Oh, he'll know. But whether he'll let the children see is another matter. I'm tired just looking at him," Joella answered. Darcy watched her father, a twin holding either hand, trot across the street. As he reached the entrance booth, he suddenly came to a stop and let go of the twins' hands.

"Uh-oh! Now he's gone and done it." Joella began to walk faster to keep up with her father. Darcy hurried after her mother. Jake was leaning heavily on the turnstile, and even at a distance, Darcy could see he was white as a sheet. He seemed to be rubbing his leg.

"Dad! Dad, are you all right?" Joella called as they pushed their way through the entrance gate. His eyes were glazed over and at first, Darcy thought he hadn't heard, but he looked up after a moment, noticed her, and forced a sickly smile.

"I'm fine, Joella, just fine. It's only my past catching up with me. Sometimes I have trouble remembering that I'm not a youngster any more. Other than that, I feel fine. I promised the kids, and I always keep my promises. I'm going to ride every ride, and then catch me a look at some shameless women." But the life had gone out of his voice. He was putting on a front for the children. Darcy knew him well enough to know that he would never admit that he was tired. She resolved to make it a very short evening.

"Well, maybe you've got that kind of energy, but I'm not sure Mom and I do, so do me a favor and take it easy on a pair of old ladies, huh? Now, I've always been partial to Merry-go-rounds," Darcy said, hoping to keep the old man fairly quiet until they could convince him to go home.

"Aw Mom, the Merry-go-round is for babies." Noah said, tugging at her sleeve, "I want to ride on the Round-up."

"Come on, Slugger. I'll take you on the Round-up," Jake said. "Your mother can take the twins on the carousel." And before Darcy could protest, they had started off.

"Meet us at the refreshment stand," she called after them, and saw their heads dip in a way that seemed to mean they had heard her. When they got off of the Merry-go-round, Darcy scoured the lot with her eyes, but she couldn't locate her strays. The twins were pulling her in two different directions at once, and Joella was too busy looking for her father to take them off her hands. Finally, Darcy squatted down, put an arm around each of her twins, and whispered, "Let's go get some cotton candy, okay? We'll do some more rides later." She stood, taking one child with each hand. "Come on, Mom. Nothing to do now but wait for them at the refreshment stand. Pop will find us there eventually, and you can at least sit for a little while."

"Not many people here I know tonight," Joella said as they walked.

"Oh, Mom, folks in town are so plain ignorant. Alice Murray was in the shop today. Told me she wouldn't come out to Morgan's Field if they were giving away free money—'and neither would any self-respecting Christian'," Darcy mocked.

Joella snorted and looked down at the children, who were busily arguing about what ride they would go on next, paying no attention to the inexplicable gossip of the adults. "Like *she's* got room to be so high and mighty," Joella added.

"I don't understand it, Mom. It all seems so strange to me. I remember telling ghost stories about this place when I was a kid, but it always seemed a strange place to be afraid of. It's not like some spooky old house. It's just an empty lot. Did you ever know why people thought his place was haunted?"

"I don't think anybody really knows, Darcy. There were a couple of kids found dead here when I was a girl, but I don't think that could be it. The place had a reputation long before that. I remember once when I was a kid, I mentioned the place to Uncle Eli. I thought he was going to have a stroke right there on the spot. He told me never to come here."

"The old curmudgeon. Never took much to set him off," Darcy said.

"Don't talk about your uncle like that, Darcy. Lord knows the poor old man has enough to be curmudgeonly about, the old weasel. Besides, he was only trying to be helpful, in his own way. I mean, if he really thinks the place is haunted.

"Oh, Mom. How could a place be any better or worse than the people in it?"

"That's the way I feel. Still, it does kind of give me the creeps being here. You hear so many stories. I'll bet your grandfather could tell you something about it, but I doubt he will."

"Oh, he'd tell all right. And tell something different the next night, and the next. Pop loves nothing better than making up stories," Darcy laughed.

"Well, honey, it couldn't have been a very pleasant time for him, what with Uncle Eli's accident and all." Joella stopped talking and began to wave to someone across the midway. "Look! There goes someone we know. Isn't that the little McCluskey kid from the drug store? Who's that with her?"

"I don't know. Cute though. Hi, Carole," she called. Carole waved, then shrugged as the boy pulled her off in another direction. Darcy didn't mention the other familiar face she'd seen so far that night. Walter Redd had been waiting in line for the Sky Diver, and the woman with him wasn't Alma. She wondered if Redd's wife knew what he was up to. *Darcy Billingsly, that was unfair,* she told herself. The whole thing was probably perfectly innocent. Small town politicians do not parade their infidelities around at public carnivals. That was what God had made roadside motels for. But he had been holding the girl's hand.

It was the twins who spotted Pop-Pop first, jumping up and down with excitement and spraying food all over as they shouted his name. Noah had him by the hand, practically dragging him along; a reluctant puppy on a leash. Darcy was torn. Keith and Alex were so excited about the rides he'd promised them; the calm ones, like Ferris Wheel, Dodge 'Ems and Swings. Noah had his turn, and it didn't seem fair for the twins to miss theirs, they had so looked forward to it. On the other hand, she was genuinely worried about her grandfather, who, in spite of his protestations of good health, did not look like he was feeling very well. He seemed much more fragile than usual, and, even less normal for the sharp-as-a-tack old man, somewhat disoriented and confused. He took the matter out of her hand.

"We are not leaving, Darcy. Not until I've taken these boys on the rides I promised them. You can go if you want to. I'll find a way to get these hooligans home."

Darcy spit on a tissue and cleaned off the boys' faces. Then, with a sigh of resignation, she and Joella stood. "It's your show, Pop," Darcy said. "Where are we going?"

2

A car stopped by the edge of the road. It was a ten-year-old Chevy with a missing headlight and a rather large collection of dents. The driver was not much older than Mei Chou herself. His face was a virulent mask of acne, and his smile revealed bits of food caught between his teeth. He leaned toward the passenger window and winked. "Where ya goin', cutie?" he asked. She didn't like the way he looked at her, but he had been the first driver to stop in quite a while.

"I'm meeting a friend," she said softly. "There's a carnival in Somerset."

"A friend, huh? Is she cute? I like a good carnival. Sounds like fun. Hop in." She hesitated for just a moment. "Come on, get in, I'm not gonna hurt you." He leaned across the seat and opened the passenger door. She slid into the seat and looked around for the seat belt. "Not there," he said. "I have to remember to get it replaced one of these days." He turned to look at her as he pulled back onto the highway, which made her even more nervous. "Hi. My name's Vic, what's yours?"

"May," she said, giving the name her school friends called her.

"Maizie, huh? That's pretty. Well, tell me about this friend you're meeting. I got a friend who might like to meet her. What do you say?"

"Please don't call me Maizie. We must ask my friend if she wants to meet this boy first," she said. She was sitting squashed against the door to keep as far away from him as she could get. "Maybe she would like that," she said, afraid of what might happen if she said no. She stared out of the passenger window, determinedly not looking at the boy who had given her a ride. This was a stupid thing to do. She had lied to Mother Chem and stolen from her, she had accepted a lift from a strange boy, and now he was expecting to go to the carnival with her. She would be amazed if she even managed to live through the night, as stupid as she was being. She made an involuntary move to grab at the dragon under her shirt, then hurriedly pulled her hand away. Suppose he saw her? Suppose he thought there was something valuable under there? If he should force her to give it to him… If he should steal it… It was no more than she deserved, being a thief herself, but she wouldn't be able to stand it if she lost her dragon. It was the only thing she had that was really hers.

The car pulled off the highway onto a dark road lined with trees, and suddenly Mei Chou was terrified. She had never been with a boy before. Suppose he tried to kiss her? She did not want to kiss this boy; the thought made her gag. Then she had a worse thought. Suppose he was one of those awful men you read about in the paper, the ones they always used to explain why girls shouldn't hitch-hike. She pushed herself even harder against the door.

"Maizie, uh… May, you don't have to be afraid of me. Come on, sit over here," he said, patting the space between them on the seat. "Should be right around here, somewhere. Want a beer?" he asked, reaching into the back seat. His hand came back clutching a dripping can which he held out toward her. Afraid not to take it, she held it in her lap while it made a wet, cold stain on her pants. He reached back for another one, and popped the tab expertly with one hand. He took a sip and held it out to her. "Hold this for me, Babe, would you?" Beer splashed into her lap. Now that they were no longer going so fast, she was ready to open the door and bolt, but she had no idea where they were.

"You shouldn't drink that while you are driving," she spoke slowly, trying to keep the fear out of her voice.

"Cut me a break, babe. I can handle it. Ah, here we are," he said. Mei Chou looked up to see a huge double Ferris Wheel towering above the car; they swerved by the side of the fence and crossed the street to enter the parking lot.

As soon as the car stopped, Mei Chou opened the door and tore across the street. She did not look behind to see if the boy was following her. She reached the ticket window and fumbled in her purse with nervous, trembling fingers; finding only a five, she shifted her weight back and forth between her two feet while she waited for change. She could see Vic now, still in the parking lot, staring after her. Afraid that he might follow, she stuffed the change into her purse and turned to run.

She ran straight into a large man who was coming out through the entrance. The man turned to yell at her. Now embarrassment as well as fear goaded her, but now she could no longer run. Too many people, not enough space. She tore a ticket off the roll and waited in line at the first ride she came to, looking over her shoulder from time to time. No one was coming. Not yet. The line started to move. The double Ferris Wheel ground slowly around, emptying and filling a seat at a time. For minutes that felt like hours, she waited while the line pressed slowly on. Then it was her turn. She walked slowly forward and sat in the seat. Her eyes were still trained warily on the entrance. Finally, the man who ran the ride slammed the seat-bar closed, just as Vic entered the lot.

3

Sam pushed his way into Dandy's office and stood in the doorway, arms folded across his chest. "So, Patch. Wanna tell me how you got her to do it?"

"Well, I thought I was gonna have some trouble with her, but the minute she saw him, it was a piece of cake. They took to each other right away," Dandy said. Sam didn't like the smile on his face or the smug, cocky look in his eyes. Dandy was up to something.

"She would," Sam said, noncommitally. "What time can I expect to have her back tonight?" he asked.

"I don't think she'll be able to work tonight. Don't look so put out. You don't really need her. Just make sure that if she brings Redd around to meet the girls, they all know how to act, okay?"

"Yeah. Sure." He could hear Dandy's laughter behind him as he walked down the steps to the lot. What the hell was Patch cooking up now? Whatever it was, Sam Dollar didn't like it one bit.

Across the way, he could see Katie and her politician at the grab joint, laughing and talking, holding *hands*, for chrissake! He felt a familiar ache in his chest. Automatically, his hand reached up to touch the little dragon through the thin material of his T-shirt, and the pain slowly melted and fell away. Still, he felt restless, chained. He needed to get away, even for a little while. Away from the damn lights and music and the lousy smell of peanuts. Off somewhere where there weren't a million people every time you turned around. Without another thought for the lot, or the show he was supposed to open in just a few minutes, he turned and headed toward the turnstile. As he pushed his way through, a young oriental girl ran past, almost knocking him over, and he turned to yell at her. "Lousy kids! Why don't you watch where you're going?" Then he turned and pushed his way out onto the macadam.

For half an hour he walked, not knowing where he was going, not even caring. What the hell was wrong with that girl, sniffing up the leg of the first man to come by? It would be just like her to run off with some lousy, double-tongued politician. He could see her three years from now, pregnant, with a brat in each arm. She'd like that. Dressing up and going to la-de-dah functions where they sipped sherry and showed their teeth for the photographers. Well, good for her, and good riddance. What he didn't understand was what Patch had to gain in all of this. Jim Dandy would never have been able to manipulate Thot like that.

"You are in love, my little bear." Thot had said that to him on one of the few nights they had managed to grab together. She had been pregnant then, and they had been making plans for the day when his hitch was up and he could finally bring her home. Her and his baby. He tugged at the leather thong, pulling his little dragon out from underneath his T-shirt. He held it in his hand and stared at it for a long time. "You would never have left me," he heard himself say, but she *had* left him. She had gone off and died, and taken their baby with her. He stared at the dragon and tried to recall her face, but though memories of Thot were sharp, he found her face growing dim, merging with Katie's until the two women almost became one in his mind. "You are in love…" He heard it again, but this time it was Katie's voice, and it was mocking him.

No! I'm *not* in love. I'll never fall in love again. Never! But he knew it wasn't true. There had always been women in Sam's life. He had even missed a few of them when they left, but none had ever preyed on his mind like Katie. Not since Thot had he allowed a woman to lay any such claim on him. The question now was, what he was going to do about it? He knew how she felt about him; knew that he could have her if he wanted her, but damn it, he didn't want to be tied down. No house in the burbs with two point five children and a brand new foreign import in the garage for him. That was the one thing she wasn't going to do to him. Sam grabbed at the dragon and held it until his pulse rate slowed and his breath came easy once again.

Far off in the distance, he could see the double Ferris Wheel spinning wildly. Time to go back. After all, he was carny, and he had a show to do.

He had managed to walk almost a mile and still stay within a few blocks of the Carnival. This time, he took the direct route, walking with purpose. There were things he had to do before he could talk to Katie. What the hell was he going to say to the Viking?

On his way back to the lot, a handbill caught his eye. It was a standard carnival three-sheet.

THE JIM DANDY TRAVELING AMUSEMENT FAIR
PROUDLY PRESENTS
GOLGOTHA: PLACE OF SKULLS!

What the hell was it talking about? Had Patch taken on a new proposition without telling anyone? Couldn't be. They would have had to block out space for it. As it was, there wasn't room on that lot for a thin man on a pogo stick. Besides, the drawings on the card, all crudely-done skeletons and ghosts, seemed to indicate a haunted house or a dark ride. They already had Bluebeard's Castle. Did they really need another one? Dollar scratched his head and shrugged. Patch's worry, not his. He crumpled the paper and started to walk. If he didn't hurry, the girls would wind up starting without him. The way things had been going between them, he knew what trouble that might be.

4

Aggie put a "Be Back In Ten Minutes" sign outside her tent. It was time for her to take a break and long past. She had wanted to call Susan as soon as she got into town, but then, she hadn't counted on being up most of the night before, or on sleeping until it was time to open, nor on having Jeff drop by for coffee. More than once, she had regretted having a mobile phone installed in her trailer—everyone always seemed to have some emergency that couldn't be handled over a pay instrument, and at all hours of the night—but she didn't regret it tonight. If she was going to ditch the show for a couple of days to see her kids, she had to make arrangements. And she had to come up with an excuse that wouldn't scare the pants off them. "Nerves" just wasn't going to do. She knew that she was going to have to tell Susan everything eventually, if she wanted the child to help, but not over the phone.

The first thing she did was put on water for tea, then suddenly found herself straightening up the room. It didn't really need it. She decided to stop putting off the inevitable and make the call. She punched the numbers, complaining all the while about the eccentricities of mobile phone service. "Susan, it's your mother. I'm sorry about not getting in touch earlier, honey, but guess where we are? Philadelphia. Well, not exactly in Philadelphia, but a stone's throw away. How's everything on your end?"

"We're all fine here," Susan said. "Are you okay? You sound a little tired, Mom,"

"I am tired," she said, grateful to have an excuse provided for her. "It's those damn circus jumps. They get to me. I'm not as young as I used to be."

"Circus jump?" Susan asked.

"Oh, hon, just carnival slang. It's where you tear down one night and have to set up the next morning a couple hundred miles away. This was a particularly long one, that's all."

"Oh, Mom, I don't understand why you have to do this. Especially if it gets to you. I don't want to open up that old argument, I just want to remind you that if you need to quit… Listen, if you're going to be that close, why don't we come down to see you?"

Aggie sighed. It was more an explosion than a shout, catching herself by surprise, and she wondered why she felt so vehement about it. She had wanted to show off her family for a long time… but for some reason she couldn't fathom, she knew that she didn't want them down here. Not now. "No, darling, that won't be necessary. I'm coming up. As soon as the show folds on Sunday. I'm going to skip out for a few days and come see you. Can you put me up for that long?"

"You know there's nothing that Carl and I would like better," Susan said.

"You're sure? It won't be an imposition?"

"We have the extra room. I'll love it. And as for Carl, I think he only married me to get close to you. Come on up. Stay for a month or forever. We'd love to have you."

"You only say that because you know I won't. How about your brother? Have you seen him lately? Do you think he could spare some time for his gray-haired mother?"

"You stopped dying your hair? It was red the last time I looked. Joey's over here every day, just about, but I'm sure he can arrange to be difficult if he knows you're coming."

"Every day?" Aggie asked. "Really?"

"It's my job to see to it that he eats right. Oh, and Mom, he's got a new girl. She's adorable. I can't wait for you to meet her. She's the tiniest woman I've ever seen, but strong as an ox, and a real sweet kid. She's a nurse at Carl's hospital. And Mom, you'll be thrilled to know she's Jewish."

Now when did I ever care about that? Aggie wondered. "That's real nice. Can't wait 'til I meet her. Okay, Susan, this is costing me a fortune, and I'll be seeing you on Monday, so… Tell Carl I love him, and give the baby a kiss for me."

"Bye, Mom. Try to relax and don't work yourself so hard," Susan said before the line went dead. Aggie cradled the phone until a dial tone returned. It was good talking to Susan again, but she was sorry she had called. Now the child was going to worry about her. Aggie was no longer sure how much to tell her. Certainly, "tired" wouldn't do for long, and "nerves" wouldn't be much better, but then what else would you call it? She'd just been a little jumpy; oversensitive. No, that wasn't it. She'd actually *seen* things, smelled things that weren't there. Had hallucinations.

Hallucinations! God, how much worse it sounded when you put a name on it.

The whistle of the kettle brought her back to the present. She made a cup of tea and sat down to enjoy it. In spite of everything, it had been good to talk to Susan again. Just two more days until she would be with both of her children again. She missed them. They were great kids. When she had decided to go back on the circuit, they had been very supportive. Even Susan, who had her doubts, wound up being behind her in the end. Joey, with strange insight for a college kid, had known that she wouldn't be happy sitting at home collecting an annuity, even though it meant that he had to move into the dorm.

She slurped the last of her tea and tied her scarf back on her head. Now that was real proof that she needed a doctor. Here she sat, reminiscing about her children, when there was money to be won. "Must be Alzheimer's," she said. She started getting ready to go back to work when she realized that she really was tired. Maybe that was what was wrong with her. Hard to get enough sleep when you had to stay up 'til all hours, and it would be a while before she could get to bed tonight. She thought about all the lovely silver that would cross her palm that evening, and decided she would rather take a nap. She *was* getting old!

5

The Round-Up whirled around at a dizzying speed, pressing Walt and Katie back against the wire mesh of the ride. There was no need to hold on: centrifugal force wouldn't let them move if they tried. With his eyes closed, Walt could feel the movement, but it was more like lying on his back being swung from side to side. With them open, it was like standing inside a Mix-master. At last it was over. He was glad to be able to help Katie down onto solid ground, though his knees still felt a little wobbly. She seemed none the worse for wear.

"What now?" she asked. "We haven't done the Dodge 'Ems or the Zipper yet."

"I think I can pass for now," he said, then added, "Unless you really want to," hoping not to give his queasy stomach away. Thankfully, she shook her head. "Then why don't you show me around a little?"

"Sure, where would you like to start?" she asked.

They were standing in front of the Ring Toss, and Walt pointed at Lucinda. "We can start with this lovely lady, if you don't mind," he said.

"Lucinda Carger, I'd like you to meet Walter Redd. Show Walt how it's done, Cinda," Katie said with a wink.

"Well, Walt, there is a little trick to it. You have to throw the rings with a little back spin, kinda like the way you'd throw a frisbee. See what I mean?" she said, giving him a little demonstration. She handed him the regulation size rings and motioned for him to try. Three tries, three misses.

"Tougher than it looks," he said.

"That's okay, Walt, go again. I know you can do it." The cheapest prizes were on blocks small enough to be looped by even the smaller rings, if the mark had a good arm, while the best prizes, like the watches and jewelry, were on blocks so large and angled in such a way that none of the rings would go over when thrown from where the customer was standing, though the agent could place a ring over a block if he had to show the mark that he *could*. The regulation rings went over the better slum like the stuffed animals. Walt got one on the fifth try, and Cinda handed him stuffed dog. Redd started to give his prize to Katie, but she pushed his hand away.

"I'd only have to give it back to Cinda. Why don't you take it home to your kids? I'll bet Jessie would really love it." She smiled. "You know, now that you're in on the secret, there's a carnival rule. The next time you go to a carnival, you have to say 'with it' whenever you pass one of these booths, so they'll know not to let you play."

"'With it'? I'll remember that."

"Okay, now this is one of Maxie's joints," she said at the next booth over. "Maxie owns about four or five of the booths on the midway, and hires college students to run them during the summer."

"Wait a minute, I'm confused. I thought Mr. Dandy owned the carnival." He could tell immediately that it had been a stupid thing to say, but Katie smiled at him politely and began to explain.

"I used to think the same thing, Walt, but that's not what people mean when they talk about owning a carnival. All Patch and Jack Martin own is the name. Sometimes the owners will own some of the booths or rides, but it isn't necessary. Think of it as an office building renting space. Patch books the lots, sets up the dates, and gets the acts together. Then people like Cinda and Maxie rent space in his carnival, only it's called 'paying privilege' instead of renting space."

"And who is Patch?" Redd asked, feeling stupider by the minute.

"Sorry, that's carny talk. A kind of nickname. A patch is the person who runs interference. He patches things up when they go wrong. Say a mar... customer comes on the lot and he's had too much to drink. Suppose what he really wants is to make some trouble. Then, it would be the patch's job to take care of him. Or say one of our people go into town and the local folk don't like his face. Happens sometimes. If he gets arrested, then it's the patch who has to see about bail and trial dates and such." She carefully didn't mention that it was the patch's job to pay the squeeze to the local bigwigs. Either Walt knew that already, or he shouldn't be told. "It's unusual for an owner to be the patch. We may be the only show like that on the circuit. But that was what Mr. Dandy was before he acquired the show, so I guess he felt comfortable doing it this way."

"I see," he said, not really understanding.

"'I see,' said the blind man. It's okay. It took me a while to figure it all out, too."

"Did you hear the one about the restaurant on the moon?" he asked Katie as they strolled along. She shook her head. "Great food, no atmosphere." At first he thought she hadn't gotten the joke, but then she began to laugh.

"Why can't women judge distances?" she shot back at him. They exchanged one liners as she took him around from booth to booth. Walter gave in first.

"I give up, Katie," he laughed. "My side hurts too much to laugh any more and besides, I'm out of jokes."

"Come on, then. I'll introduce you to some of Pritt's people."

"Pritt?" he asked, half expecting another joke.

"Short for Pretty Pictures. You'll understand when you meet him," she said.

"Surely that's not his real name," Walt said. She answered stiffly, and he realized that there had been an edge of criticism in his tone.

"No, it's not. Now look, Walt. There's one thing you have to understand about carnies before I introduce you to anyone else. You must never ask a carny personal questions. Not even little ones. If he—or she— wants to tell you, that's fine. Now, some of these folk will tell you their whole life history if you give them half a chance, but you must never ask. It's considered bad manners, okay?" He nodded solemnly, feeling like a schoolboy who's just had his knuckles rapped by the teacher.

"What about you, Katie? Can I ask you?"

"Nothing to tell. Kathleen Hanlon's my real name. I grew up in Marblehead, just a little north of Boston. My folks had a little money, but that all went to my brother when they died. I majored in journalism at U of P, and went to work for a little paper in Georgia. Met up with the carnival when I was doing an article, and decided that it was better, any day, than punching a time clock. Been with it ever since. Capsule life history. Satisfied?"

"Does it ever bother you, what you do?" He hadn't meant to imply any moral outrage with the question, but he could see right away that she was offended.

"Hell no!" she said haughtily. "When Randy Bottoms gets up on that stage, honey, she feels real good about herself. And when I finish my act and I'm just plain Katie Hanlon... Hell, I feel good about myself then, too."

"Please, Katie. I didn't mean to imply... I only meant... Oh, hell, Katie, I'm sorry. I only meant that you seem so quiet and shy and really rather... I don't know... cultured."

"Whereas all strippers are loud and vulgar and cheap, right?" He was digging the grave even deeper. He bit his lip. They had at most a few hours together. The last thing in the world he wanted to do was make her angry. He knew the best thing he could possibly do was to go home and never even look at her again, but he couldn't bring himself to do it just yet. In all his years with Alma he had only cheated once, and that was a drunken one-night-stand, easily forgotten. But the feelings he was beginning to have for Katie were very dangerous and quite delightful. He wanted to hang onto them for just a little while, and now he had spoiled everything. He couldn't leave while she was mad.

"Now, Katie, I didn't mean it that way at all. Please don't be angry." He put his hand on her arm, caught her looking at his wedding band, and drew it back again. She smiled at him then, sweetly, sympathetically, almost as if she knew what he was thinking. He wanted desperately to kiss her, but he pushed the feeling back.

"It's okay," she said. "Come on. I'll show you around the ten-in-one."

6

"Dad, will you *please* stop pacing. You look like a caged cat," Ron Billingsly said to his father.

"Just working off some energy." Arthur Billingsly replied. "You know, even as we speak, my little business is in the process of expanding."

"The carnival? Nothing's going to happen there, is it? Darcy's there tonight. And the kids," Ron said. There was an edge of sudden panic in his voice.

"Darcy's there? Oh, good. When she gets home, you can ask her if she saw any members of the Junior Council there. I hear one of them has a new girlfriend." Billingsly broke into a chuckle that was half a cough, the butt of a half-smoked cigar hanging wetly between his fingers.

"But nothing's going to happen on the lot, is it?" Ron asked again, urgently.

"Nothing that will affect your wife and kids, though maybe they can be of some help… if they happen to be looking in the right direction." Billingsly looked at his son, and shook his head in disgust. "What do you think this is? Some sort of shoot-em-up or something? Do you think I'm Al Capone? I'm not sending a bunch of hoods over there with uzis to mow the good councilman down. I have a much subtler plan than that." Billingsly laid his cigar in the ash tray and started to laugh. "This time tomorrow, everyone in Somerset is going to know that our Mr. Redd is having an affair with one of the girls from the carnival. And we're going to have the pictures to back it up. Doesn't matter that there's no shots of them in bed together. Everyone knows what she does for a living. They'll fill in the blanks. Then, no matter what his legal position is, it's good bye Mr. Boy-scout. Who's going to believe his anti-smut campaign after that, huh?"

Ron's worried look slowly changed into a smile. "You're right. That is subtle. I'm not quite sure how it's going to get you the zoning, though."

"Oh, with Chips and Veransky on our side, and everyone believing that Redd has some personal axe to grind, I think we can manage, don't you?"

Noise and music from the bar suddenly spilled into Billingsly's office as Mary opened the door. "Mr. B., things are really quiet tonight and Rosa wanted to know if she could have the night off? She's got this fella she wants to see."

"Mary, when are you going to learn to knock?" He answered grumpily. "Okay, Rosa gets the night off. Hey! This guy isn't a customer, is he? I don't want her giving out any freebies."

"Nah. He doesn't even know what she does." Mary was the perfect picture of a floozy, jaw working away at a piece of gum, head just a fraction too high. She placed the back of a hand haughtily on one hip, blew Ron a kiss, then turned and walked through the door, shutting it behind her.

7

She was the prettiest girl there. He liked the way she laughed with her head thrown back, and that cynical twinkle in her eye. Jeff's hair was still a little damp from his last dunking, and he was painfully aware that he had to go back into the box in a couple of hours. Not much time to cut one girl from the herd and have her waiting for him when he came out. Now, at least, he knew which one he wanted.

He watched them get into line for the double Ferris Wheel. This was going to be easy. He pushed through to the front of the line, and spoke to the roughie on duty. The deal was easily made, at the cost to Jeff of two green pills. Now he waited until the girls reached the front of the line. He watched as the ride-boy directed the girls two by two into the seats. "But there's three of us," Jeff's blonde said.

"Sorry," the roughie told her. "Ain't safe for more than two gals to a seat. Take the next car" He swung the bar down and moved the seats along. When she was seated, Jeff popped in next to her as if he'd been standing behind her all along.

"Hello," he said as the bar swung down over their laps. "My name's Jeff. What's yours?"

"Carole," she said, without looking at him.

"You live around here?" he asked.

"Yeah. And you?" Her tone was stiff, and she turned around trying to spot her friends in the next car up.

"No. I'm with the carnival," Jeff said, as matter-of-factly as he could. It was his chief ammunition, but he had other tricks in the bag if this one didn't get her attention. He needn't have worried. Not only did she turn and look, but she flashed a terrific smile, and her eyes sparkled.

"With the carnival? Really?" she said. "Wow, that's terrific! What do you do?"

"Mostly, I take baths," he said, then noting her quizzical expression, he pointed out the Bozo Joint on their next downward swing. "I'll show you when we get off," he offered.

Carole looked excited, then hesitant. She looked up toward the car just ahead. "Well... I don't know," she said.

"Oh, they can come, too," Jeff said. After all, he could lose them later. The first part was to make her feel comfortable. "What is it that you do, Carole?"

"I work in a drug store. Not very exotic. Not like working for a carnival. It must be fun."

Was it fun? Sometimes yes, sometimes no, but he knew what she wanted to hear. "Sure, it's terrific. Much better than being in school, which is what I do in the winter."

"Oh, a college man," she said. He could see the rest of her tension melt away. Axe-murderers and rapists never went to college. She would feel safe with him now.

From the top of the double wheel, the whole town was visible. Jeff had Carole point out the sights while he romanticized about his job, leaving out the sleazier elements. It was a long ride. Much longer than the usual three minutes, because Jeff had arranged for it to be that way, but eventually the wheel slowed and started letting people off. They were the last car to be emptied, and Jeff thanked the ride-boy in front of Carole to give her an idea of his influence. It always paid to let them see how much more fun it was to see the carnival with a carny.

Once they had made their way back to the midway, Carole introduced him to her friends, who seemed too anxious to stick with them for his comfort. Easy to take care of. He knew that what they wanted was an inside tour. He took them first to the G-top, and had them wait while he went inside. It was fairly easy to locate the college kids when they weren't on duty. Horny bastards would be glad to find a couple of girls without having to handle the preliminaries. The deal was that once he introduced them, they were to split off as quickly as possible. He brought the fellows out and introduced them.

"Sharon and Barb, this is Luke and Stoney. Luke works over at the String Joint, and Stoney is a caller for the ten-in-one, what you ladies would call the freak show, I guess." By the time they reached the Bozo Joint, he was happy to note that they were comfortably alone.

"Well, well, well, look at that arm. You ain't gonna hit nothin' with that, Mister. Bet the most exercise you ever get is turning pages," the crudely painted clown called to a bookish little man who was throwing balls at the targets on the side of a cage. The clown was perched on a wooden slat that was suspended over a tank of water inside the cage.

Three throws for a dollar... three misses. "Go back to the library, Mister. I don't want anybody gettin' a hernia," Larry shouted from behind his bozo make-up. The mark bought another three balls. "Now follow the sound of my voice, fella. I don't want you throwing that into the crowd." The bars twanged as the first ball hit the side of the cage. The second one was right on target, hitting with a clang of bells. The platform split in half, dumping the bozo into the tank. He climbed back onto his perch again, dripping. "Whew, I needed that! Hot tonight. Nice accident, Mister. Bet you couldn't do it again in a thousand years," Larry goaded, but the mark, a big smile on his face, handed the last ball back to Maxie, who was agenting the pitch, and walked off down the midway.

"Well, Carole, this is what I have to do in about, oh, two more hours," he said, pointing at Larry. The crowd, happy to see someone else humiliated, as crowds often are, was laughing. Carole smiled and took Jeff's arm.

"It looks dangerous," she said proudly. "What do you do when it's cold out?"

"I wear a wet suit." He treated her to tales of the dangers of working the cage, some made up out of whole cloth and others basically true, while he walked her around the lot, going on the rides without having to wait in the lines or turn in tickets. She laughed a lot, in all the right places, and he really liked the way that her eyes shone, but it was getting close to work time and she showed no signs that she was ready to take a look at his trailer. "Look, let's go get a couple of cokes and talk about what you want to do," he said, in the vain hope of getting her alone.

8

For the fifteenth time in half a hour, Essie peeked out through the front flap of the tent. Where the hell was Sam? In all the years she'd known him, she'd never seen him miss a show. He always liked to stay close by in case he was needed. There were a couple of times in recent memory when that had turned out to be a good idea. Now he had not only missed a whole turn, but he was about to miss another one. She wondered if it had anything to do with their little scheme with Katie. She hoped so. The sooner Sam came to his senses, the better. The Viking was even more full of herself than usual, picking the moment when Sam was gone to turn on the juice. They weren't supposed to work that strong in this burg. Especially not with Mr. Junior Council strolling around the lot. Who knew when Katie would take it into her head to introduce him to the girls?

"I didn't take your Goddamned lipstick, bitch, but if you want mine you can have it!" Essie heard Glory's voice raised in anger. There was the sound of a chair falling over, followed by a scream. In a flash, Essie tore down the aisle and into the back. Her first reaction was to laugh. The Viking was sitting in the dust, all six feet of her, a bright, carmine X across her face. Essie suppressed her laughter and pushed Glory back.

"All right, both of you. You too, Glory. That'll be enough. Viking, we have a show to do in five minutes, so get that crap off your face. *Now!*"

"Essie, she's tryin' to get us all in trouble. I ain't goin' to jail on account of her," Glory said.

"Right. Viking, you want to serve lunch, get a job as a waitress. Tonight, it's a straight strip, got me? No pulling any stunts, no grabbing center stage. No bullshit. Just remember, Sam'll be back sometime, and I guarantee he won't like it."

"Got away with it, didn't I?" the Viking sneered. "You would too, if you weren't afraid to do your job the way you're supposed to. So you can just stop trying to push me around. I take my orders from Sam. Not you. Besides, I know what you're up to. You're just trying to get Sam back for your little friend. As if she could ever hold a real man."

Essie smiled and said nothing.

"What's all this about real men?" Sam asked as he walked in through the back flap. All of the dancers looked away. None of them spoke. "You know, I could hear you all the way down the damn midway. What happened to your face?" he asked the Viking, his tone softening. Her eyes squinted, and she looked over at Glory, who was sitting before a mirror, fixing her make-up without a care in the world.

"Someone bumped into me while I was putting my lipstick on," she answered prudently. Essie smiled. Maybe there was hope for her after all, but no... she was just too worried by what Essie had said to goad anyone into telling Sam about what she had done.

"Speaking of hearing things all the way down the midway, what was that?" Essie asked, as a piercing shriek echoed through the tent. Sam shrugged. "You'd think I'd be used to it by now, Sam, wouldn't you? Always somethin' noisy happening out there. Now, listen, Sam," Essie said softly, taking his arm. "Let them turn the tip without me tonight. You and I need to have a little talk."

"Damn it, Es. We're short one girl as it is," Sam answered.

"Not the show, Sam. Just the Bally. They can do that without me just fine." She led him over to the chair in front of the mirror, and waited patiently for the girls to go outside, but the Viking seemed reluctant to leave. She stood by the tent flap and looked as though she were about to say something.

"Viking, go to work," Sam said, his voice sounding tired and annoyed. The blonde reluctantly turned and left. When Essie heard the pitch begin, she started to speak.

"Sam, I've known you ever since you were old enough to walk. You're a good man, Sam Dollar, but sometimes you let your hormones get in the way of your good judgement. This girl just isn't carny, Sam. Never will be. You're gonna have to let her go."

Surprisingly, he gave in without a fight. "I know, Es. You're right. You usually are. It's just that I hate to just throw her out in the middle of nowhere. She's really not a bad kid. Just greedy. Give me a little time. I want to break it to her gently."

"Take your own sweet time. I just hope Katie's still there when you come to your senses," Essie threw in as a parting shot as she left to do her act.

# # #

Katie continued to chide him, shaking her head as she pulled him out of the ten-in-one. "...I cried because I had no shoes... Now you sound just like a mark. Don't feel sorry for Randall," Katie said. "That lovely lady in there with the long, black beard happens to be his wife. His disability has not only provided him with a pleasant way to make a living, it's provided him with friends who understand him better than any outsiders ever could."

"You don't think he would elect to be normal if he could?" Walt asked.

"What is normal, Mr. Redd?" Katie answered.

The politician shrugged. "Yesterday I would have answered that. Today... I'm not sure," Walter shot back, more because he knew it was what she wanted to hear than because he really believed it. Nothing she said would ever really convince him that he wasn't better off than Randall the Gnarly Man. The Bearded Lady might have a beautiful soul, but he wouldn't want her kissing him first thing in the morning. Now, Katie was another matter... but guilty images of Alma made him push that thought further back in his mind. "Okay, Miss Hanlon, you've made your point. Where to now?"

"How about a soda. No, a real soda this time, I promise," she said in response to his wary look. "I don't know about you, but I'm tired," she added. He followed her through the back of the enclosure and between two tents back onto the midway. It seemed far more crowded now than it had when they entered the ten-in-one. She took them back to Lutzy's, and this time saw to it that he received something drinkable.

"You know, we haven't done the Zipper yet, and I really want to try that," Walt said, pointing a little way down the lot. She turned, following his arm to see what he was pointing at, and stopped dead in her tracks, as if she'd just walked into a wall.

Against a flat black background, the dripping, blood-red letters read GOLGOTHA: PLACE OF SKULLS. In the center of the platform, almost two stories high, was the re-creation of a human skull; not the lurid, hokey design most of the carnival's signs and posters followed, but a gruesomely-realistic piece of work. It's mouth was open a distance of about six feet, and it was through this that the tracks for the ride's cars were laid. Those cars were also black with crimson seats, with a smaller version of the skull design painted on their sides. Four of them waited their turn in line on the platform. As soon as an empty car came through the spiderwebbing over the exit to bump gently into the car at the end of the line, the first car took off, mounting the short hill to the entrance with a rusty little rattle and disappearing into the gaping mouth. No passengers waited, no roughie stood by to take tickets; there was only the dim red glow from the tunnel entrance and the movement of the cars to let people know that the ride was indeed open.

"What... where?" Katie said. Walt was confused by her reaction. She looked truly frightened. He looked again at the ride and wondered if perhaps someone was supposed to be there taking tickets. He could understand why that might cause a reaction, but not the one she had just gone through.

"Katie, what's wrong? Is there anything I can help you with?" But she looked around, almost surprised to see him there. He could see that she was making an effort to pull herself together.

"Uh... no, nothing's wrong. That is, it's just something minor. Nothing you need to worry about." She took a deep breath and smiled, but he could tell that she was still troubled. "Why don't you wait right here for a moment and I'll take care of it, okay?"

"Well, all right, if you want me to. Maybe I'll take a ride while I wait," he said, teasing her. He had hoped that maybe he would get a laugh out of her, to calm her down.

"No!" she said with surprising force. "I mean... there's nobody there to take your ticket. That's one of the things I have to see Patch about. It's a little dangerous to leave a ride untended." She looked like she was going to cry. "Better yet, meet me at the kootch tent in about five minutes, will you?"

"Kootch tent?" he asked.

"The girly show, you know, where I work. I want to introduce you to the girls."

When she was finally out of sight, he walked over to the ride to get a closer look. What on Earth had upset her like that? No one to run it? That might be a little dangerous, but it certainly wasn't the only thing troubling her. She had been badly frightened. The ride seemed ordinary enough to him. A little tasteless perhaps in its choice of names, but she certainly must be used to tastelessness by now. He mounted the three wooden steps to the platform. They seemed to be in good repair. In fact, to his inexperienced eye, everything seemed quite new. He walked over to look into the tunnel, but all he could see was a vague hint of red light, and that looked fairly far off. It seemed a little warm near the entrance, and he wondered if she had seen smoke or some other tell-tale sign of a fire, but if that was the case, her reaction had been very odd indeed. He looked around the ride itself, but there was no evidence of smoke or flame. He sniffed the air, but the only aroma that assailed his nostrils was the oversweet scent of cotton candy and popcorn… overlayed with a trace of ozone.

A man stepped out of the exit and stood over near the row of cars. He was short and well-built, dressed all in black.

"Ticket, please," he said, holding out a gloved hand. His voice held a trace of some foreign accent.

"Is everything okay here?" Walt asked him.

"Everything," the man replied, "is exactly as it should be." Walt looked down the midway for Katie, but she was nowhere in sight. He knew that she would be angry at him for not listening, but his curiosity was peaked. Besides, there was someone in attendance now. He would like to be able to tell her that everything was fine, so that they could resume where they had left off. Anyway, she couldn't expect him just to sit there and wait. He pulled a ticket off the string she had handed him, and pressed it into the waiting palm. One last time he looked for Katie on the midway without success, then took a seat in the first car. Odd, how the metal bar snapped loudly across his knees without his having to touch it. He could feel his excitement mount as his car crested the little hill and began the long slide down the skeletal throat.

Part Five

THE BALLY

1

By the time the Ferris Wheel came to a stop, Mei Chou had relaxed. After all, he was only some pizza-faced kid from the sticks: what could he possibly do to her here, in front of all these people? Anyway, she couldn't see any trace of him now. Perhaps he had given up on her and gone home. She waited patiently as the ride moved and stopped, moved and stopped, emptying and filling the cars two and three people at a time. She had kept a sharp eye out for people she knew while she scanned the crowd for the boy, but she hadn't seen any of her school friends, either. The boy on the ride with her had made no attempt at conversation, and neither had she. Mei was content to leave it that way.

Finally her car was on the bottom, the lap bar was opened, and the ride boy put out his hand to help her down. She was glad to be back on the solid earth once again.

Her legs still a bit unsteady, she walked away from the Ferris Wheel. She moved along the narrow corridor with the jostling crowd, looking all around her for her friends, still keeping a wary eye out for Vic. Abruptly, she stopped dead in her tracks, as though turned to stone, barely noticing the people bumping into her as they squeezed past.

In front of an opened tent stood a huge, bear-like man, wearing jeans and a T-shirt. And he was wearing her dragon, on a chain around his neck! Her dragon! How did he get it? Somehow, he had stolen it! She stared at the big man in amazement, and then fury began to mount inside her. How could he steal her dragon? Her special dragon. Her mother had given it to her, and it was hers. She had managed to hold on to it through all the hungry times, and there were all those terrible things she did rather than part with it. She certainly wasn't going to lose it now.

"How dare you!" she screamed again, as she pushed through the tent flap, tears of frustration clouding her eyes. The man looked at her blankly as she rushed at him and tore at his dragon. He held her at arm's length, and she found that she was unable to hit anything but his wrist. He even managed to keep her from biting his hand. She tried with all her strength to do some damage to him, until despair and frustration got the best of her. She was crying in earnest now. "Please give it back to me. Please!" So much a habit was it for her to reach for her dragon whenever she was unhappy or in pain, that she did so now, unconsciously. And it was *there*! There it was, right there under her shirt, hanging on a chain, exactly where she had put it.

"Great, just what I need today, another lunatic. Would you mind telling me just what it is I supposedly took?" Sam asked, but she was already tugging on the stolen chain that held her precious property. She flipped the little carving out from inside her shirt, and looked back and forth between the two of them. She felt a sweat break out on her forehead and her knees began to buckle, but she managed to ease herself gently to the ground. Fortunately the ground was soft. Before she could push herself into a sitting position, the man was bending over her. "I'm okay," she started to tell him, but it was not her safety that seemed to concern him. He was looking intently at her dragon. Too weak and tired to fight any longer, she allowed him to examine it.

2

Dim blue light scattered through the darkness like luminescent clouds in the night sky. The chill, lifeless crust of the Earth opened like a hungry mouth and sucked all warmth and energy into its cold, black depths. For a long time, there was nothing, just the dizzy sensation of falling, whirling down, into the unknown emptiness. Then there was nothing at all. The eternal nothing of death. Suddenly there was a voice, lightning bright throughout the void.

"I must go now," it said.

"You are not ready yet," another voice answered, and this one was as deep and dark as the Earth itself.

"But I must go," the lightning said. "Can't you feel them? They are dancing on my very bones."

"Their time will come," the dark thunder replied. "They will be ashes. They will be clay. But you must wait. You have done all you can do, for now. Gather your strength. You do so even as we speak. Wait. If you do not wait, you will not be strong enough."

"Who among them can stop me?" the voice of fire asked, calm and arrogant.

"There is one. There is always one, if you go before you are ready. I cannot help you more than I have."

"And if I wait?"

"You will grow stronger."

"Too late. It has already begun." The lightning flashed brightly, and was gone.

Aggie sat bolt upright in bed, her body bathed in sweat, her pulse racing and her heart beating so hard it felt as if it would tear right out of her chest. For a moment, she had no idea where she was. In panic, she reached out and fumbled for a lamp. It took her trembling hands a while to find it.

With the light on, she could sit up, take a deep breath and try to relax. It was not the content of the dream that scared her. It made no sense to her at all. But the void had been so sinister, and the voices so cold and unearthly. It had almost been like listening to the devil himself.

Sounds of the carnival began to intrude on her consciousness, and she suddenly realized that it could not be the middle of the night, as she had first thought. The travel alarm clock showed that she had been asleep for less than half an hour. There was still lots of money to be won, if she could manage to go out and win it. Certainly, she wasn't going to get back to sleep any time soon. In fact, if she was going to have that dream again, she might never want to sleep at all. In its own way, it had been worse than the hallucinations. Worse than the odd things that had been happening to her for the last few days. There had been a sense of unreality about those other experiences, but this was so real that she could almost believe that she had been physically transported somewhere in her sleep. Probably all these things had the same cause, though. And it wasn't overwork and exhaustion, either. There was something really wrong. Something physical, she hoped; something curable. She'd read about chemical imbalances and the strange things they could do to your mind. She wasn't quite sure, but she thought doctors could do something about *them*.

Whatever it was, she wasn't going to become a burden on her children. She'd take a whole bottle of those little red pills before she'd let that happen. Somehow, the thought made her easier in her mind, as if it was important to know that there was a way out. Not that she'd ever seriously considered suicide, but she had always been aware that there were some things that were worse than death. Hell, when she was a kid, she'd thought being this age was one of them.

She straightened her costume and went back to the lot. Time to tell some young kid that he was going to burn like a flame and die gloriously.

3

The old man saw the ride before the kids pointed it out to him. He saw it, but he hadn't read the name. Then he noticed, and it hit him in his gut like a well-aimed blow from trained prize-fighter. *GOLGOTHA: PLACE OF SKULLS*. It was a blaspheme to give that name to an amusement ride, but it wasn't the blasphemy that bothered him. Jake had never been much of a churchgoer. Not even after Eli's accident, when he had prayed more than he ever had before or since. But that name… that horrible name. It had been the name that Morgan had called his house. The house that had stood right there on that very spot, all those long years ago.

Instinctively, Jake drew the children back. They could not be a part of this. He would get rid of them somehow. But how to get rid of them without having to go home himself. That wasn't going to be very easy. Joella and Darcy were watching him like a pair of birds nesting their young. He knew he hadn't been fooling them with his forced cheerfulness and pretended energy. Ever since he had first entered the lot he had felt every one of his eighty-five years. That frightened him more than anything. Not only the tiredness, which was happening more and more often of late, and which was unfortunately natural for a man of his age, but his leg was hurting. Why, he hadn't had any trouble with that leg since he was a little older than Noah. A little arthritis gave him twinges from time to time, but that was only natural. This was a different sort of pain. Strange that coming back here would make him relive that remembered injury of so long ago.

"Darcy, I'm going to sit this one out. Why don't you take the twins on the Dodge 'Em Cars. Joella, you can ride the Shooty-Shoots with Noah," he said. He didn't really believe it would work.

"Noah's perfectly capable of riding the Roller Coaster alone, Dad. I wouldn't ride that thing if Monty Hall gave me half a million to do it," Joella said. She pulled out a handkerchief and wiped her neck.

Jake forced a chuckle. "Now how am I going to sneak off to the girly show with you hanging around?" he asked.

"You don't need to go to no girly show, Pop," Darcy said. "The excitement would probably kill you."

"A fine way to talk to your grandfather," he answered, using mock anger to hide the true emotion. He watched Darcy cart the youngsters off while Noah, ticket tucked tightly in his sweaty fist, ran off in another direction. Joella seemed content just to sit and watch the passersby, but Jake knew his daughter. She would be disappointed if she didn't manage to pick up some little bit of gossip for the "girls" to cackle over at her next hen party. But then, he was sure she'd find something.

"Joella, I'm tired," he said, putting his newly developed plan into action.

Joella looked him up and down in surprise. He knew it was not a statement she expected to hear from him. "Doesn't surprise me," she said at last. "It's okay, we'll go home right after this ride."

"No, well, that's just the point. I don't want the kids to know. I don't want to spoil their good time. Tell you what… I'll just get a cab, and you can tell the kids I had to rest. Then you all can stay and have fun." He crossed his fingers behind his back. After careful deliberation, he had decided that this was the only way. If they took him home, he would have the devil's own time getting out of the house again, and there was no way they would ever leave without him. But if they thought he had already gone, if they weren't constantly keeping an eye on him, he could simply find a place to hide out until they left. They wouldn't stay long once he'd gone. He was sure of that. Then he'd be free to do whatever needed to be done.

"Dad, you're not going to catch a cab. How do you think we can play around at a carnival knowing that you don't feel well? It won't hurt the kids to think of someone else for a change. It'll do them good." She crammed her handkerchief back into her purse with a motion that seemed to say "and that settles that," but he didn't think it was settled.

"Well, in that case, I won't go," he said and started moving off in the direction that Noah had taken.

"Dad, you stop this right now!" Joella could be a drill sergeant, but Jake was tougher.

"Joella, I won't have you treating me like a child. If you won't let me go home by myself, then I'm going to have to stay, and that's that!" he said. He was amazed to hear himself talking that way to his daughter. Joella had always managed to bully him, but not tonight. This whole thing might just be a strange coincidence, probably was, but he couldn't simply ignore it. There was a feeling in his gut that told him something was wrong. No matter how silly it might seem, he wanted to be sure.

He wished there were some other way to get Joella and the kids out of here. He felt a little guilty about the aggravation he was giving her. Now she really would worry, it was so unlike him to act this way. Perhaps it would have been better to let them take him home and then sneak out and come back, but what was done was done.

Joella eyed him strangely for a moment, then heaved a sigh and said nothing.

"I'll tell you what. Since you're so worried about me, I'll go to Eli's. Then, if I should get taken deathly ill, Mrs. Duffy will be there to look after me. How's that?"

"It's your life, Dad. Do what you want," Joella said with a resigned sigh.

Jake had no idea where Darcy and the children were, but he had to take a chance that they wouldn't spot him. He walked toward the exit until he was sure that Joella's view was blocked by the crowds. Then, almost as if he had practiced all his life, he slipped quickly between two of the game booths. In the narrow lot, the booths were pushed almost up against the fence. The area in the back was a narrow tangle of cables and trash where Jake could walk the length of the lot with little chance that he would be seen by anyone. Here he rested for a moment, leaning up against the fence. That overwhelming rush of fatigue was gone, erased by adrenaline. He made his way to the rear of the lot until, blocked by the side of a tent, he could go no farther. From this vantage point, he could see nothing but the sides of the booth and tent that surrounded him and the massive crowds moving on the lot. But he could hear the voice of the barker announcing a show to the tinny sound of an ancient record once the rage with his granddaughter's generation.

"Lookey, lookey, lookey! Ain't she sweet, fellas? This is nothing to what you'll see inside! This is no show for the family. Only red-blooded men need apply. She's gonna move it like you never saw it moved before, so step up, boys..." Jake moved around the front of the tent to get a better look at the offering. An hour ago, he would have been pleased just to sit here and watch that tall blonde grind, but right now he was too wrapped up in the business at hand. Still, it was a good place to hide out until the kids left. If he was never sure of anything else, they certainly wouldn't be walking into this place. He merged into the crowd, careful not to draw attention to himself as he bought a ticket and waited in line to get inside.

4

Katie knocked on the door to Dandy's office, waited, and knocked again. She was just about to turn and leave when the door opened. "Where's the baby you're supposed to be sittin'," Dandy asked, punctuating the sentence with an arched eyebrow and an amused smile.

"He'll keep. *This* is important," she said, pushing past him into the interior of the Winnebago. "Someone's gone and left a ride untended again."

His expression changed immediately to one of concern. "Which ride?" he asked.

"It's the new one. The dark ride—which, by the way, is going to cause you a lot more trouble than you bargained for."

"What the hell are you talking about, Katie?" Dandy asked, looking at her as if she had lost her mind.

"That new ride on the lot. The one with the biblical name, not Noah's Ark… damn," she chewed at a thumbnail. "Golgotha: place of skulls." That was it. "Hell of a name for a dark ride."

"Katie, you been hittin' them pills of Pritt's," Dandy said. "I ain't put no new ride on the midway since the beginnin' of the season." Katie stopped dead and stared at him, her mouth hanging open, then decided he was pulling her leg. It would be just like him to do that.

"Well, whoever put it there, the cars are running and nobody's watching it," she said, sidestepping the issue.

Dandy shook his head and rolled his eyes up. "Okay, Princess. Show me what you're talkin' about."

Katie led him across the lot to a spot between the Bozo cage and the ten-in-one, where, for the second time that day, an untended ride was going through its paces, one car at a time. It was unlit, save for the red glow emanating from the skeletal mouth, but it was plainly visible in the light from the rides across the way. Katie had expected Dandy's usual attitude of cool amusement, or perhaps one of concern about the potential danger, but she hadn't expected the look of dumbfounded astonishment on his face when she pointed out the ride.

"Now how the hell did that get here?" he said, and his voice was so harsh that for once Katie believed that he had not known about the ride.

The thought frightened her. Who would put up a ride in the carnival without permission? How could they do it? "Katie, go cover the Bozo for a minute. I want to have a word with Maxie."

Katie halfheartedly took the tendered dollar bills and handed out balls to the marks that Larry was insulting, but her concentration was on the two men over by the dark ride. Between the crowd noise and the bozo's catcalls, she could not make out a word that they were saying, but the longer they talked, the redder Dandy's face got, and the more Maxie shook his head. Then it was over. Maxie slowly walked back to his proposition while Dandy ran across the lot shouting, "Get someone over here to close this damn thing down. And I do mean pronto!"

"What's going on?" Katie asked Maxie in the carny lingo.

"I don't know. I ain't had time to piss, let alone watch the lot for him." Maxie muttered as he took the bills from her hand. "What does he think this is? That's his job."

"But how could somebody move the joint without you seeing them, Maxie?" Katie asked.

"Nobody moved me. That much I do know. Been here all night and I din't see nothin' unusual. That stupid Spider 'us there this mornin', but the roughies moved that to the back earlier. That left a pretty big hole. Musta been more room there than he thought's all."

Katie started to question him further, but the Bozo agent was already back at work, so she walked back to the untended ride. A chair made its tortuous way from the exit, its wheels shrieking against the metal rails, to land with a loud smack into the back of the line. With a hideous groan, the first chair began to move, and the others all banged their way up one place. As a dark ride, it would be very effective. Just looking at it sent shivers up her spine. She couldn't believe that Walter had wanted her to ride it.

Walter! She had promised to be right back, and it had been at least half an hour. She hoped that he would still be waiting for her.

5

Sam Dollar held firmly on to the dragon, and looked up at the girl who wore it. Her face displayed an expression that might have been embarrassment at her mistake, but there was something else there, too. She looked back and forth between the two dragons, as if unable to believe that they weren't the same. On close inspection, it was easy to see that they were not *quite* the same. They were posed in slightly different positions, and hers had a light discoloration on the side that looked like a trick of the shadows until it was moved into the light. Still, there was something so similar about them that Sam was convinced that they were carved by the same hand. He remembered the night Thot gave him the carving, a tender smile on her face and the gentle swell of her pregnancy pushing against his chest. "There, my soldier," she said as she tied the leather thong around his neck. "My father carved this. It is for good luck. It will keep you safe." She tucked the dragon into his shirt, and kissed the top of his head. He had protested that she should keep it, but she only laughed. "Why would I need it when I have you. See this?" she said, holding up another carving. "This one is for him." She rubbed her belly.

"Where did you get this?" he asked, pulling the child close with the chain, but the child no longer seemed frightened. There was a look of excitement in her eyes, and she smiled up at him. Sam wasn't sure why that made him uneasy.

"My father," she said, almost reverently.

Sam was startled. Anger boiled up in him, so deeply that he was afraid of what he might do. He dropped the dragon and walked away. "My daughter is dead," he said at last, his emotions barely in check. "Wanna see proof? I can show it to ya." He moved forward menacingly. "She's dead... and this," he grabbed the girl's dragon once again, "it's hers. Where did you get it?" He yanked at the carving, breaking the gold chain. The child cried out in pain, but Sam didn't care. She was a thief and a liar. "Did you steal it?" He waited for a response, but she merely stared at him wide-eyed. "Well?"

"It was my mother's," the girl said. He could see that she was terrified, but what happened to the little bitch was no concern of his.

"Your mother's?" he asked in astonishment. "And just who was that? Do you even know? Some Saigon whore? Huh… huh? And where did she get it? Some john give it to her? Oh, never mind. Just get out of here!"

The child reached down and picked up the chain, but she didn't leave. There were tears in her eyes while she looked at him. "Give me my dragon," she said, thrusting out her hand. It was shaking.

"Get out. Now!" he said, his voice gone dangerously soft, and he raised his arm as if he was about to hit her. She threw the broken chain at his face and ran out through the flap.

Sam shook his head, wondering what the girl had been up to. But the image of the girl stayed with him. Her lantern jaw and thin lips, the aquiline nose that looked rather strange seated between the epicanthic folds of her eyes. The same nose he saw every time he shaved.

No, that was a trap. Mei was dead. He knew that she was dead. He hadn't wanted to believe it, and it had taken a lot to convince him, but he had seen the report with his own eyes. So this little bitch had the dragon. So what? Anyone could have looted the rubble that had been all that was left of the village after the raid. Nothing was sacred in that God-forsaken hole. And if the girl happened to look a little like him, hell… he had a common face. *She* was some other ex-GI's problem.

He heard the sound of footsteps, and tucked the dragon into his pocket just in time to have it hidden when the Viking walked in through the curtain. She had not a stitch on, and she slinked about the back room as if she were still on the stage, but he found the performance more annoying than erotic.

"Oh boy, was I good tonight!" she said.

"You're supposed to work in a G in this burg," he said, his voice flat and emotionless. He picked up her robe from the back of a chair, and threw it at her. She seemed surprised. Sam reflected that it would be just like her to think that the mere sight of her body would have him too aroused to yell at her. The thought made him laugh. It was not a pleasant laugh. He watched her expression turn to one of anger, and he was all set to counter the barrage when Essie interrupted.

"What the hell was all that noise? Some kinda rube goin' on here?" Essie asked. She was putting her bra back on as she came through the curtain, Magda and Glory tight on her heels. All were topless, sweat-shined from their labor, and all wearing their g-strings. "You won't forget our talk?" Essie whispered as she passed him, her eyes riveted on the Viking.

"Oh, all of you, go take a break!" Sam roared. A raised voice from the usually soft-spoken Sam was enough to make the girls all grab their robes and flee. Nobody argued with him when he was in a bad mood. At least, no one who knew him.

Women! He was sick of all of them, big and little. He reached up and clutched at his dragon, but the still-sharp memory of the girl was all it brought to mind. Angrier than ever, he ripped it off, ignoring the huge welt the parting leather had raised on the back of his neck. "Damn," he shouted, and threw it across the tent.

6

Dandy ran around to the back of the ride muttering a string of curses under his breath. He had never heard of such a thing. Rides occasionally disappeared from the lot without anyone being notified, but appearing out of the blue? To his knowledge, it had never happened before. And what the hell was he supposed to do about it? Pick it up and move it? It would have to be a dark ride, and a rather heavy one at that. He found the rear access door and tried it, but of course it was firmly locked. He pressed his ear against the door. Many sounds, vague and jumbled together, could be faintly heard through the thin plywood. He could make out the scraping of metal on metal as the cars groaned their way along the track. He could hear what he thought might be scream, but whether it was a part of the act or some marks enjoying the show, he couldn't tell. He could also hear something that sounded vaguely like laughter.

Through the crack in the door he could see what was holding the door closed. It was either a very thin bolt or a hook and eye latch. Just in case it was the latter, he slipped his knife open and slid it through the crack. The results were unproductive, and he made his way back to the front of the ride.

Maxie was fumbling with the wires, searching for the plug that would shut the ride down. "Hold that a minute, Maxie," Dandy called. "I want to check inside. Make sure we aren't locking anyone in there. You stay here and ferkrissake, don't let anyone in."

"Don't take too long, Patch. Nobody's mindin' the store," Maxie said, pointing at the untended Bozo joint. Dandy mounted the platform and made for the entrance. It was warm inside. He could feel pulsing waves of warmth from the interior, as though someone had turned the heat up too high. There was nothing much to see. The dark was broken only by a dim red light which seemed to be some distance away, and his eyes could follow the track only a past the door. There didn't seem to be much of a walkway. Dangerous. He entered the gaping mouth and walked carefully down the long descending grade.

A little way in, he passed through some slimy webbing that felt almost like the real thing. His skin seemed to shrink from its touch. He had never paid much attention to the rides, but he was sure that the clumsy effects in Bluebeard's Castle were nothing like this. Farther on, the floor leveled off. He came to a tiny alcove covered with some sort of gauzy material. Behind the gauze, a demon was illuminated in dull green light. The tracks screamed. A chair began the rickety descent into the ride. Dandy ducked into the alcove to let the chair go by. On a rickety track of its own, the demon moved forward and began a series of complicated movements so realistic that Dandy had to touch it to satisfy himself that it was just a machine.

More alcoves littered the way, each inhabited by its own strange creature. One large smoke-breathing dragon prompted the carney to wonder how much the ride cost in terms of gasoline for the generators. He couldn't feel the breeze of an air filtration system, but the place seemed well enough ventilated that the smoke didn't hang in the air, though he could smell it distinctly. It was an odd illusion that the floor seemed to be steadily sloping downwards, though the drop from the entrance platform to the ground couldn't be more than six feet. He knew that it could be done in the way that the walls were decorated and the slant on the platforms of each alcove.

Finally he found himself in a cul-de-sac. The tracks entered, did a little loop and exited under the wall. If he stared at the wall long enough, he could just begin to make out the crack between the double doors that opened to admit the chair. To one side was a sign that read PLEASE DISEMBARK HERE, but there seemed to be nowhere to go. The heat was oppressive, and his mouth was beginning to feel dry. More than anything, he wished he had brought his bottle. Things were very queer. One good, long drink would go down pretty well about now. He pushed at the double doors, but they refused to open to his touch. Then, just as he was about to give up and start heading back, he heard the approach of a chair. It ambled slowly into the chamber, slid half-way around the loop, and came to a stop. The sign lit up, and beneath it a door slid silently open. "You will please step carefully out of the car now," a deep bass voice rumbled softly from the chair itself. "We will now begin the walking tour of *Golgotha: Place of Skulls*." The voice faded out into mad, Hollywood-villain laughter as the chair rumbled away through the double doors. Dandy laughed. Not bad for a two-bit carnival. He turned and walked through the door that had opened behind him.

Almost immediately, the door slid shut. The walls lit up, and red flames crackled around him. Hell, he could smell the sulphur. Also, he could feel that the room was moving; moving so slowly that he couldn't tell if it was going up or down. Then the fire died down to a mere ember. Just before the door opened, the room went dark; then Dandy stepped out of the elevator into a place so bright it took his eyes a moment to adjust.

He seemed to be standing on a catwalk that extended from rock face to cliff wall miles above a distant barren plane. He was inured to heights, working as easily at the top of the Ferris Wheel or Roller Coaster frames as he did on the ground, but even his stomach felt a lurch when he looked down. The catwalk couldn't possibly be this high. Not only was the building too small, but he simply hadn't been in the elevator that long. A careful inspection of the wall behind him showed how the illusion was done. He was actually only about four feet up in the air, looking down upon a carefully constructed miniature. Every detail was perfect. Perfect not only in the feeling of height, but in the vast looming emptiness, the harsh beating sunlight that somehow didn't cast a shadow, the illusion of being outdoors inside a relatively small building. At the far cliff the catwalk turned a corner and ran across a gorge that would have done well in the Grand Canyon. Below, in the depths of the gorge, a giant lay face down among the rocks. No, that was wrong. Four feet away a body was sprawled across the miniature landscape. Dandy sprang over the side and ran to his aid.

At first the showman thought that Walter Redd was dead, but the body was warm, and a touch revealed that he was still alive. There was barely enough room for Dandy to move aside while the politician shook his head and slowly regained consciousness.

"Are you hurt? Can you move? Do you need a doctor?" Dandy asked, while threats of lawsuits flashed in his mind. It was bad enough when it was somebody's kid, but this guy could really take him to the cleaners. Redd's look of surprise and confusion did nothing to ease Dandy's mind.

"Where is my house?" Redd asked. Then he seemed to notice Dandy for the first time. "Sorry. I'm okay now," he said, sounding almost surprised, then added, "I think," as he managed only to heave himself into a seated position.

"Well, what the hell happened?" Dandy asked.

"I'm not sure," Redd replied, shaking his head weakly. "Actually, what I'd really like… is there some place where I could lie down for a minute or two?" He reached out a hand to Dandy, who helped him to his feet.

"Sure, we can go to my office," Dandy replied.

7

"This is where I live for the season. Larry takes the front half and I have the back. Have a seat and I'll get us some brew. Unless you'd like something a little weaker? We have some soda." Carole shook her head, and looked about for a place to sit. There was a mattress on the floor, but no chairs. She leaned back against the wall.

Jeff knew she was waiting for him to make the first move. He had known many women like this one, shy or coy; she was excited, ready for almost anything, but too afraid of rejection to initiate it on her own. It might even be something she'd been waiting quite a while for. There weren't many safe chances in a small town like this one. Someone always knew what you'd been up to, and sooner or later the news got out. It had taken Jeff a long time to figure out why women found him so much more attractive as a carny in the summer than as a student in the winter, and when the answer finally came to him, it was so blindingly simple that he almost blushed. Jeff the carny would be gone in the morning. No one to leak the rumor to the history teacher or the hairdresser. No one around to hate her in the morning. Still, he would have to make the first move. A seductress she wasn't.

"It must feel crowded in here by the end of the summer," she said.

He popped the top, spritzing them both, and handed her the can. "Not too bad," he answered. "We don't spend a whole lot of time in here." Before he opened his own can, he rolled it gently down her sweat-stained back. "Feel good?" he asked. She sighed. He could tell by the way she responded that it felt wonderful. He could feel parts of her body tightening up in response to his touch, and he hoped that she wouldn't make him waste too much time. It was hot in the little box of a trailer.

Jeff reached out and stroked her shoulder with two gentle fingers, and Carole covered them with her hand, following the contour of his arm with fingers of her own. He gave her a sudden kiss on that shoulder, then pulled away. He walked to the door, closing and locking it, increasing both the heat and the privacy.

It was very hot in the trailer. So hot that there was a dream-like quality about the whole affair. She was real—he could feel the supple skin as he pressed his mouth against hers, running his hands down her body and easing her out of her clothes—and yet he saw the whole thing through a haze. Not quite like being stoned… or maybe even more so. And somehow he was moving without volition, as if someone else were pulling the strings. He crushed her to him roughly, ripping the strap of her bra when it wouldn't slide easily over her shoulder. She tried to push herself away, but it was a feeble attempt. "No, Jeff… not so hard, honey. No." Then, suddenly, she was pushing him away, telling him to stop. But he couldn't stop. The more she pulled away from him, the harder, the nastier his pursuit. He felt her teeth bite into his shoulder, and his hand came up in response, slapping her hard against the side of her head. She cried out, and he slapped her again, and yet again, hitting her harder each time. She was quiet after that, letting him do what he wanted. Pulling, pounding, pinching, grinding… He found his fingers digging tightly into her skin, his mouth hard against hers. He ripped the clothes from his own body, and mounted her roughly, totally absorbed in his own fulfillment. With fevered thrusts, he relieved the ache inside of him—a dog biting holes in its own leg to remove an itch—aware only distantly that Carole was even there. Then suddenly, with one last painful jolt, it was over, and as his sweat-soaked body rolled loosely aside, he became aware of her once more.

Carole was sobbing softly. "Carole," he whispered, and felt her pull away from him. Already, bruises were starting to show on her body. "Oh, God, I'm sorry. I'm so sorry." What had made him behave that way? He had never been like that before. Never. And this had been her first time, too. He'd wanted to make it so special for her.

She pulled the sheet up over herself and rolled against the wall, crying so quietly that he had to watch the gentle quaking of the sheet to see it. He wanted to grab her, to hold her and comfort her, to tell her that he wasn't like that at all. But he had been like that. How could he deny it? He'd been an animal.

Disgusted, he stood and thrust his legs into his pants There was nothing he could say or do. Not ever. Jeff Petticola, rapist. He could feel the tears stinging behind his eyelids, but he couldn't bear to show them. "I… I'm sorry. I gotta go. The bathroom's through there," he said. She didn't answer, and he went quickly out of the trailer.

8

Gregor put the cover plates back on the motor, wiped his hands on the greasy rag, and slammed home the lid of his tool box. It was the most baffling problem he'd ever run across in his life. There was nothing wrong with the ride, it just wouldn't work. Obviously, it had to be a short in the wiring. Nothing else could account for the fact that it had started running all by itself. No, damnit. That wouldn't explain it either. The motor was off, the brake was on. Even a short in the wiring couldn't account for that. Well, he'd just have to replace the wires and see what happened. What a time for the lousy thing to quit on him. And it was always one of the most popular of his rides.

He turned and watched the spinning glow of the rides on the midway. Most of them were his, and they were doing well enough. He'd get by. He picked up the tool box and started to head back to his trailer, then stopped. The box slipped from his fingers and landed with a soft thud on the ground, still he continued to watch as a lone figure detached itself from the crowd and headed toward the back lot. She was beautiful. The grace of her movements, the way her hair flowed softly around her, always made her appear to be floating in a sea of air. He waited until she was nearby, then picked up the box and started toward her.

"Not at work tonight?" he said. He hadn't meant to startle her, but from the way she jumped, her mind must have been a million miles away. "I'm sorry. I didn't mean to frighten you. I thought you saw me."

"I'm not seeing much of anything tonight," she said. Now that she was close, he could see how nervous and distracted she looked. Of course it was Dollar. That asshole. He was the bane of her existence. If he, Gregor, had a girl like this in love with him… he thought briefly of his wife. No, that had been different. She had chosen to let him go. Besides, he was older now. Smarter. Smart enough to know that for Katie, he was only a friend. Why did women always seem to fall for the very men who would give them the hardest time? And what about Dollar, all prepared to let her go and at the same time jealous as shit over a man Katie couldn't care less about? Well, he'd gladly be her friend if that was all she wanted.

"Things not going so good tonight?" he asked. He thought for a moment that she was going to cry, but she bit her lip and blinked back the tears.

"Patch told me to keep this local politico in tow, and now I've gone and lost him," she said.

"You've lost a whole politician? Maybe you've tried looking under a rock?" he asked.

"No, he's really a very nice man actu…" suddenly she looked at Gregor and began to laugh. "I know. Silly, isn't it? He must have left when I went to get Patch. I don't know why, though. We were getting along so well."

"Any man dumb enough to let you out of his sight, who needs him," Gregor said.

Katie smiled. She threw her arm around Gregor's shoulders, and kissed him gently on the cheek. "Thanks, pal," she said. "You know what I'm gonna do? I'm going to go to work. If Patch has anything to say to me, he can find me in the tent." As she turned to go, she looked up at the broken ride and shuddered. "God, that thing looks gruesome! Like a giant, dead insect."

Gregor looked up at the spider and shrugged. It was a huge, hulking bite of frustration, and it was going to cost him a lot of money, but— gruesome? What could possibly be gruesome about steel, wires, leather, and a bit of black paint. "You! You cost me a fortune, you. How you can be so bad to me when I treat you so good? This I will never understand." He slapped one of the chairs and watched it swing freely on a well-greased hinge. Behind him, Katie laughed, and he smiled to know that for a moment he had made her smile. As for the Spider, he'd worked on it enough for tonight. Tomorrow he would rewire the whole thing, and with any luck at all, it would be back in service before they left this burg. In the meantime, he had other things to think about. He picked up his toolbox, then, almost as if he were worried that the ride might have been insulted by the remarks, he gently patted its steel frame.

9

Any other day, Jake would have been pleased to watch the show. He would have pushed his way right up to the front row and plunged his head between those long creamy thighs, just the way Bill Damler was doing. Even now, distracted as he was, he found himself from time to time soothed into near-forgetfulness by that sweet golden thatch and those lovely pink nipples sitting like sundae cherries on top of those ice-cream breasts. Like an issue of *Playboy* come to life. The others had been a treat, but this one almost made him forget about the stomach-churning reason he had run out on his girls.

Not completely, though, and when the fifteen minutes he'd promised to allow himself was up, he let himself out of the tent in the middle of the performance.

Jake peered cautiously out through the tent flaps, then eased his way behind the tent for a good look down the midway, just to be certain that Joella and Darcy were really gone. Not that he really needed to. He knew that they wouldn't have stayed any longer than was necessary to be sure he was on his way. He might have been able to blackmail them into letting him go off by himself, but he knew they wouldn't leave him alone any longer than they could help it. Now he had to act fast, because sure as he stood here, they would be back as soon as they found him gone.

He stepped out onto the midway and located the ride that had troubled him. He had felt in his bones that there was something wrong, and now he was sure. Oh, the ride was running. There was still that red glow in the mouth of the skull, and the black chairs still made their slow circuit, but now a man stood on the platform, turning back all the interested patrons. That made things difficult, because he had to get inside.

Years ago, on this very spot, he lived through a night of terror. A night that in its own way had left him almost as maimed as his brother. He never remembered much about it, but he always knew that it hadn't quite ended. Now he could feel it, echoing back through time, calling to him. It was almost as if that ride had his name on it. He would get inside, and when he did, his childhood would come back to haunt him.

He made his way to the Bozo cage and stood at the back of the crowd, waiting for the moment that he knew was coming. He didn't have to wait very long. One man, insulted by the clown in the cage and anxious for a chance to get even, picked up several balls without having paid for them.

"Maxie!" the clown called. It was the man on the platform who answered. Jake watched him. It was obvious that he was trying to be in two places at once, but greed won, and he ran over to the cage to protect his investment. The platform was empty.

Jake had no idea how long it would remain empty. He wasn't very fast on his feet, but he took the chance. After all, what could they say to him if they caught him? But they wouldn't. This was *meant*.

10

"And now, ladies and gentlemen, if you will step this way, we have here an exhibition…" Randall watched the last of the stragglers follow Pritt to the next partition. It had been a bad show. Three lousy fliers was all that he had sold, and his wife hadn't done much better. It was a good thing they were getting out. He squared up the stack of paper and put a rubber band around it. Inflation was part of the problem. When he first started in the business, the little biographies they sold at the end of each show were the hottest part of the night. Even at the cost of "one thin dime, one tenth of a dollar," he had made much more money than he had ever made at the exorbitant price of fifty cents. Of course, then they had been something to read. Tragic fiction of the trashiest and most popular sort. All about how his poor, pregnant mother, falling innocently into a toad-infested pond, had given birth to Randall. The public didn't want that sort of thing any more. At least, that was what Pritt had told him, though the headlines in the tabloids didn't seem to bear him out. Nowadays, at least in Carger's ten-in-one, the leaflets were a simple discussion of the medical conditions that had caused his appearance and the tragic life he suffered because of it.

On the whole, that tragic life had been a lot of fun. Certainly he wouldn't have married such a wonderful, sexy, talented woman as Sally if he'd been forced to spend his life working in an office. Besides, nothing was really any different. People always gawked at him with looks of horror, or even worse, pity. But here, they had to *pay* for the privilege. What sweeter revenge was there anywhere?

Of course, the prim and prissy, socially conscious do-gooders would much rather see him living on state aid than earning an honest living. It was *immoral* for him to exhibit himself. Illegal too, in many communities, thanks to their helpful interference. He was among the last of a dying breed. Still, he suspected that those prissy attitudes were only a small part of the reason. Times change.

"Randall, aren't you coming for dinner?" Sally called him out of his reverie. He followed her out of the tent and back to his trailer. Stew had been simmering in a crock pot all afternoon. It filled the place with a delightful aroma when the lid was lifted, and made his mouth water. He kissed his wife on the cheek, running his fingers through her long, full beard.

"It smells wonderful. Let's eat," he said.

"I'm going to take some over to Emma Mae before the show." She poured stew into two cracked and mismatched bowls, and set them down on the flowered place mats.

"This is good," he told his wife. He ate the meal quickly, tearing chunks from a loaf of French bread to sop up the gravy, happy to see how much his delight in his wife's cooking pleased her. "I don't know if there'll be enough left for Ella Mae," he said, going back for seconds.

"I don't know if there was enough to begin with," Sally said, then hid her face in pretend shame. "I shouldn'ta said that. And her my best friend and all."

"No, you shouldn't, and she'd have been the first one to say it herself," Randal added with a smile. Then suddenly his expression became serious. "Sally, do you really think we ought to wait 'til the end of the season to pack it in? Things have been going so badly, maybe we ought to just cut our losses and split."

"And do what? At least I have hobbies. What the hell would you do with yourself all day? I can see it all now. Just like Ed Willars, who took off the beginning of the season and was back before the season ended. Do you remember what he said? 'There's only so many times a day you can mow the lawn, Sally,' he told me. I keep telling you, Randy, we have to think about starting up a business."

"Okay, Sal. You're right, as usual. You decide what we ought to do. Whatever, it's okay with me. Just promise me one thing. Whatever we decide to do, please, honey, *please*, don't shave."

11

It was hot in the tent. Sam wondered why he hadn't noticed it before. Sweat dripped into his eyes and pooled around the neckline of his shirt, making a large dark stain on the thin cloth. He lifted the hem of his shirt and wiped his face with it. It was almost too hot to breathe. He walked outside, hoping for a bit of fresh air, but the breeze had deserted him. It was almost more oppressive out in the open. He looked at the crowds that covered the infield and wondered how they could stand it.

On the back lot, Katie and Gregor were talking. The thought crossed his mind that perhaps he should go over there, but he wasn't quite sure why. To hell with them both. To hell with everyone. And yet, without any volition, his feet were propelling him in that direction.

Like a fever dream, his mind noted—without taking notice of—everything that he passed along the way. The Viking sat dejectedly on the steps of the trailer, her canary yellow robe spread open at the waist, revealing that she was, in fact, a natural blonde. Far down, along a row of cars, three kids stood peering through the fence, egging each other into taking the big climb over it. An old man, as wizened as Methuselah, was hiding behind the G-top as if the FBI was hot on his trail. A strange, hazy mist or weird enveloping patch of fog loomed in the air behind Dandy's Winnebago, turning slowly in a breeze that Dollar never felt. He shook his head to try and clear his mind, but nothing helped. His marshmallow brain refused to focus.

"Where's Mr. Redd?" Sam asked. He meant it to sound mocking, but with his customary bravado it was just a question. Katie looked at him oddly, bit her lip, and paused for a moment before answering.

"I seem to have lost him," she said a little nervously.

"Does that mean I can expect you to work the next show?"

"You all right, Sam?" she asked. There was no mistaking the sudden concern in her voice. He wanted to shout at her. He wanted to tell her what she should have been able to see. He wanted to tell her that it was all gone to shit. Dandy, the girls, Thot, and most of all, her. He wanted to grab her and shake some sense into her dumb, college-educated head, but he didn't have the energy. His anger died as quickly as it had flared, long before the first harsh word could escape his lips. He turned and walked away.

The Viking was still on the step. For a moment he stared at her. He knew there was something he wanted to say to her, but he couldn't remember what. It all seemed so long ago. Her lower lip protruded in a pout, and she pulled her wrapper close around her, but said nothing. Finally, he reached over her and pulled the door open with a roughness that would have knocked her off the step if she hadn't moved out of the way fast enough. "You're not going on tonight," he said as he disappeared inside. He locked the door behind him.

Her clothes were strewn all over the room. He gave a thought to throwing them out after her, but the gesture would cost more energy than he could spare. She was calling after him, banging on the door, as he threw himself across the bed. It was easy to block out the noise. Block out everything. No sooner did he close his eyes against the light than the world went away. The jungle closed in. Strange noises whispered through the dark, and distant flames threw smoke across the horizon. Thot's face, distant and hazy, swam before his eyes, but in the effort to bring it close, it changed and mutated until he saw before him the girl in the tent. A scream escaped his lips. He forced his eyes to open, bringing back the dimly lit surfaces of ceiling and wall, and with them came the carnival sounds of laughter and music, all hideously intertwined with the dull groans of machinery. He stood and walked slowly over to the refrigerator and took out a can of beer. This he pressed to his forehead and against the back of his neck before he returned it, unopened, to its shelf.

If the heat in the lot was oppressive, inside the trailer it was unbearable. The Viking was no longer pounding on his door; and the cool can had cleared his head a little. It was safe to go out. It was still stunningly hot, even when he moved away from the narrow alleys between the homes and out into the open. Nor had the fog dissipated. It hung suspended high in the air; if anything, it was more solid than ever, his own personal cloud in an otherwise unbroken sky. No harbinger of the blessed relief of rain, it seemed more like the desert clouds that promised nothing but hot wind and blowing sand that would scour dry everything in their path. Almost, he could see a shape in it, like some large animal hanging over the Earth. It followed him to the midway, staring over his shoulder as he peered between the tents for another look at the girl.

Twice he thought he saw her among the crowds, but it was difficult to be sure. So many young girls walking through the dust. So many dark-haired girls. Could she really be his?

From somewhere off to his right came the discordant blare of loud speaker feedback, followed by the scratchy strains of an old forty-five. Like an old milk-truck horse, his feet followed the sounds of their own accord, and he found himself standing in front of his proposition. Already, Essie and Magda were out on the stage, going through the first few motions of their dance, and surprisingly enough in the turgid heat, a small crowd was beginning to gather. He tried his customary vault onto the stage, found himself unable to spare the energy, and climbed stiffly up the stairs to the platform.

"For all you gentlemen out there…" he began, running through his spiel without the usual zip. "And here we have Magda the beautiful, Magda the amazing. She can shake it up one side and down the other…" The patter came without thought, but his head was whirling. The cloud floated low, just over the audience, taking on even more solidity and form, and the heat had returned worse than before. He never lost consciousness. Not quite. But he could feel his body droop and the light fade from his eyes as though a curtain had descended. Only his ears gave him contact with the world—then even they refused to function.

Part Six

TURNING THE TIP

1

Katie heard the commotion while she was still backstage. Only half in costume, she tossed a robe over her shoulders and rushed out to see what was going on. All she could see were backs, bending over something or someone, but she couldn't make out what it was. She moved around for a better look.

Sam! It was Sam! And he looked awful. No, he looked worse than awful; he looked dead! Her throat swelled to a tight little knot and her knees grew weak. She knelt down by his side and took his face in her hands. "Sam!" she begged in a hoarse whisper. She saw his eyelids flutter; heard a sigh escape his lips, and her body relaxed just a little. "Somebody help me get him back to the trailer. Maxie! Pritt! *Anyone*, please help!" she called, though she knew they couldn't hear her above the noise of the infield.

"Could I help, lady?" A young man presented himself at the edge of the platform. He was tall and well-muscled, but Sam was a large man himself. Katie doubted that one man alone could carry him. The kid seemed to read her mind. "I can handle him," he said. Sam was now awake enough to help, and he leaned on the boy's shoulder as Katie led them through the narrow space between the tents and threaded them through the twisty alley of cars, trucks, trailers, and campers parked any-which-way. Katie never saw what hit her as the Viking came out of nowhere, knocking her aside.

"Sammy!" The Viking ran to his side, getting in the way, though Katie had to admit that the boy didn't seem to mind. "Sam, what happened?"

"I think he passed out," the youngster volunteered, while Sam shook his head woozily. Katie was back on her feet and ready to direct her helper, but the Viking brushed her aside.

"This way," she said, trying to take Sam's other arm. Now Katie was really angry. Almost angry enough to forget Sam, the boy, everything.

"Out of my way, *bitch*!" Katie said. The blonde gaped at her, but said nothing as Katie opened the door of the trailer and motioned the boy inside. He reappeared a moment later, empty-handed, and Katie thanked him with a free pass to the show, but before she could enter the trailer herself, she felt a hand grab her hair and yank backwards, straining her neck.

Katie wasn't a brawler. She had always thought of physical violence as something only low-class people indulged in—but this was just more than she could stand. It had been building up all season. No matter that she had never been hit, never learned how to throw a punch; instinct took over, and she landed a solid right to the Viking's head. There wasn't time for her to glory in her triumph, however. Almost instantly, the tall blonde was upon her, hands and feet flying, trying to hit, scratch, bite, and kick all at the same time. There was only enough time for Katie to be surprised that she was neither frightened nor slow. The world rolled by in a swirl of action-reaction, with her on top and then underneath and then on top again, until a pair of hands on her shoulders pulled her away while she was still trying to get in another blow.

"All right, you two!" It was the boy who had helped carry Sam. Pritt was holding the Viking, and Katie just had to laugh when she looked at her. Her robe was twisted around her arm, and there was nothing underneath except a scratched and bruised Viking. There was quite a crowd outside Sam's trailer, but no one seemed to mind the Viking's appearance. Katie found it very funny. She laughed until her stomach ached and she grabbed at the pain, only to find that, except for a g-string, she was dressed exactly the same way. In fact, her robe had been ripped off entirely, and lay in a heap by the steps to Sam's trailer. Dressing like this when she danced was one thing; out here, it seemed indecent. Her cheeks grew warm with embarrassment. Quickly, she snatched up her robe and disappeared into Sam's trailer.

"That's some shiner you're gonna have," Sam said. Katie looked at herself, bruised, scratched, and almost totally naked, and then she looked at Sam. He was covered with sweat and still a little shaky, but his color was starting to return, and the way he was looking at *her* was a sure sign that he was getting better. She began to laugh, and in a moment he was laughing with her. "What a pair," he said at last.

She flopped down next to him on the edge of the bed, and threw her arms around his neck. "Oh, Sam," she sighed. He put his arms around her and gently stroked her spine. There was no getting around it. He was the antithesis of everything she'd ever wanted in a man—and there was no one else in the world for her, no matter how difficult he was. He would be difficult, too. He always was, whenever he was close to showing any emotion, but she was ready for it, all of her armor carefully in place. But when his next remark did come, it was not at all what she was expecting.

"How can you tell if a child is yours?" he asked.

"What do you mean, you *lost* him? How the hell do you lose a full-grown politician. You tell the people of this country how to pull off that one and you can get rich!" As Arthur Billingsly spoke, he gestured with the cigar, stabbing it repeatedly through the air. Gaylen Schuster dodged his head away from the live coal that seemed to be aimed right at his eye.

"I don't know. They just disappeared. I found the girl again a little later, but by then she was alone. It doesn't matter though. I have enough of what you want right here," Schuster said, waving a small black canister in the air. But Billingsly was a mile ahead of him.

"Disappeared for a while, eh? I can just imagine what they were doing. The shots you could have gotten." He snatched at the canister. "I'll take care of that. No. On second thought, maybe you'd better do it. Mary!" She must have been right outside the door, for she appeared almost instantly. "Schuster, if those pictures come out the way you say they will, you may find yourself in for a bonus. Mary, show our guest out, please, then go home yourself."

Once Billingsly was alone, he tried to put this new piece into the puzzle. So Walter had disappeared. It must have happened quite some time ago, because Schuster swore he'd looked for him before he left. Well, Redd hadn't gone home. He'd had someone call the house to make sure. Where the hell would a stuffed shirt like that wind up at this time on a Friday night? Well, Billingsly didn't really think anything was up—Redd had always been too careful to get caught, if he'd ever pulled this sort of thing before—but just in case there was, he definitely wanted to know about it. Caught in the act was a hell of a lot better than second-hand photographs, any day. There was only one thing to do. He would have to go to the lot and see for himself. Besides, it was a good excuse to check the land out. He was very certain it was going to be his before too much longer.

Mei Chou left the kootch tent determined to get her dragon back before the night was over. Only then would she worry about the big man. He had been mean to her, but she didn't really think he was a mean man. Even when he was yelling at her, there was something about him that she liked. His face was nice. Anyway, she had nowhere else to go, nothing to do. After stealing from Mother Chem, she certainly couldn't go back there. Mother Chem wouldn't have her. She had only been another pair of hands at the restaurant, and now those hands weren't to be trusted.

She crept behind the nearest tent and watched. It wasn't long before the man emerged, but when she tried to follow him back into the area behind the carnival, an older man appeared out of nowhere. "You can't go back there, honey," he said. She didn't answer. She stood her ground for as long as she could, looking after the man who could well be her father. Finally, when she hadn't moved away, the older man herded her gently back to the midway. She circled the lot quickly and tried again. This time there was no one to stop her, but now it was too late. The big man was gone.

For half an hour she poked around in the little paths between the trucks, looking into windows when she could, ducking out of sight whenever she saw anyone around. There was no trace of him. She knew that any one of those homes could be his, or even worse, that he could have taken one of the cars and driven off into the town, or even to the city. It didn't matter. The one thing she did know was that he worked at this carnival. That meant that sometime before it left, he would be back. She could wait. Even if it meant that she had to curl up under the stars and spend the night, she could wait. She'd slept in worse places. In the meantime, there were many things she could do.

One ride would just about use up the money she had left, and it wouldn't keep her busy for very long. There were places where she could get something to eat, but she wasn't really hungry. Besides, she wanted to find something that would use up a lot of time. She looked around at all the wonderful things there were to do, and then she spotted the side-show. Those colorful posters bulged with the wind like magic sails, almost forcing her to stop for a moment to read them. It might be fun to see the sword swallower, or the Magnificent Madam Galena. Mei had never seen a bearded lady. There was just enough left of the money she'd taken to buy a ticket and still have a little left over. She made her purchase and entered "THE WORLD OF THE STRANGE: THE UNUSUAL".

It was very different inside from the way she'd imagined it. The light was dim, the areas partitioned off by plain, weather-worn canvas, and most of the sights weren't very spectacular. The first act they showed was the giant. He wasn't really very much taller than the average basketball player, but to Mei he seemed like a character out of a storybook. The snake-charmer's costume was stained and rather tacky, and she seemed quite nervous about touching the snakes. Chou wasn't scared of snakes. She knew which ones to keep away from, and some of them were very good to eat. There was a tattoo place two doors from the restaurant, but even there she had never seen anyone to match the tattooed man in the show. Why, he was so completely covered with tattoos that he looked clothed even where he wasn't. The bearded lady wasn't just bearded, she was hairy everywhere. At first, Mei thought that she was a man in a woman's dress, but her hands were tiny and delicate, and when she spoke the child lost any doubts. The gnarly man just made her sad, and the girl turning into a gorilla looked phony even to her unjaded eyes, but the sword swallower, the contortionist, and the magician were fun, and the fat lady was very fat indeed. Each one had something to sell after his turn. She wasn't really interested in the little pamphlets, but the giant sold rings that fit his finger, and they were big enough to make into a key chain. Mei dipped into the last of her money. It was worth it for such a wonderful thing. The magician was selling magic tricks, and she would have liked to have one, but she was out of money by then, and moved on quickly to the next performance. The whole thing didn't take very long.

The lot seemed very bright after the darkness of the tent. She blinked once, and looked around for somewhere to go. Without money there wasn't much to do at a carnival. Then she spotted the big man. He was walking through the lot arm and arm with a woman. Mei wondered if the woman was his wife. That could make things a little difficult if the man did turn out to be her father. She had never considered the idea that he might be married. She was just wondering if she ought to take a chance and approach him when the lights winked out.

4

Jeff slammed the trailer door behind him and leaned back against it. What the hell had he done. He could remember it, every dirty little move, but not with the reality of something that just happened. It was more like remembering a movie that you saw a long time ago. As if it hadn't really been him at all.

After a while, he felt Carole moving around in the trailer, and quickly started walking away. He had no direction in mind, but he had caused her enough pain for one night. Seeing him now wouldn't help her at all. What could he say? "Sorry Carole, I don't usually beat girls up and rape them; I don't know what came over me?" Somehow he didn't think that would do much good. He hadn't consciously picked a direction, but when he found himself standing outside the G-top, he knew it was the best place to go. A place where he could be alone while everyone else was working. A place where *she* wouldn't run across him. Even more important, a place where he wouldn't run across her. He could have time to think here. It was past time for self-recriminations: he had to be ready in case she called the cops.

Would she report what happened? He thought the whole affair over carefully, and as he thought about it, the whole thing began to come back to him with more insight. He had hit her, all right… hit her hard. But it was more than that. He had enjoyed it. Enjoyed hitting her. With stunning new clarity, he realized that the simple act of clubbing her across the face with the back of his hand had been more enjoyable than the orgasm that followed. Why had she done this to him? The bitch. He could see now that it was really *her* fault. She had wanted it, practically begged for it! No, that wasn't right. He couldn't allow himself to think like that. Tears sprang to his eyes, but he blinked them back, and for a long time he stared at the side of the tent and thought of nothing at all.

It was a strange sound that brought him back to reality: the collective oohing and ahing of the infield crowd, as though someone had been setting off fireworks for the marks. But he hadn't heard any fireworks. He wasn't really interested in the cause, but it did make him realize that he couldn't bear to be there alone any longer. Right at the moment, he was his least favorite person. He had to find someone to talk to. Oh, not to explain things. He wasn't ready for that yet. Maybe he wouldn't ever be. No matter, he had to have company. There was only one person who would do. He had to find Aggie.

He left the tent confused, frightened, unhappy, but on the midway, another kind of unease took over. All the way to Aggie's tent, he fought the desire to stop every few feet and look back over his shoulder. Something was wrong. Something else beside himself. It was as though the whole world had suddenly gone crazy. Or was it just that he was going crazy? Only when he finally reached his destination did he allow himself to stop and look around. Even then, it took a few minutes for the whole thing to sink in. Jesus! It was impossible. It couldn't happen. Yet it *had* happened, somehow. Every light on every ride and every pole and every string around every booth had suddenly turned red.

5

Eli knew instantly that something was wrong. He had always had that power where his brother was concerned. He had always known. He remembered quite vividly the day that Jake first started working with Werner Morgan. Eli had known then that it was trouble. He had ignored the feeling. He had never liked Morgan, and he told himself that he was just jealous because it was the first time his brother had ever done anything without him… but the premonition had been there. Then, even after Jake began to change, to do things Eli knew his brother would never do on his own, Eli continued to ignore his instincts. On the night of the accident, he had the same feeling he was experiencing now. Only then it had hit his gut strongly enough for him to sneak out of his parents' home and go to the Morgan place. And he had been right. Morgan would have killed Jake that night, if Eli hadn't acted. Now he had that same feeling again. Pain-ridden and nearly immobile as he was, Eli didn't know what he could do… but he had to go.

Mrs. Duffy was safely tucked away in her room. He knew she would try to discourage him if she knew he was going out—or worse; she might try to go with him. Somehow he knew that this was something he'd have to do by himself, without any interference from Mrs. Duffy. If he just called a cab, then by the time it drove up to the door, it would be too late for her to stop him.

There were only two cab drivers in all of Somerset. Not only was the town so small that most people could walk wherever they went, but they almost all had cars anyway if they did decide to drive. Eli was one of the few patrons that the minuscule cab company had. But that was good, because even if Mrs. Duffy did try to interfere, he knew whose side the cab driver would take. It wasn't long before Frank Cousins came to the door in his company jacket. "Where we going tonight, Mr. Jefferson?" he asked.

"Yes, just where are you going?" a voice called from the hall steps.

"Out, Mrs. Duffy, just out," he replied.

"Frank, you're not to take him anywhere," she said, but Eli knew that the cab driver would stand behind him—he knew which side his bread was buttered on. The cab driver looked uncomfortable, and shrugged his shoulders in response. Mrs. Duffy tried again from another angle. "Eli Jefferson, you're not going anywhere. Sick as you are," she said, and took hold of the handles on his wheelchair.

"Mrs. Duffy, do I look like an adult to you? When I want your permission, I'll ask for it," he said in a hard, flat voice, without turning his head around to look at her. He felt it when she released the chair, and immediately wheeled himself down the ramp that led to the street.

"All right, Mr. Jefferson," Mrs. Duffy said stiffly. "I can't keep you here if you don't want to stay, but don't expect me to be waiting to take care of you when you get back. I can't work with a patient who won't follow the doctor's orders." Eli nodded in response. He didn't think it was anything he had to worry about. He had a strong suspicion that he wasn't coming back.

"Take me to 235 Wilson Street… no, take me to Morgan field," he said, changing his mind without knowing why. It was Jake he had to worry about. Surely Jake was home from that silly carnival by now. Yet, somehow, the carnival was calling to Eli, the same way he had been called to those same grounds all those years ago.

6

Dandy started to reach into the refrigerator for a brew, then decided that the occasion called for scotch. "I think maybe you could use a drink. Hell, for a minute there, I thought you was dead." Dandy took a bottle from his desk drawer and poured an ample amount of the amber liquid into two tumblers, keeping the fullest for himself.

"Dead?" Walter Redd repeated, as if the word offended him.

"Well, you were out cold, anyway. What happened in there?" Dandy asked. He downed his own glass and refilled it, barely noting that Redd had not touched his yet.

"I don't remember," Redd answered. Dandy didn't believe him. He could always tell when someone was lying, and this man definitely was. There was something strange about him. Something different. Something that set Dandy's teeth on edge. He had changed, changed in some way that was undefinable, and yet, somehow unmistakable. Dandy downed the new glass and filled it one more time.

"Maybe we oughta get a doctor to have a look at you," the carny said.

"I don't need a doctor," Redd answered slowly. He stood up and walked around the room as though he was testing his legs. "No, I don't need a doctor. I'm okay, *now*," he added. He looked at Dandy, and the pitchman got the feeling that Redd could see right through him. Redd's eyes were the eyes of a feral creature, a fox or a wolf, hard and opaque as rubies. "Not very safe, these rides of yours," Redd said after a moment, with a sly, slow grin. "Someone could have gotten hurt. I could have gotten hurt. I did get hurt, in fact, didn't I? I must say that it makes me quite angry." He stared stonily at Dandy. "No, Mr. Dandy, I'm afraid that some things around here are going to have to change." He smiled a razor-thin smile at Dandy, barely moving his lips.

A sudden confused uproar of sound from outside caught Dandy's attention. That was all he needed. It had to happen now. Well, whatever it was, he was going to have to take care of it, Redd or no Redd. Be good to get away from Redd for a moment, anyway; all of a sudden, the guy gave him the creeps. "Excuse me a minute, please. I'd better go see what's going on."

"By all means," Redd said in that same calm voice. Did the man mean to give him the impression that he already *knew* everything that was going on? Redd was better at this than Dandy had thought. He just didn't seem like the same dumb Honest John who'd had his tongue hanging out over Katie a few hours ago. This Redd seemed like a man who knew exactly what he was doing, full of self-confidence; unshakeable and calmly arrogant. But, damn it, now that he'd made that impossible deal with Billingsly, he needed him. If he didn't shape up and take control of this conversation, Jim Dandy was going to find himself in a world of trouble. Thoughtfully, he put his drink down and stood up.

The minute he stuck his head out the door, Dandy saw what had caused all the shouting, but it took a minute for the implications to sink in. It wasn't possible. It simply couldn't happen. All the little colored lights on the Ferris Wheel had somehow been changed to red. And the same thing had happened to the Carousel, and the string joint and Maxie's joints, and the grab joint and even to the main lights that stood high up over the infield. Red—all of them had turned red. But that was impossible! No one could have changed all of those lights this fast. It had to be... It had to be... No, he couldn't think of a single rational explanation for what had happened. It *couldn't* have happened, but it had. It made the hairs rise on the back of his neck.

The marks were cheering and applauding. They thought of it as a deliberate effect, some sort of magic act to impress them, but those agents he could see around the lot knew better. Everything had come to a stop as Cinda, Pritt, Maxie, and Shingo-Shango stood gaping around them in amazement with their mouths open. He ran to find Gregor, but as he moved across the lot, his people called after him with questions for which he had no answer. What the hell was he going to tell them? What the hell was he going to tell anyone? This was all he needed, on top of everything else. The only bright spot he could find was that at least this wasn't something that Redd could add to his list of grievances. However this had happened, it certainly wasn't *Dandy's* fault.

7

It was all out in the open now. Sam had given Katie the whole story. He hadn't wanted to tell her, but she'd pulled it out of him bit by bit.

"Katie, it's hard for me to talk about my time in Nam. It was a different world there. We were all different people. I was very young, and I had spent most of my life working with my father and the dancers who worked for him. Sure, I knew some of the girls I went to school with, but I never really had a chance to spend much time with them. And then I met Thot, and she was so different from everyone I knew. Maybe that's why I…" He saw the look of confusion on Katie's face, and patted her hand. "Maybe I'd better start at the beginning," he said.

"When I was stationed at headquarters, I worked with a local translator named Pai Som Trinh. This man and his family sort of took me in. I never had that sort of family life, and I liked it. It was different. Anyway, Som had a daughter named Thot. She wanted to learn to speak English, and I used to do a little bit of magic and juggling that I'd picked up here and there. She wanted to learn that, too. I thought it would be fun to teach her. She was such a cute kid. And then one day I realized she wasn't a kid anymore. I never meant to fall in love with her—there was her father, and there was the war—but things just happened." He felt Katie stiffen, and he stopped talking. She smiled and put her arms around him and pulled his head down next to her own.

"Go ahead," she said, gently.

"Things got pretty desperate toward the end. Both of her parents were killed. She was pregnant by then. I really wanted to marry her, to bring her and the child back with me when I came home, but there was a lot of red tape involved in that sort of thing. The Army made it as hard as possible."

"Married?" he heard Katie say under her breath. He knew she hadn't meant for him to hear, but he hugged her tightly and continued.

"I only saw the baby once. There were rumors that there was going to be a big offensive, and all leaves were cancelled. Then the base was shelled pretty heavily, and I wound up in the hospital. It was a pretty bad injury. For a while they didn't know if they were gonna be able to save my leg."

"That scar on your thigh?" she asked. He nodded in answer.

"When I finally did get out, I tried to find them, but they were gone. Most of the town had been wiped out in the offensive, and the survivors had been relocated. Later, I got word they were dead."

She took it well—much better than he would have expected her to. There was more to Katie than he usually gave her credit for. A lot more than most women. Whatever she felt about the story he'd told her, she remained both sympathetic and practical. It was a new feeling for him, hard to get used to, but he was beginning to be glad to have another head helping him sort things out. His own didn't seem to be working very well lately.

"Well, how reliable was your source? Could it have been wrong? If you're certain that the child is dead and that this girl couldn't possibly be your daughter, then just forget about the whole thing; your problem is solved. On the other hand, if you think there's a possibility that she might really *be* Mei—then, we'll just have to work it out. For instance, is she the right age? Does she really look that much like you, or could she be any mixed-blood child? What does she know about her mother?" Katie massaged his shoulders as she spoke to him. If she was shaken by any of the story, she didn't let it show.

"*Could* Mei have survived? That's just it, Katie, how can I ever *know*, for sure? The word I got was that both mother and child had been killed, but things were pretty screwed up over there toward the end of my hitch. They got worse after I left. The whole country was in chaos. As far as the other questions go, well, we'll just have to find her. Maybe she can tell us something." He walked over to the window and leaned his head out. The heat was worse than ever, as though some foul giant was breathing down his neck. And that weird cloud still hung motionless in the air, looming over the lot. It almost seemed to be more than a cloud. More solid than it had been before—a white and terrible thing that seemed to be taking the shape of a giant beast. "And there's something else, too," he said, whipping his head back inside. "Haven't you noticed it? There's something the matter with Patch. He's, I don't know—different somehow. He's not in control any more. It's… there's something wrong. He's losing it. I can feel it."

"How, Sam?" she asked, unable to keep a hint of worry from showing in her voice. Sam caught the sound right away, and knew that it wasn't really Patch that she was concerned about.

"No, Katie," he said with a laugh as he backed slowly away from her, "*I* haven't lost it. Not yet. But I've been in this business for a long time. Gets so you can tell. He's fucked up. He's drinkin' too much. And he's nervous; *scared* of somethin'. I'm tellin' you, somethin's wrong."

Katie shrugged. "Sam, you're changing the subject. There isn't time to worry about Patch now, or the show either. If you want to find out about this girl, you'll have to find her. Now! She won't be around tomorrow. This can't wait. Let's take a walk around the lot, right now, keep an eye out for her while we talk. Whatever's wrong with Patch, if anything is, it will keep." He had to agree, however reluctantly. Whatever he'd told Katie in the unbearable heat of the night, he certainly couldn't tell her that there was something deadly and menacing waiting out there for him, some power not of this Earth. That was the one thing she just wouldn't believe.

They strolled across the lot arm in arm like lovers, each of them keeping a watchful eye on their surroundings. Sam knew that Katie was searching the face of every passing child for the little girl that he might claim as his own, but although he did want to talk to the girl, most of his own his mind was elsewhere. "Katie, look at that," he said, pointing at the... cloud, except that it no longer looked like a cloud to him. It was solid now, frighteningly, undeniably real, and its form was quite distinct. Scales scalloping down its back, red eyes that seemed to glow balefully from within, snakelike tendrils curling from the sides of its awful mouth... It might have been his own little dragon grown to monstrous size, except for a large yellow stain down its side. It waited just outside the lot, completely motionless, seemingly content just to watch him... for the moment.

"You mean the Zipper?" she asked. "Is she there?"

"No, I mean the..." He paused, then shook his head hopelessly. Somehow, it didn't surprise him that she couldn't see it. It wasn't *her* problem. It wasn't after *her*.

That was when all the lights turned red.

8

Aggie put on her costume with special care, making sure that everything was exactly right. She would probably never get a chance to wear it again. This life had been good to her, and she hated the thought of leaving it, but there was no room for sick people in this gypsy existence. It took life and energy to read a mark and tell him everything he wanted to hear. When she left for Susan's, she was fairly sure that she would have to pack it in for the rest of the season, if not forever. Yet even a season seemed like a long time at her age, and she wanted to do something that would make this night special. The last thing in the world she wanted was to remember this life as a series of frights, frustrations, and bad dreams. Whatever she did this evening, it was going to have to serve her memories for quite a while.

But much though she wanted the evening to be pleasant, things had not gotten any better. She was feeling very old and more than a little unsteady. Infirm. Fragile. The nervousness that had plagued her ever since they left Virginia was with her still. If anything, it had gotten worse. All day she had fought a desire to run off, leave right away, leave *now*, without finishing out the date, but that wouldn't be fair to anyone. Besides, she had to give herself this time to say goodbye. Who knew if she would ever be "with it" again? It was this sudden surge of nostalgia that brought her out to the lot for a last look around, a moment or two with Lutzy and Cinda and the rest before she opened the camp.

She was there when it happened.

The lights didn't simply turn red. First, everything went dark, and night descended in earnest upon the carnival. It lasted for just a second. None of the rides stopped spinning. The constant hum from the generator continued as if nothing unusual had happened. It was just a blink; not even long enough for the marks to be disturbed. Then the lights came on again, but it wasn't quite the same. It was dimmer, darker, more sinister. It was as though the power had gone off and not come back quite all the way. A brown-out. But no, that couldn't be it. The rides were turning at full speed. Yet everything looked red. The lights were red. They were *all* red. A collective "Ah" went up from the crowd. The marks found it impressive, but whatever kind of trick it was, Aggie wasn't pleased. Patch should have warned them. It wasn't right. None of it was right. With trembling hands and a heavy heart, Aggie made her way to the Mitt Camp.

She arrived at the Mitt Camp in time to find someone entering the tent before her. The dim red light gave a ghastly look to the intruder; a demon entering its nest. Things had been going so badly that she was almost prepared to believe that it was a demon, until it turned around and she saw that it was just Jeff. Just Jeff… and yet, there was something different about him. Something that couldn't be accounted for by the strange lighting alone. "Aggie," he whispered hoarsely. She jumped. A feeling in her legs and spine and deep in her stomach told her to run. But it was only Jeff. It was her friend.

"Jeff, are you okay?" she asked. He whirled to face her.

"No, Aggie. I'm not okay. No one is okay. Don't you feel it? Something strange is going on. It's everywhere I go. Look at the lights. *They* know. Whatever it is, it's something bad, Aggie. Whatever it is, it frightens me." She fought back an uncontrollable urge to laugh, not that anything was funny. It was just nerves. Somehow, Jeff's hysteria seemed to mesh with her own, putting into words what she hadn't even been able to admit that she felt. And there was something about his face, the way his eyes had sunk back in their sockets, that made him look like a death's-head. She had seen him that way before, and she closed her eyes. "Oh Lord, please not again," she said, but when she opened her eyes, she saw it was just a trick of the light.

"Jeff, calm down. You have to calm down and tell me what's happened. It's just the lights, you know. They took me the same way for a minute, but it's really okay. Just a few simple lights."

"Do I sound crazy to you? I think I must be. Something awful is happening to me and I don't know what to do," he said. His voice sounded desperate, and now that she could see him up close, she could tell that it was more than just the lights. It seemed as though he had spent the last few days reading her mind, and now he was playing it all back for her. Maybe there *was* something happening. The atmosphere around the show had been so very different of late, so… evil… yes, *evil*. That was the word for it. No, that was silly. There wasn't any such thing as a cosmic, all-pervading evil. Still, she had to admit that if it was affecting Jeff too, it couldn't all be in her mind.

"Perhaps..." she started to say. Even Jeff looked hopeful. She wanted to believe it. Anything, as long as it meant that the things that were happening were being caused by something outside of her. She wanted to believe it more than anything, and for that very reason she rejected it. "No, Jeff. This is silly. There is nothing unusual happening. Just the heat, getting on people's nerves, that's all," she said with conviction.

"You're wrong, Aggie. There *is* something happening. There's something evil out there. I know you've felt it too. Something evil, dangerous, and malignant. I can feel it, clutching at my mind. Working its claws into my brain. I don't know how much longer I can fight it. I'm not even sure that I want to fight it any longer."

Aggie stared in horror at Jeff. There *was* something... She could feel the vision starting to come again. No, it mustn't. She couldn't stand it. Not again. Not ever again! Without another word to Jeff, she turned and ran out of the tent.

9

There were no spaces left in the parking lot, but Billingsly didn't care. He pulled the huge bulk of his Mercedes right up onto the sidewalk in front of the main entrance, and eased himself out of the car. He sailed grandly up to the gate, handed the ticket taker a ten dollar bill, and swept on through the turnstile without waiting for his change.

Damn the carnival. Red lights might make it look interesting from a distance, but here on the midway you could barely see where you were going. Fortunately, he already knew where the office was. That would be his first stop. He found Dandy outside, surrounded by underlings. He was barking at them ineffectually, issuing orders that they were ignoring, practically whining. Billingsly didn't know what it was all about, but there was a definite lack of control here that made the fat man wonder if that aura of competence he'd noticed before was only something Dandy managed to put on from time to time. No matter now. "Mr. Dandy," he said, just loudly enough to be heard over the din. Dandy looked up, then went back to what he was doing. Billingsly was annoyed. He was not used to being ignored. "Dandy, right *now*, in your office!"

Dandy glanced up again. This time he looked Billingsly up and down as if he were some strange kind of creature he had never seen before. Then he smiled. "You don't want to go in there," he said. "That's where your friend is."

Billingsly barked out a laugh. "Redd, do you mean? Fantastic. Just the man I wanted to see."

"Go to it, then. I'll be along in a minute," Dandy said.

Billingsly shrugged and opened the door to the trailer. He'd wanted Dandy to be with him simply because sometimes a witness—even one as questionable as a carnival grifter—was useful in getting to the Redds of this world. Still, he had to remember that he had the photographs, and he had Gaylen Schuster. He really didn't need anything else. There was nothing about Redd that worried him. If ever there was a little man who was designed from birth for stomping under foot, it was Redd.

"Hey, Walt, having a good time?" he asked as he entered the office. Redd looked up at him without lifting his head, and smiled. It was a smile

Billingsly would have sworn that the councilman didn't even have in his inventory. It was the smile of a man who had everything under control. Well, Arthur Billingsly could play that game as well as anyone. For a moment, the two men stared at each other, without exchanging a word. Then Billingsly took the seat behind the desk, giving himself the upper hand, and put his feet up.

"I've been waiting for this moment for a long time," Billingsly said. "For years I've had to listen to you preach about how I deal in sin and corruption, about how I pollute the town. Well, you talk a good game, Mr. Redd, but I've got the goods on you now. I know what you've been up to, and I happen to have the pictures to prove it." The speech was carefully designed, and he was fairly sure of the reaction it would get. He expected confusion, concern, possibly even outraged protestations of innocence— but nothing he'd imagined matched the reaction that he actually got.

"And just what do you intend to do about it?" Redd answered coolly. His expression hadn't changed at all.

"I intend to make the biggest stink you've ever heard, unless you give me what I want," Billingsly answered.

"And just what is it that you want?"

"You know damn well what I want. I want this land, and you're going to give it to me. Do you want to know why?" Billingsly asked, ready at last to play his trump card.

"This land? No, I'm sorry, this is *my* land," Redd said.

"Oh, so *that's* what it is. Son of a bitch, I finally get the picture. All this highfalutin, self-righteous talk, and it turns out that you won't sell me the land because *you* want it. Well, buster, you've got another think coming. You're *going* to sell me this land, because if you don't, everyone, including that jealous little wife of yours, is going to see the pictures that prove you've been having an affair with that little carnival girl. Get me?" Billingsly leaned back in Dandy's chair, took out a cigar, and went through the ceremony of lighting it.

"Sir, this conversation is beginning to bore me," Redd said. He stood slowly, walked around the desk, and clapped a hand on Billingsly's shoulder. "You don't want that cigar," he said, taking it out of Billingsly's hand. He took a puff on it himself and then, slowly, deliberately, blew the smoke in the fat man's face. "Especially not when you're feeling so poorly," he added. Billingsly looked up at Redd in stunned surprise. "Oh, yes. You *are* feeling bad now, aren't you? Double vision... and it's getting difficult to breathe." Billingsly drew in a ragged breath, then another. His eyes were starting to bulge.

"You can't have this land," Redd said in a calm, reasonable tone. "No one can have this land. This is *my* land, and people are going to treat it with respect. You respect me now, don't you? Poor man, I know, you're feeling ill, so very sick, but at least your heart is still beating. You can feel it, can't you? Perhaps I can help," he said. He laid his hand on the older man's back and stroked gently. "There now. Feel your heart slow down. Slower, slower, slower... now *stop*," he added suddenly. Billingsly lurched spasmodically to his feet, clutched at his chest, and slumped back into the chair. "There, *that's* better," Redd said brightly. He laughed. Then he turned with a smile and walked out of the office.

10

When the Viking entered the trailer, Essie resisted an urge to smile. "What happened to you?" she asked.

"That bitch! That lousy bitch! And he isn't any better," the Viking said through great gulping sobs.

"You mean *Katie* did that to you?" Magda laughed. "Maybe there *is* some justice in this world." Essie motioned her to silence, but she was too late to stem the tide. The Viking flew at Maggie in a rage. But Maggie was not the novice to fighting that Katie was. In a moment or two, she had the tall blonde down on the floor, and was administering open-palm blows to her face that left angry red welts behind. "This is for Glory! And this one's for Katie! And *this* one's for your lousy fuckin' attitude…" Essie grabbed Maggie's arm before she could deliver another blow.

"All right, Maggie, enough. I think she gets the idea." Maggie backed off and let the woman stand.

Sobbing and cursing incoherently, the Viking pulled her suitcase out of the closet, heaped all of her clothes on the cot, and began to alternate between tossing the clothes into the bag and clumsily struggling into the ones she wanted to wear. Essie chased Maggie and Glory out of the trailer before something was said that might make the Viking decide to stay. She knew when to back off. Besides, though she had no use for the woman, there was no sense kicking her when she was down. She left the trailer to a string of curses that the Viking spat out through puffed and quivering lips.

She fought an urge to go check on Sam and Katie. If they were back together, she would find out in time. The last thing they needed right now was any outside interference. Still, she smiled, feeling just a little responsible for the whole thing. And if the Viking was truly leaving, that was one more weight off her shoulders. But Katie wasn't the only one who would be glad to know that the Viking was leaving.

Cinda was at her usual place in front of the Ring Toss. The crowds had thinned out, and she wasn't very busy. "What's with the lights?" Essie asked.

"I don't know, Es. Some mighty strange things been happenin' here tonight, and I don't mind sayin' it's scarin' the piss outa me. The marks've been rangy as hell, an' then there was the lights. Pritt's been havin' trouble with the animals, they're all spooked. There was Sam passin' out, and that strange ride that no one seems to know where it's come from. I'm tellin' ya, Es, I'm ready to pack it in right now."

"Come on," Essie scoffed. "You been with it long enough to know there's always somethin' going wrong. It's just that tonight it's all goin' wrong at once, that's all. There'll be an easy explanation for it all, too. You'll see." Essie was worried too, but for a different reason. Dandy hadn't told her much of what he was thinking, but she always knew. He'd been counting a lot on this weekend. It wouldn't help him to have all this funny stuff happen right now. Two marks walked over to Cinda's store, and Essie left her to do her job.

Essie went to the office. She had put off seeing Dandy all night, afraid of what this string of disasters would be doing to him. He could be cruel when things were going wrong for him. Not that she minded so much, but he tended to blame her for his problems, and that she really hated. She heard the voices as soon as she neared the office. Neither of them belonged to Dandy. Curious, but not wanting to interfere, she stepped up onto the Winnebago's first step, and leaned over to look in the window. She recognized the men—both of them had been on the lot earlier—but it took her a moment to realize what was going on.

"Double vision… and it's getting difficult to breathe," she heard Redd say, in the calm and quiet voice of someone telling a child not to be afraid of the dark. Billingsly looked like a man having an attack. His eyes were straining wide and his skin was turning blue. It was almost as if the younger man was *making* the whole thing happen. Why didn't he do something? She watched transfixed, wanting to interfere, but somehow afraid to move. Afraid to even make a sound. Afraid to call the man's attention to *her*.

"You can't have this land. No one can have this land. This is *my* land, and people are going to respect it. You respect it now, don't you? Poor man, I know, you're feeling ill, so very sick, but your heart is still beating. You can feel it, can't you? Perhaps I can help. There now. Feel your heart slow down. Slower, slower, slower… now *stop*." Essie watched the old man die. There was no doubt that he was dead. He slumped down in the chair, eyes staring lifelessly ahead. She heard the other man laugh. A cold, terrible laugh, a laugh to turn your bones to ice. She jumped quietly down from the step, and ran to find Dandy.

11

He stretched his arms, took a deep breath, and laughed. It was good to be alive again. Alive and young and strong! And he would grow stronger still. Too long he had been in the dark and the cold, waiting... Now the wait was almost over. Soon he would have such power as he had only dreamed of. Power enough to make him invulnerable, unstoppable. He took a good look at the body that stared lifelessly up at him from the chair. That had been easy. Poor thing. Struck down by a heart attack in the prime of his life. A pity. Billingsly might actually have been useful to him, but he wanted the wrong thing, the one thing he could never have. They had to learn. This was *his* land. It had been given to him, as his reward... he would not allow it to be defiled.

Yes, he had been a true and faithful son, and he had been given a second chance. He would grow even stronger. This was a good body; he would be used to it soon. Already, he could feel his influence stretching out like groping tendrils. Now he must gather strength from those around him. Their fear was food and drink to him. Their struggles against him an exercise for his will. Some, he knew, were already under his control; others felt only the effect of his presence, but he would have them too, in time. Then he had some unfinished business to take care of. He had called his adversaries to him. The battle had already begun.

Without a backward glance at the blob of already-spoiling meat left behind, he walked out of the trailer to make ready to do his work.

12

It was too hot to bother with the damn ride any longer. His clothes, his hands, even his face and hair were covered with grease. What Gregor needed was a long, hot shower, and maybe even a little nap to make up for the sleep he'd lost that morning. He tinkered the thing back together and closed the cover plates. He thought of the rides as children. Sometimes they got sulky, and there just wasn't anything you could do with them. Idly, he flipped the switch, and the motor blazed to life as if there had never been anything wrong with it. Gregor uttered a curse in Hungarian and turned the motor off.

"Ah, you been playing with me," he said, patting the motor case just as if it were a tiny head. "Tomorrow it's back to work for you." Not taking any chances after the earlier fiasco, he set the brake and locked the motor, even though he knew it couldn't possibly run until it was opened up. Now he could go have that shower in peace.

Even with all the windows opened, there wasn't a breath of air in the trailer. He turned the shower on, letting it work up as good a head of steam as it ever did. For years now he had promised himself that one of these days he was going to spend the night in one of those roadside places where the showers were hot, the beds freshly made, and you could have breakfast in bed at the lift of a telephone. Now he resolved to do so the following night. He wasn't going to let any damn carnival aggravate him to death. Meanwhile he stripped off his clothes, looking forward to any shower, even a tepid one.

The knock on the door couldn't have been at a worse time. Gregor threw a towel around his waist and pressed his dirty face against the window screen.

"Gregor, on the lot, *now*!" Dandy called.

"Hey, Patch, have a heart! I'm just taking a shower. I'll be there in a minute."

"Now!" Dandy said. There was a quaver in his voice that told the mechanic that he meant business. But Gregor had taken enough for one day.

"Yeh, yeh, yeh," he said sarcastically as he threw the same dirty clothes on over his sweaty body. "Be right there." He took his time getting dressed, turning off the water, even tidying up a little bit before he left the trailer. It had been a lousy day, and he enjoyed making Dandy sweat. Then, finally convinced that he had wasted as much time as he could get away with, he let himself out of the trailer.

He didn't need to examine Dandy's sweating palms or the wild look of excitement on his face to know that something really major was wrong this time. What's more, he instantly spotted exactly what the trouble was. Without waiting for instructions from Dandy, he ran toward the lot.

It wasn't just that only the red bulbs remained lit, as he had first thought. Gregor could almost have convinced himself that there was some reason for *that*—but this? There was *no* explanation for this. All of the bulbs had turned red, as if some magic spell had been placed on the lot. Gregor felt the hairs prickle on the backs of his arms. Only God or the Devil could do something like this. Gregor was not a religious man, but in his native Hungary he had heard stories, even seen things that couldn't be explained. Back there, when he was a boy, people still wore sacks of garlic and silver charms to ward off the devil's work. He had long considered it nonsense… but now he wasn't so sure.

Then he noticed the strange new ride, sitting right where his Spider had been, and he knew for certain that all this wasn't God's doing. This was the Devil's work. The evil one was at work, tonight, here! Gregor had never been so frightened in his life. Not even as a small boy during the war, when he had come close to death many times. But that was nothing next to this. The mechanic crossed himself. He felt an urge to run and, with difficulty, fought it down. Not even at the risk of his immortal soul would he be shown a coward in front of these people. He chided himself for his silliness. He was a rational man, after all, a modern man, not a simple peasant from some little superstitious village.

"Mr. Patch, how…?" he started to ask.

"That's what I wanted you to tell me," Dandy said. "How? How on Earth could every light suddenly turn red like that? Jeezus, it's like witchcraft!" Gregor looked at the man's eyes, the hands that trembled ever so slightly, so that he had to keep them in his pockets to keep them still, and he realized that Dandy was every bit as frightened as he was. *More* frightened.

It was at just that moment that Essie ran, up looking sweaty and hysterical. "Patch! Patch!" she cried, and threw her arms around neck. She burst wildy into tears.

Katie spotted the girl before Sam did. He had been unable to take his eyes off the thing outside the fence. It was as real to him as the solid little dragon that he held in his pocket, so real that he was surprised that everyone on the lot wasn't pointing and screaming. It seemed to be waiting patiently; waiting for what, he couldn't tell, although he had the sick, uneasy feeling that its eyes were fixed on him wherever he happened to go. So strong was the conviction that it was watching him, and so preoccupied had he been by it, that he hadn't even noticed when the lights changed to red until Katie pointed it out to him. It had just seemed to be another episode, like the one he'd had earlier. He could tell that the changing lights frightened her a little, but he didn't have the energy to be scared of anything else, and once he put his arm around her, Katie relaxed a bit as well. It was then that she spotted the child.

"Look, Sam. There she is," Katie said. At first it looked like the child might run away, but Katie was good with kids, and it was she who talked to the girl, soothingly, the way you gentle a frightened horse.

"He's like a bear sometimes. He likes to growl. But underneath he's really a nice guy. I think he has something of yours," she said to the child.

"My dragon," Mei Chou said, growing excited.

"Yes, you'll get your dragon—but first we have to go someplace quiet. Someplace where we can talk," Katie said.

Mei Chou looked at Sam through large, solemn eyes. Eyes that reminded him of Thot. "He's waiting for us," she said. Katie looked confused, but Sam smiled and took her by the hand.

"I don't think he means us any harm," he said. He walked her back to his trailer.

What do you say to a girl who may well be your orphaned child? *What kind of life have you had? Who are you living with now?* "What do you know of your mother?" he asked her finally.

"I never knew my mother," the child replied. "She died, I think, when I was very small. I don't know who cared for me after that. Different people, I think. I stayed longest with a Chinese family in Saigon; they gave me my name. Then, when Mother Chem wanted to leave the country, they put us together. You see, families got first priority. It was done a lot." She told him about her life in this country, about her school and the people she knew. On the verge of some great emotion, she searched Sam's face, and he knew that one word from him would push her into either ecstasy or great despair, but he didn't know which word to say. "Tell me about my mother," she asked at last.

Sam heard Katie draw a sharp breath. "Honey, how…" she started to say.

"She was very beautiful," Sam interrupted. He felt Katie's hand clasp his shoulder in support. "Come on, let's go find that chain you took, and we'll take you home."

"Home? I don't have a home. You can't take me back there! I won't go!" Tears sprang to her eyes.

"Oh, Christ, what do you want from me? You can't stay *here*." Sam said. "This is no place for a kid. I wouldn't know what to do for you. What about school? Do you even know what I do for a living?" Sam threw his hands in the air, and looked at Katie pleadingly. "I won't have it. You just can't stay with me. You have to go home!" he said.

On the horizon, the dragon seemed to stir, to move its great head menacingly, and Sam was pierced again with an icy shaft of fear and unease.

Part Seven

HEY RUBE

1

Jeff watched Aggie run out of the tent. He knew what she was thinking. He could see it in her eyes, the way she looked at him. She was one of the few people he thought of as a friend, but obviously *she* didn't feel that way. Oh, no. Now he saw the truth. She thought she was much too good to even go near him. He had wanted, hoped that she would tell him everything was all right, a mother kissing away the hurt from a scraped knee. Well, she wasn't his mother, thank god, so—so much for her. So much for all of them. Who did she think she was to judge him like that? There was nothing wrong with *him*. "Damn you! Damn you! Damn you!" he shouted, banging his fists against her flimsy card table until it bounced and fell, flinging its contents across the tiny tent. Rage boiled inside him. He hadn't done anything wrong. It was *her*. Her and everyone like her. She was just like Carole, both of them pretending to be so nice and kind and good, and all the while they were looking down their snooty little noses at him. Them and their high and mighty attitudes. What did they have to feel so superior about? He assigned Aggie's face to the overturned table and kicked it soundly one more time. "That's for *you*," he said, then stalked out of the tent.

The infield looked foreign, as though he was no longer welcome there. The cloyingly sweet smells of caramel corn and cotton candy sickened him, making him want to gag. Even the tinny music, barely audible over the bustling crowd, sounded harsh and mocking. He was no longer a part of the carnival. It had rejected him.

Well, so be it. He wouldn't stay where he wasn't wanted. But before he left, he would make a noise that they would hear from Maine to Mississippi! They wouldn't soon forget Jeff Petticola.

"Howdy, Jeff," Cinda called as he passed the Ring Toss. She was outside the booth, leaning back against the counter as the agents often did while waiting for customers. She held three rings in her hand, banging them impatiently against her thigh. She was another one. He could hear the condescending tone in her voice, see the look of hatred in her eyes.

"Fuck you!" he replied, walking past without a backward glance.

There was a long line in front of the ten-in-one. He could hear them all clucking and snorting as he nudged his way to the front, slipped under the restraining rope, and ducked inside. Here, at last, there was some peace; the tent, as usual, being empty between shows. The curtains between the little alcoves were pulled back, making one long room, and giving the individual, wood-crate platforms almost the feel of furniture. Here at last he felt at home. This was where the freaks belonged, and he was king of the freaks. He jumped up onto one of the wooden display platforms and did a little dance. "Here I am, world!" he shouted to the empty tent. "You hear me, freaks? I'm one of you now."

Randall poked his head in through the back flap and looked around. His expression was angry until he spotted Jeff, then he brightened. But Jeff could see through that pose, too. Even the damn freaks thought they were better than he was. Here was Randall, a squat little toad of a man, with those disgusting lumps hanging all over his body, and he had the nerve to feel superior. Well, at least Jeff knew what was what and who was better than whom. "Oh, hi, Jeff," the Gnarly Man said.

"Oh, cut the crap, you ugly little two-faced hypocrite! I know you hate me. You all hate me!" He jumped down from the box and ran toward the entrance, then whirled and faced Randall, his finger pointed at the man who, even now, had the gall to pretend to be shocked. "But you'll all be sorry, you know. Yes, you will!"

All sign of Carole was gone when he got to the trailer, except the blood stains on the sheets. Too bad there weren't more of them, but at least she was gone. That was good. He would only have had to hit her again if she were there. In fact, now that he thought about it, that might not be such a bad idea. It would have been fun to punch her around a little. It was all her fault, anyway. People wouldn't be giving him such a hard time now if it wasn't for her. What a fucking little bitch she was to come sneaking into his life with her promises of sex and maybe even something more, and then to do *this* to him. He wished she were there right now. He'd give her something to cry about. He pounded his fist into the wall.

He looked in the mirror, amazed to find that the face that stared back at him was the same one he always saw. From the way people had been looking at him tonight, he'd wondered if he'd grown horns or fangs or something. Well, that was easily taken care of. Instead of the usual clown face he wore to work, he applied the greasepaint in great big swirls of white and black, until he resembled nothing so much as a living skull, dead and deadly. Two eyes peered, small and dark and feral, from within the blackened sockets. Then, to complete the picture, a flash of scarlet that made it look as if his throat had been cut from ear to ear. The grotesque effect it produced in combination with his simple clown costume of baggy pants, suspenders, and a T-shirt pleased him greatly, and he stood for a long time admiring himself in the mirror, trying it with and without the orange wig, and deciding that without looked better. Scarier. And they had every right to be scared of him tonight. Yes, sir. Now he saw himself as others saw him. A demon, a creature of the night. A monster. Now he was ready.

The shocked looks on people's faces as he walked to the Bozo cage did not seem to him very different than the looks he'd been getting all night long anyway. Even Maxie—Maxie who'd always pretended to be so fucking kind and fatherly—looked right into his soul and saw the horror there. Well, Maxie too could go straight to hell and roast on a fucking spit... but not now. Not yet. Now, he needed Maxie's permission to get into the cage.

"You sure you want to go on tonight, kid?" Maxie asked.

Jeff bit back the response that came to his lips, and answered instead, "Sure, where else would I want to be on a night as hot as this?" Even so, he noticed Maxie's reluctance as he let Larry out of the cage so that Jeff could get in. And Larry must have noticed how much Jeff was looking forward to working this night, because suddenly he seemed reluctant to leave. Larry, who rarely wanted to work at all. He bit back his anger. That was for later. Right now he *had* to get inside the tank. "Hey guys, I'm only trying to match the decor," he said, pointing to the skull on the ride next door. He knew they didn't quite buy it, for even after Larry left the cage, he spent a moment whispering to Maxie in a way that made Jeff wish that he could tear into them right then and there. But there wasn't time. If he didn't hurry into the cage, Larry just might talk Maxie into letting him do another shift.

Jeff rushed into the cage, and took his seat on the perch. There, he thought with relief. Nothing could stop him now. From up here, he could survey his surroundings, the rides, the little asshole agents, the crowds of fucking stupid marks strolling by, gaping dumbly at him. Slowly, he smiled. *This is gonna to be fun,* he thought.

2

"I'm not going back! I'm not. You can't make me. If you don't want me, I'll find someplace else to go. I don't need you. I can take care of myself," Mei Chou thrust her chin out, folded her arms across her chest, and looked away from them both.

"Listen, you. If you're my daughter, then I can damn well put you over my knee and teach you what's what. No kid of mine is going to be a thief and a runaway. I can't keep you here. You can't stay with me, so you're goin' back and that's that." He moved menacingly toward her. "You're gonna take back the chain and the money and you're gonna apolog—" Suddenly, he felt all of his strength flowing out of his body, as if someone had opened a drain. He stuck his arm out and caught the wall. It was all that kept him from falling.

Katie rushed to his side, but he couldn't let *her* help him. He didn't even want her to see him this way. Using what little strength he had, he twisted out of her grasp and found himself pressed against the window, the metal fittings biting into his arm.

It was out there. He didn't need to see it to know that. It pressed on his consciousness the way a bandage pressed on the skin. He raised his eyelids, saw it—the dragon, towering against the sky—then tried to look away, but he couldn't find the energy to turn around. It held him spellbound, unable to look away, and yet somehow he knew that staring at it was the worst thing he could do. Looking at it, acknowledging its presence, seemed to give it even more form and substance—as if it were his own willingness to give it power over him that *gave* it that power. He closed his eyes. It was all he could do. Until now, his only fear of the dragon was that he saw it at all, but suddenly all that had changed. Suddenly he realized that it was not merely watching and waiting. It was there for a *purpose*. If he could only lift the veils of gauze that clouded his mind, he would know what to do. Instinctively, he reached for the little carving under his shirt, but it wasn't there. Then he remembered. He had torn it off his neck and thrown it across the kootch tent—and suddenly the welt on the back of his neck where the leather thong had bitten into it ached unbearably. The weakness, the fatigue, the confusion, it had all started then. He began to have an inkling of what he had to do. It was his dragon, angry and jealous that he had deserted it. He had to get it back—he had to wear it again. Make it once again his protector.

"I have to go," he said, but Katie was on him in an instant, holding him up, helping him toward the bed.

"You're not going anywhere," she said, firmly.

"You don't understand, Katie. I have to. If you love me at all, you won't get in my way." The words came out in a hoarse whisper, but there was a force behind them. He saw the reluctance in her eyes, but she bit her lip and backed away.

"All right," she said warily, "but we're coming with you."

He didn't want assistance, but he found it difficult to walk without her aid, so he was forced to allow her to help. They did their best to make it look as though he merely had his arm around her, but she actually took quite a bit of his weight as they stumbled across the lot to the kootch tent with Mei following behind. The dragon followed, too. Close enough for him to feel its searing breath on his back. He let himself turn and look, though he wanted to ignore it with every fibre of his being. Katie, he knew, was confused and worried, but she didn't ask questions, and she didn't interfere. She helped him to the tent, seated him in one of the folding chairs, and backed away.

"Now what?" she asked. He reached for her hand, and took a moment to push a strand of hair behind her ear, then he put his hand behind her neck and pulled her gently to him for a kiss.

"We're looking for a tiny carving of a dragon. You've seen it, Katie. It's the one I always wear." And for the first time since his childhood, he found himself saying a silent prayer. "Please God, let me find it in time."

3

Dandy patted Essie gently with one arm, and shrugged at Gregor with the other. This was embarrassing, her throwing herself at him like this in public. He would have liked to herd her off someplace a little more private, but she was holding on to him so tightly that he couldn't move. His repeated suggestion that they go back to his office only made her more hysterical. What's more, he couldn't make heads or tails out of the few words she managed to gasp out. She talked quickly in a high-pitched and ragged voice that she interspersed with deep gulps of air. There were even moments when no sound came out at all. It would have been funny if it wasn't obvious that she was very badly shaken.

Finally, he got her as far as Lutzy's joint, and sat her down on the bench. He managed to get a few sips of coffee into her, and she was able to speak more clearly, but even then it all sounded like nonsense.

"Patch, it was murder! That… that fat man… in the office. I saw him. I heard him. He made him have a… he made him have a h… heart attack. He did! I saw him," she said, her words all rushed together incoherently, separated by long pauses for breath. Dandy fought back an urge to laugh.

"Essie, calm down!" he shouted. She looked up at him, her face strained and drawn, but her breath came a little more naturally. "Now come on, woman. Start making sense. What on Earth are you talkin' about?"

Essie took a deep breath and started again. "I came lookin' for you. I know things ain't been goin' so good tonight and I thought… I thought maybe I could h… help. I got to your office, and I heard these strange voices inside. Oh, Patch, it was awful." She started to cry again. "It was that guy, the one you fixed up with Katie, and he was there with that fat man, you know, and he was… he…"

"Redd?" Dandy asked. He couldn't picture that asswipe civil servant hurting anyone. "Or do you mean the other one? Calm down, Baby, and tell me what he did to ya."

"Not to *me*. It was the other one. He made him have a heart attack!"

"You mean the two of them were arguing and one of them had an attack?" Dandy was really concerned now. Not so much on behalf of the sick man, but Essie shouldn't be *this* upset. She'd weathered far worse things without even batting an eye.

"No! I mean what I said. Oh shit. I can't explain it, but he did. He *made* him have a heart attack. Just by talking to him. It was awful. Oh, Patch, I've never been so frightened." She made an effort to calm herself, taking a large gulp of coffee and several deep breaths. "I'm better now," she said, and meant it. "Listen, I know it sounds crazy, but he was like some kind of demon in there. Like he had some sort of magic powers." She explained to him what she had seen and heard.

"Okay, now listen carefully, because I want you to do exactly what I say. I want you to find Aunt Aggie, and I want you to take her back to her trailer. Have her give you a cup of tea, and ask her if you can stay the night. Got me? I want you to go right to bed, and stay there until the morning."

"No, Patch! I don't need... I can't go. I gotta stick around. You can't deal... you can't... Patch, please don't send me away. I want to help!" she said. He could see the effort she was making to stay composed.

"Essie, if there's a murderer runnin' around here, then you saw him. I don't wanna have to worry about you, too. The best help you can be for me is to do what I say. Go to Aggie's and keep outta my way. Okay?" He looked into her eyes, saw her resist, then agree, reluctantly. He patted her on the arm, and she headed for the Mitt Camp tent. Poor girl was coming unglued. It had to be something in the air. Everyone was acting crazy. He headed over to the office to see if he could begin to make any sense out of the story she'd told him. If even part of it was correct, there would be a dead body in there. Just what he needed. Another mess to work his way out of.

There was a body in the office, all right. He checked to make sure Billingsly was actually dead. He was. Dandy knew that he ought to call the police right away, but it was only another hour or so until closing time. The dead man wasn't going anywhere. It was silly to have the cops running around on the lot while it was open. Think of all the money they'd lose. He did wonder a little about the story Essie had told him. Surely there was a simple, rational explanation for the whole thing. Dandy decided to find Redd if he could. Maybe he could have the whole thing straightened out by the time the cops showed up.

He found Redd on the lot. The politician had been surprisingly easy to spot in the thinning crowd. He wasn't quite sure just what to say to him, but Redd took the whole matter out of his hands.

"Ah, Mr. Dandy. Just the man I wanted to speak to," he said loudly. Then he put an arm around Dandy's shoulders and whispered, "There's been a tragedy. Mr. Billingsly seems to have had a heart attack. I'd like to handle things with the police on your behalf. I think that would be best, don't you? I know that carnival people aren't always given the best treatment by law-enforcement men, and after all, you are our guests. Now, if you'll just cooperate with me, I'll see to it that there aren't any repercussions for you or your business. I have some Glenfiddich with me. Perhaps you'd like to relax and have a drink and let me take care of things for once. Oh, but maybe we ought to lock the gates first."

Yes, the gates. Why hadn't Dandy thought of that? "It might be more difficult if the police get here and people have left the lot," Redd added.

Dandy nodded. It *would* be better if the gates were locked. Good thing Redd was taking care of things now. He would never have thought of that on his own. He hurried away, feeling a real sense of urgency about getting it done.

Somehow, he knew that it was very important.

4

Eli's cab pulled up at the main entrance to the carnival, and Frank helped the old man into his chair. There was a young girl just outside the gate. She was leaning against the fence, crying, hugging herself into near invisibility. Eli almost didn't see her at all. He didn't know her, but then he didn't often have occasion to leave the house anymore. She looked so unhappy that he had to go speak to her. "Are you all right?" he asked.

She jumped when she heard him, and hugged herself even tighter; when she looked up, he could see the bruises starting on her face, traces of dried blood in the corner of her mouth, and the stains on her torn blouse. "Do you need help?" he asked. She looked him over warily, then shook her head. "Are you from around here?" he tried again. This time she nodded. He really wished there was something he could do. "Why don't you take the cab?" he said. Again she shook her head.

"No money," she said in a soft voice that held all the sadness in her face.

"I'll pay for it," he said. He handed Frank a five and told him to take the girl home.

"Want me to come back for you, Mr. Jefferson?" the driver asked.

"No, Frank. I don't think I'll need you," he replied.

He had some difficulty going through the turnstile. It must have looked very odd, a twisted old man in a wheelchair, feeble and obviously in pain, trying to force his way into a carnival, but the woman who took the tickets helped him through with no more than a quizzical glance. It wasn't much better inside. The paths between the rides were narrow and still fairly crowded, despite the hour. No one was in a big hurry to make way for him. And as he made his slow progress along the midway, he kept watch for his brother. Surely, another old man wouldn't be so hard to spot among all these crowds of high-spirited young people, but there was no sign of him at all.

The first thing that hit Eli was the smell of raw sugar that permeated the air. Everything looked strange and oddly distorted in the dark red light. Shadows were green, the hollows and lines in peoples faces exaggerated until they almost seemed like walking caricatures, or perhaps walking corpses, and somehow, in the bally in front of the sideshow, the exhibitions seemed more normal than the customers. Eli laughed to think that he, with his mutilated frame, his lined and wizened face, must surely look like something out of a late-night television movie, an ancient mummy come to life.

Strange how the lights, the action, the difficulty in getting around, all distracted him from where he was. The last time he'd been here, things had been very different. It was right over there, where the big tent with the pictures of the fire-eater and the tattooed man now stood, that he had lain for minutes of agony that seemed like days, slipping in and out of consciousness until the ambulance came. He could remember clearly how Jake had stood over him, crying, hysterical, while he listened, unable to answer or even to move. All he could do was lie there and force himself to keep on breathing, while flames consumed the house, and Morgan himself danced like a madman in the upstairs window, twisting in the flames, until the very timbers of the house fell through.

Funny, how calmly he could think about it now.

Slowly, he made his way over to where the house had stood, and found himself blocked by a six-foot platform without a ramp to give him access. It was a strange ride, with an odd name that was somehow connected to the Morgan affair as well. Vaguely, he recalled Jake telling him something once. Something about how Morgan called his house "The Place of Skulls." The same name as the ride. That couldn't be just a coincidence.

He pondered it until he found himself distracted by a death's-head clown in a cage nearby. The clown was surrounded by the largest crowd in the carnival, and he taunted them mercilessly as they watched without enjoyment. Without knowing why he did so, Eli wheeled as close as he could get, and settled down to wait. Someone pressed up close beside him. He felt the gentle scratch of paper being stuffed into his hand. It was a five dollar bill.

"I sent the cab home, Mr. Jefferson. I couldn't leave just yet," Carole said. "There's something I have to take care of."

5

Jenny had gone to sleep right after dinner. The child never slept well during overnight travel, and Pritt had laid down the law. Now, suddenly, she found herself sitting bolt upright in bed, and she wasn't sure what had awakened her. She had the distinct impression that someone had shaken her, but a quick check showed her that she was alone. She decided that it must have been a dream. Still sleep-fogged, she stretched out again, pulling the covers up over her head. It was in that first, easy, floating stage right before sleep comes, that it happened again. Something hit her on the back and bounded away. This time she threw off the covers and sat up, dangling her feet over the edge. She was completely awake.

The answer to her mystery skidded across the floor, banged into the wall with a painful sounding thud, and took off in the direction from which he'd started. "Diablo!" she screamed. She raced after the kitten and picked him up. "That was bad! Bad cat," she said, and let him squirm out of her arms. Then she opened the cabinet and poured some Little Friskies into his bowl. Perhaps that would keep him quiet for a little while. Not that she had any hopes of getting back to sleep. This was one of the rare times when Jenny regretted her parents' vagabond life. There was no television, and she had already read the few books they were able to carry with them in the camper. She had never been one for dolls or toys, and most of the games that could be played indoors required at least two players. She wanted to get dressed and go out on the lot, but Pritt had been very clear about that. "You get yourself into that bed and don't let me see your face until morning," he had told her. Only once had she ever disobeyed a direct order from her father. She wouldn't do it again.

Out of sheer boredom, she sat herself down at the table and watched the cat for a long time. He was very playful tonight, running back and forth within the cramped quarters, stopping occasionally to chase his tail. And then he did something strange. He stopped dead on the floor right in front of her and began to stare at a spot right over her left shoulder. She looked behind her, but there wasn't anything there. Diablo continued to stare. Suddenly, he inflated, each hair standing straight out from his tiny body until he was almost twice his normal size. The cat hissed. Jenny was frightened now. The cat growled, backed up, then hissed again. Something had scared Diablo. Something that she couldn't see. All of a sudden, she didn't care about her father being mad. She grabbed her robe, slid her feet into a pair of sneakers, and ran for the door. "You'll be all right here," she said to the cat, who by now had gone back to playing as if nothing had happened. "Really, you will."

The lights had all been turned off in the ten-in-one, and many of the joints had closed their awnings, so she knew that it had to be very late, but there was still a large crowd on the lot. That was unusual at this time of night. What's more, they all seemed to be gathered around the Bozo. Without hesitation, she bypassed the side show and ran to her mother's store.

6

Essie didn't go to Aggie's place. About halfway there, she began to calm down, to realize that Dandy had only been trying to get rid of her. What on Earth was he up to? She would simply follow him, not without being seen, but there were ways to do these things. One thing the carnival didn't lack was platforms, towers, tall structures. Lots of high places where she could hide and keep an eye on what was happening. There was, for instance, a place in the Roller Coaster tunnel that the roughies used for maintenance… and occasionally for other things, but that was too dangerous when the ride was in use. There was another place the roughies went. Sharing a trailer six or seven ways, they were very well chaperoned, but teenage boys will always find *some*where to go if they've got someone willing to go with them. This place would make a particularly good observation point, because it was right out in the open, yet screened from prying eyes by a wooden facade and an overhead awning. It was the top of the trucks that made up Bluebeard's Castle. From there, she could watch the whole lot without being seen.

She was almost spotted climbing the ladder, though. Pritt came out of the ten-in-one just as she put her foot on the very first rung. "Hi, Esmerelda. Strange night, huh? Maybe the strangest one *I've* ever seen. Been in this business a long time, and never seen the like."

You don't know the half of it, she thought. She leaned up against the ladder casually, as if that had been her only goal. He offered her a cigarette, and she took it gratefully. "Good thing Emma Mae's on the light side. I've been in some shows you would have had to call a crane to get the fat lady back up on her feet," Essie said.

"Yeah, but what about the lights?" Pritt said. Essie drew a deep drag on the cigarette. She didn't want to get into that again. "Why the hell is the boss man playin' around with the lights? You can't hardly see nothin' in the tent anymore." He squinted up at the string of red bulbs that surrounded his tent. "Well, time for one last show. Then Cinda and me and Jennie're gonna catch one hell of a good night's sleep." He sauntered away.

Essie breathed a sigh of relief. Let Patch take the weight for the lights. She only hoped that most of the rest of them would blame Dandy as well.

Any explanation was better than none. As soon as Pritt was out of sight, off went the shoes, then seven, eight, nine, ten steps, and she was up the ladder before anyone else could notice her.

It was an odd view of the lot from up here. People on the Zipper slid past within a few feet of her. Their expressions ranged from wild excitement to outright terror. Essie never could understand why people did that to themselves. There were some places she could only see through spinning steel, or when the ride wasn't running. Part of the back lot was obscured by the tops of the tents. It took a long time to spot Dandy, but that was because he wasn't where she expected him to be. He wasn't near the office, and he wasn't alone. He had gone all the way to the back of the parking lot, and he was speaking to some guy. She could tell just by their intimacy, the set of their bodies, that their talk was supposed to be a secret, but it wasn't until a few moments later, when they separated, that she recognized the man. Redd, she realized, feeling a thrill of apprehension.

Dandy punched Redd in the arm as they separated. It was a friendly gesture, accompanied by a laugh. Essie could not see the other man's expression, but there was a real feeling of camaraderie on Dandy's side. She'd known Patch a long time. He was placating Redd. Redd! A man who—even if she *had* been wrong about what she thought she heard— had at the very least stood calmly by and watched another man die without lifting a finger to help. Her eyes followed Redd as he walked back toward the infield, then went back to watching Dandy. She couldn't really tell what he was doing. He was walking along just inside the tall fence that circled the property, and seemed to be checking it for something. Then she realized that there had been a gate in the section he had been checking, and what he was doing—it was obvious now that he had moved a little to one side—was putting the padlocks on the gate. Closing and locking it. He moved around to another gate and locked that as well. Essie was puzzled. They needed those extra exits. Why, they would be closed down faster for lack of exits than for all the naked women, broken rides, and gaffed games in the world. She watched in puzzlement for a long time, but when she became certain that he was heading for the main entrance, she knew that she had to interfere.

She half-slid, half-climbed down the ladder. The shoes she forgot about completely until the taffy apples, caramel corn, and half-crushed cigarette butts under foot forced her to return for them. She tried going around the back way, behind the booths and rides along the fence, but the cables, trash barrels, and other debris blocked her way behind almost every store, so she went through the midway. But there, frustratingly, the crowds were almost too thick to push through. By far the largest concentration of people were gathered in front of the Bozo tank. Turning quite a tip tonight… but there was something odd about the patter, and she paused to listen.

7

"Susan, I've got to get out of here right away," Aggie said. "Now. Tonight. I don't know what's happening to me. I think I'm losing my mind." She was instantly sorry that she'd said it. Now Susan would panic, and that was the last thing Aggie wanted, but she knew she couldn't manage even another night of this. It didn't seem to matter that she knew it was all in her head. That only made things worse. In doubting her sanity, she actually began to wonder if Jeff really had said those strange things to her, if the lights really had turned red, or if it was all in her mind. How many of the bizarre things that had gone on in the last few days had really happened?

"Okay, Mom. Try to relax. It's probably not all that serious, so don't worry. Mark and I will be down to pick you up in a couple of hours. Just sit tight, okay?" The voice on the other end of the phone was calm and collected. Susan didn't believe her; probably thought it was a bid for attention. Aggie was sure that was what Mark was telling her. Not that it mattered. They were coming for her. That was the important part. Later, she could send David down to collect her stuff. Later she would worry about later. She had to get out of here, *now*.

She was really going! The thought filled her with a kind of joy she'd lately forgotten she could even feel. For a moment, she felt as light as a feather. She didn't know why. Whatever was wrong with her, it certainly wouldn't stop just because she left the carnival… or would it? *Forget about it,* she told herself—but even if she didn't make any plans for the future yet, she still had things to do. She had to make arrangements for someone to fold up her tent and pack the trailer. Someone should probably move it off the lot and find some local parking for it, too. Ordinarily, she would have asked Jeff, but he had done so much for her lately, and besides, right now he seemed to be having problems of his own. Maybe Pritt would help her.

Aggie got to the ten-in-one just as the last show was ending. She found Pritt out in the back and put the question to him. "Gosh, Aggie, I'd like to help, but I'd hate to promise. I got this tent to do, and I have to help Cinda. I barely had time to scratch today, and who knows what it'll be like tomorrow. Tell ya what: you see if you can get anyone else, and if not, let me know and I'll try."

She thanked him and left. It was a big operation, and she had done things for most of the other carnies at one time or another. Even Sam's girls could do it, if push came to shove. There was no reason to depend on Pritt if he was that busy. Or she could just say "the hell with it" and leave it up to Dandy. She was sure he wouldn't strike the lot and leave her stuff sitting here unprotected. He would have to find someone to move it for her.

Most of the infield was empty now, except for a crowd that was gathering around the Bozo cage. Maxie was probably raking in a bundle tonight. In a way, it was a shame, because she'd hoped to get a chance to say goodbye to Jeff before she left. She was still feeling uncomfortable about the way she had left him. But Susan would be there soon, and Aggie knew that she had to be packed and ready when her daughter got there, but maybe… just maybe, if she went over there now she would get a chance to talk to him for a minute.

The dragon eluded them. Even Sam, as tired and used-up as he felt, got up from his chair to help in the search. They checked under and on top of the makeup tables, and under the edge of the tent, even reaching under the back of the dance platform on the other side of the partition. They found almost everything, from used gum to a broken key, but they didn't find the little dragon. And they had to find it soon. Sam could feel the large dragon's presence now more strongly than ever. He knew that it was just outside the tent flap. Every once in a while, the tent would ripple. Perhaps Katie attributed that to the wind, but he knew what it really was. Mei knew it too, though she showed no fear, for she would look up whenever it happened, and then renew the search with increased vigor.

"Wait, Sam," Katie said at last. "This is a waste of time. Let's try to do this the sensible way. Tell me where you were standing when you took it off, and which direction you threw it." Sam stood and walked to the center of the room. It was hard to remember. Especially when he heard the sound of claws on the canvas, and felt a hot blast of air rushing in through the back flap. Why hadn't he given more thought to what he was doing at the time? Still, he thought he remembered, catching a glint of the purple curtain as the dragon flew across the room.

The three of them tried again, piled together at the back of the curtain that cordoned off the stage from the dressing room. "We've got to hurry," Sam said.

"I'm going to check the stage. Just in case it was kicked into the other room. We've been trotting around here like elephants for a long time," Katie said. She pulled at the curtain. It came open about half-way, and then refused to budge. She reached up to push the rings aside on the curtain rod.

"Sam, it's here! I've found it! The thong is all wrapped around the curtain rod." Katie solemnly untwisted the dragon and pulled it down from the rod. She held it up for Sam to see.

Jeff squared himself on the perch and looked over the marks. Normally, he would pick on the ones who would play the longest, taunting them just enough to get them playfully anxious to avenge their honor by dunking him in the water, escalating his jibes little by little... just enough to keep them going. Usually, it was a good-natured game he played, fun for him, fun for the watching tip, and even the mark enjoyed it once he was no longer on the hot seat. Jeff was good at his job. He knew the line and he never stepped over it—but tonight was different. Tonight there was blood in the air, and Jeff went for it like a hungry cat. Every single person out there had secrets, innermost fantasies, hidden fears, things that—no matter how innocuous they might seem to the person next to them— haunted them late at night when the if-onlys came around. Somehow Jeff knew that tonight, he could tap into those hidden corners. He had always been good at reading a mark, but what he felt as he sat there on this special night was very different. More like tuning a radio into the dark recesses of their souls. Oh, he would get them all for those looks of pity and revulsion; their damn superior attitudes; the way they sneered at him and looked down on him. Not a single one of them had any right to think themselves better than he was. He knew he had the ammunition to gun them *all* down. He licked his lips and started in.

"Hey, Chubby," he called to a heavy-set man in the front row. It was best to start slowly, to sound as normal as possible, setting up his pins before he knocked them down. His spoke into the microphone, and the voice that came through the speakers was tinny and distorted, adding an even more taunting edge to the words he spoke. "I can see you have a problem with inflation. This man has a king-sized bed... his wife sleeps in the guest room. Come on, Fatso. Put me in the water." The man laughed and bought a set of balls. They always did. It was partly embarrassment, and partly an effort to look like a good sport. The man took three throws and missed the target three times. "I'm high and I'm dry," Jeff taunted. Now he really went after him. "Bet your wife don't know how much you *like* children. If she did, she never would have given you any." Bingo! Jeff could tell from the man's suspicious look that he had pegged him. The crowd laughed. Even if they had no idea what Bozo was talking about, it was fun to see the mark embarrassed. "Your definition of a virgin... a little girl who can run faster than you can." Bullseye! The man ran for the cage, a murderous glint in his eye. Maxie stepped in the way, speaking softly to the mark while signaling frantically for Jeff to cut it out. Jeff ignored him. This was what he lived for. And Maxie? Maxie would get his, too, before the night was over. He whooped and started in again.

"Hey you, Mama, in the blue print dress. Quite a looker here. Bet your husband thinks you got promoted for your *overtime*. Baby, you got a sharp tongue... really know how to deliver your boss a low blow." The man with her got the point. He turned and gave her a murderous look. Jeff saw her shrug, and knew by the man's response that he had really scored. The man yelled something at his wife, turned to the man behind him, and punched him square in the face, making his glasses fly off in a spray of blood. They scuffled, exchanging blows, then fell to the ground and began to roll over and over, tearing at each other. People backed away from the fight, but no one tried to stop it. A few even seemed to enjoy it.

Jeff laughed like a madman. He took the rest of them by turns. The crowd stirred and murmured angrily, their eyes gleaming, but though many of them were frightened, none of them left. He watched their faces as they watched him. Never before had he turned a tip like this. He could feel their horrified fascination. They grumbled among themselves, the noise getting so loud that he had to raise his voice to be heard even with the microphone, and still he went at them. It made him smile to see fists clench, relax, then clench again; to see tics jumping in peoples faces and eyes that grew small and red. To see them sweat.

They watched him the way people stare at a deadly traffic accident: angry, disgusted with themselves for staying, but totally unable to leave. That was fine with him. He didn't care *why* they stayed, as long as they did stay and he got the chance to tear into them. The heat grew more and more unbearable as the night wore on, and for once he was actually sorry that no one had managed to dunk him in the water.

Then something else caught Jeff's eye. The noise from the rube had brought several of the freaks out to see what was happening. Jeff looked at Randall, and a strange feeling came over him. A sudden calm washed over the hate raging inside him. He looked at the crowd again, and noticed that all eyes were on him. On *him*, not on the fight that by now had drawn several other participants. He had something to offer them. Something they needed. He smiled.

"You!" he said, pointing at an old man in a wheelchair. "You!" he said, and pointed at Randall. "You!" he said, pointing at Maxie. He picked out several members of the tip individually. He knew what they wanted, and somehow, he knew too that they knew he could deliver it.

It was the noise that drew Randall out of the tent between performances. This was something he'd never done before. Still, he could have sworn that he was familiar with every kind of sound a carnival could make. This wasn't one of them. Oh, he'd seen fights before, but Jeff's pitch was something totally different. Torn between wanting to do something to help and protecting his wife from the ugly crowd, he chose the latter, knowing that the minute he left her she would be right in the thick of things, trying to do what she could.

"Gentlemen, Ladies. Your future is at hand." It was the voice of the bozo, amplified and echoing through the cheap PA system. The same voice that Randall had heard a thousand times... and yet now it held a certain evangelical majesty, a compelling authority that tugged at the soul. Jeff gestured with his hand to encompass the crowd, and his voice was soothing oil on the rough skin of Randall's body. "You have all heard. The time for vengeance is at hand. You *can* redeem yourself. You *can* be rewarded. But first, you must help me to smite these offenders. Anyone who is not for you is against you. I offer you the world. The world and anything in it. You have only to fight for it," he said.

Suddenly, an image slipped into Randall's mind. It was himself—but himself as a young man, strong and healthy, blond and handsome, with perfect skin bronzed by the sun. An offer. Somehow, Randall never questioned Jeff's ability to deliver; Jeff—or whatever power was speaking through Jeff. This was something he would have sworn he had never wanted. All his life, he had said that he was glad not to be like everyone else. He had meant it. He knew he had meant it... or had he? To have a body like that. To walk down the street and know that the stares were stares of admiration and not of sick fascination, to be able to be like everyone else... to be *better* than everyone else. His heart lurched with desire. Then he turned to look at Sally. She stood next to him still, staring off into the distance. There were tears in the corners of her eyes. He wondered what dream it was that she had been offered. Her hand gripped his tightly. Would she want him like that, golden and perfect? Perhaps if she were golden and perfect, too. But he didn't want *her* that way. He wanted her just as she was. With all his strength, he turned slowly away from the bozo and took her in his arms. "I'm happy the way I am," he said, but now he knew that he would live for the rest of his life with the knowledge that this wasn't quite so. Sally threw her arms around him, clinging so tightly to him that he could feel her fingernails bite into the tender skin of his back, and he wondered if she were afraid of being swept away by the wind of desire.

"Randall, you love me, don't you?" Sally said, her voice shaky, uncertain. "You love me just the way I am?"

"Just the way you are," he said.

Sam spotted the rube from inside the tent. He left the dragon with Katie and Mei, and told them to stay where they were. Then, weak and tired though he was, he waded into the crowd, grabbed two men by their collars, and began knocking their heads together. It was easily the worst rube he'd ever seen on the lot, and it needed to be broken up. Now! But suddenly, in the midst of battle, a strange feeling came over him. An ache of longing, deep in his middle. The kind of ache that only came late at night when sleep was elusive. He looked at the bozo.

"Fight!" Jeff shouted into the microphone. "Anything worth having is worth fighting for," he said, raising a fist above his head. Sam turned, and all at once, there was Thot. She was standing before him, so real that he could almost reach out and touch her. He started to touch her.

Behind her, a movement caught his eye. The dragon was there. It reared up on its hind legs and raised a threatening paw in the air. Sam backed away, all visions of Thot momentarily driven from his mind. And when he looked back, she was gone.

The Viking heard the call even from the back lot, and like pin to magnet, she was drawn to the sound. The mud melted away into bright, floodlit concrete, her kimono into a silk, designer gown. There were flowers in her hand, and reporters waiting in front of her limousine. Hanging tightly on her arm, Sly Stallone smiled down at her worshipfully.

She smiled. This would be hers. She had always known it. Always been prepared to get it, no matter what it took.

"Fight," Jeff called. She was ready. It was Katie she wanted, but Katie was not in sight. The Viking spotted Glory, and, without any warning, punched her in the throat.

Like some glorious, technicolor fever dream, an image appeared, whole and perfect in Essie's mind. A little house with palmetto trees, and Dandy sitting on the front step. Herself on the lawn, gardening, and beautiful roses everywhere. A beautiful image, right out of one of her better dreams. Yet, it was more than just an image. Somehow, she knew that it was a promise, an offer, and she *wanted* it. Wanted it more than she had ever wanted anything else in her life. So badly that her insides twisted and ached with that desire. To live like real people, in her own little house, and to have Dandy—not the fast-talking boss-man of the carnival, but the sweet gentle man who made love to her at night—to have that Dandy all to herself. Sometimes in the darkness she would have that dream, and she would turn to Dandy and say "Patch, I wouldn't change a hair on your head," but she knew that she would. But no—it was *her* dream, not Dandy's. Never Dandy's. She loved him too much to do that to him. Shaken and dazed, she shook the feeling off and turned away.

Out of the corner of her eye, Essie spotted Jimbo vaulting over the counter of The Swinger. She wondered what he was doing. It was unusual to see the lot guard out while the show was open, and she supposed he was there to help stop the fight. He picked up the bowling pin, and without looking further, he slipped over the counter and back onto the lot, but he didn't head into the fray. Shingo-Shango was standing out beside the booth, keeping a careful eye on the restless crowd. Jimbo snuck up behind him, the pin raised like a club. Essie screamed, "Look out!" even though she knew he couldn't hear her. Once, twice, three times the pin descended on the back of Shingo-Shango's head. The carny fell in a heap of plush and stuffing, and his body began to shake. Even before Essie could get there, Shingo-Shango's face had begun to turn blue, and his seizure grew more intense. Then, suddenly, he went rigid, eyes rolled back in his head.

Jimbo turned, spotted her, and started after her. The look on his face was strange, not at all like the Jimbo she knew, and yet, he was undeniably the same man. He had her backed up against the booth, back bent halfway over the counter, no place to run. Jimbo rushed at her, raising the club, but before he could hit her, she kicked out, catching him squarely in the groin, feeling the shock of impact run up her leg. She watched with mixed emotions as he doubled up and fell. Her first impulse was to see if he was okay. Then she looked again at Shingo-Shango's bloody face. Poor Shingo-Shango had never harmed anybody, and this son-of-a-bitch had *killed* him! Cold blooded murder. Essie felt the blood drain out of her face. Jimbo was struggling to rise; he had made it to his knees, still clutching the pin feebly. In an instant she was on the day guard, all teeth and nails. She wrestled the pin from his grasp and hit him as hard as she could in his face with it. She heard a sickening crack, and blood washed down from his forehead to cover his entire face. Then she jumped back, staring down at him, clutching the pin, daring him to try to get up again. But this time he made no attempt to move. He stayed on the ground, clutching his face in his hands, curled up and moaning.

What was happening? Essie felt empty and sick.

My God, what's happening to us all?

10

All that Jake could see was the darkness, lit by a deep burning red that gave off no illumination. All that he could hear was the pounding surf of the blood coursing through his veins, the deafening thunder roll of his own heartbeat. He could feel nothing, nor could he move. Trapped, like a small boy in a closet; a prisoner, locked up in one small corner of his own mind. A prisoner, banging repeatedly on the bars, Jake concentrated all his will on trying to move just one little finger. Once before he had been like this, but he had been younger and stronger then; better able to fight. There! He felt his finger twitch. He was sure of it.

"Jake, be quiet, relax," a voice said. "Conserve your strength. Why do you fight me? This is the way it was meant to be. Remember? We were more than just friends." It was a familiar voice, soothing and relaxing. Jake felt that voice caress and enfold his body. It was barely whispered, yet it echoed from everywhere at once, bouncing off the walls of his mind and mingling with the sounds of heart and blood and breath as though it was a part of him—and Jake relaxed in spite of himself, his will to resist gone.

His mind emptied, and memories flooded in. Memories of a lonely child, with only his brother for a friend. Memories of the older man who had taken him under his wing, given him somewhere to go after school, someone to talk to, somewhere to be something other than Eli's brother. Morgan had taught him chess and a few simple magic tricks. In time, they began to study together, pouring over ancient books of arcanum. Jake knew that Eli hated Morgan, but the older man had told him that it was jealousy, and Jake was sure he was right. The friendship was overwhelming for a naive young teenager. Jake was not quite sure how they became lovers, but when it finally happened it was a bond so strong that even Eli's constant derision could not make a dent. And Morgan taught Jake such power as young boys only dream of. When Tommy Bowen broke Jake's bicycle, it was Morgan who not only taught him to stand up for himself, but gave him the means to do it. Or perhaps it was only chance, as Eli later said, that Tommy's own bike threw him, causing the boy to break his leg—but Jake remembered a night with Morgan; a night of chanting and prayer—a bird that flew down out of the trees by its own will so that Morgan might lay its heart out on the table; a heart that continued to beat in Morgan's hand. "There can be no forgiveness," Morgan had said, and "Vengeance is all." And Eli... It was Eli who murdered Morgan. And with that memory came a rush of hate that Jake hadn't felt in more than half a century.

"Good, Jake," Morgan's voice poured through his mind. "Good!"

"Oh, Jake, don't fight me," Morgan said sadly. "It won't help. You've become soft over the years. You've forgotten the first rule. There can be no forgiveness, Jake. Not for anyone. Certainly not for Eli. Don't fight me, Jake. I can do so much for you. You're an old man, Jake. You don't want to be old, do you? You don't have to be so old, Jake. Just relax... and you can feel your muscles grow strong, Jake. That's right, Jake. Now feel your body grow hard and firm. And young. A body that can do *more* than just lust, Jake. A body that can act! Feel, Jake. Feel all the things you haven't felt in years... Then, if you want to move, Jake, move for me." And Jake felt himself begin to move. With each step, the weariness drained from his body. With each step, the pain in his joints lessened, and he felt his body grow strong and hard. Through a dark tunnel he went, walking without volition at first, but as the new vigor in his limbs grew, he pushed himself onward more eagerly, faster and faster, toward a red light that neither grew nor brightened as he went. Suddenly, he somehow knew that Morgan was there with him, though he never felt a touch, or saw a shape, or heard a voice. Still, he *knew*.

11

Aggie marveled at the looks on the faces around her. She knew that look. She had seen it in her nightmares these past few nights. Whatever it was they saw or heard, she felt none of it. The only thing she was really aware of was Jeff, obviously emotionally disturbed, shouting at all of them through a tinny loudspeaker. He seemed to be driving them all mad somehow, although what he was saying had no effect on her; seemed almost silly, in fact. She noticed a young girl, walking purposefully through the crowd. It seemed she had seen her before, walking with Jeff, though the puffy bruises on her face made it hard to tell. She was pushing her way calmly through the crowd, seemingly oblivious of the fighting that was breaking out all around her.

Strangely enough, she skirted the Bozo cage and approached it from the side. Aggie wondered if perhaps, in his wild state, Jeff had mistreated her. Aggie was certain that she couldn't feel any more frightened than she already was, but something about the girl's calm, deliberate movements, the sense of purpose in her eyes, was alarming. Aggie wanted to stop her, wanted to send her home, but she move very quickly through the jostling crowd.

Carole walked up to the target on the side of the cage, reached out, and pressed it. Sirens whooped. Bells rang. With a look of astonishment on his face, the bozo splashed into the water. Then, with a strength that Aggie wouldn't have credited to such a slender woman, Carole yanked loose the thick black cable, which came free in a shower of sparks. She approached the cage, the spitting wire held in front of her like some sort of slowly twisting snake, just slowly enough to allow the bozo to see what it was she intended to do. He rushed to the bars and opened his mouth, but before he could beg for his life, she thrust her arm between the bars and plunged the live cable into the water.

The two of them danced like stuffed monkeys on a stick. The reek of burning meat permeated the air. It seemed to go on for an endless amount of time, though it couldn't have been more than a moment. Aggie pushed free. She rushed behind the cage, found the plug, and pulled it.

Grinning in rictus, his eyes like glass, the bozo slid beneath the water and disappeared. Carole, her arm caught between the bars, dangled loosely, halfway to the ground.

The bars seemed warm to Aggie's touch as she opened the back of the cage and reached in for Jeff's body. She touched it under the water—repressing a surge of nausea as it seemed to move in her hands—and tried to haul it out. It was much too heavy for her. She left it for Sam and Dandy.

She couldn't stand it any more. Here were two nice young people, dead, for no reason that she could fathom, and here was a whole crowd of people, marks and carnies both, too busy wrangling to even notice. Her eyes filled with tears, her hands shook as she hurriedly wiped them away. All she wanted now was to leave. Leave and never set foot on a lot again. Once her bags were packed, she wouldn't even have to wait on the lot. She would go out front and wait by the gate for her daughter.

She was so lost in thought, so bent on a single purpose, that it took a while for the smell to enter her consciousness. It was just as she passed the G-top. She stopped, sniffed, and turned around. Smoke! By the time she noticed, the number 2 generator was a blazing inferno.

Part Eight

THE BLOWOFF

1

Intense heat split the generator casing, and a line of burning gasoline spread out toward the tent. The canvas caught quickly, with a rush of flame that lit up the night sky and cast eerie shadows all along the midway. Nobody seemed to notice. Men and women in groups of two and three and seven fought each other with any weapon that came to hand, from bare knuckles to knives to pieces of wood and rock. The alignments were random. Marks against marks, carnies against carnies, carnies against marks; and behind them all, the fire was growing. Soon it would encompass the whole tent.

Katie was watching Sam and chewing her knuckles. She wanted to help, but was afraid of getting in the way, so she stood, poised, ready to run in any direction that might seem needful.

Aggie's scream was barely loud enough to pierce the noise out on the lot. Katie wasn't quite sure she'd heard it. Only when it came the second time was she certain enough to tear her eyes away from Sam and look around. By that time, one whole side of the tent was burning, and the flames were rapidly working their way around. Katie looked for Mei, and saw the child was safe for the moment. Dandy was nowhere to be seen.

"Sam!" she called, as loud as she could. It wasn't good enough. "Sam!" she shouted again, and still she wasn't heard. Slowly, she neared the crowd, her heart pumping so hard in her chest that she could feel it beat. "*Sam!*" This time he looked up, but he hadn't spotted her yet. She felt someone grab her arm and pull her roughly aside. This time she screamed in earnest, straining until the muscles of her throat felt raw. She fell to the ground, and her attacker went on to someone else.

"You okay, Katie?" Sam asked. He was standing over her as she sat alone by the edge of the melee, undignified, but uninjured. It could have been worse. Unable yet to speak, she pointed toward the burning tent, which was now blazing well enough to be seen from anywhere on the lot.

"Jesus!" Sam said. "Katie, take Mei off the lot. There's a pay phone down the street. Call the police and the firemen, and don't come back until this is over." Sam was heading toward the fire even as he spoke. Katie found the girl, grabbed her arm, and pulled her toward the main gate, doing her best to keep out of the way of the fight.

She could tell the gate was locked before she even reached it. Several lengths of chain had been wrapped around the gate top and bottom and secured with heavy padlocks. She wasted no further time with it. The back gates were almost certainly open, they were left open all night long. Again choosing her route carefully, she led the child across the lot, but her luck proved no better there. Both back entrances had been carefully padlocked, and the sixteen-foot fence was much too high to climb. Katie did not give up easily, but this time she knew she was defeated. She wasted no time looking for a safe haven among the cars and trailers of the back lot. That was something she'd learned early on. With tanks of gas and diesel and propane every few feet, it was the worst possible place to be in case of a fire. There had to be some place safe where she could leave the child. Someplace open, where fire was little threat, but someplace where she would be safe from the rioting mob as well. Unable to think of anyplace better, she took the child to Lutzy's joint and sat her down on the bench, but Katie had no intention of staying there herself. She could help. Katie ordered the child to wait there, then she opened the counter and entered the kitchen. It took precious minutes to find where Lutzy kept his utensils. There were several knives. Without wasting minutes to sort through them, she grabbed a handful, and started running.

The air was full of smoke and noise and little pieces of burning canvas that swirled on the wind and rained down all over the lot. People were running in every direction, and bodies—dead or unconscious, Katie couldn't tell which—were strewn here and there across the ground. The brawl was continuing to rage unabated—in fact, it was spreading out all over the lot—so that there were few people available to fight the fire. Two men were fighting so close to the blaze that their sweat-slicked bodies ran with rivers of soot. She could see Sam now, standing next to Gregor, as the two men started stripping the canvas, oblivious to the smoke and the cascading sparks that fell around them. Katie circled the fire and headed toward the kootch tent. When she got there, she threw the knives down in a pile, selected one, and started working on the ropes that held the tent in place. With all her strength, she hit the rope, using the knife like a machete, but it bounced off the taut-stretched hemp without doing any damage. Mei was there with her now, but Katie didn't waste time trying to send her back. She stopped for a moment, looked over the assortment of implements she had brought, selected a heavily serrated knife, and started sawing away on a rope. The child picked up another knife and started working on the next rope over. The work was heavy going. It had taken the combined labor of several roughies, used to lifting and pulling, over an hour to get the tent up, and the ropes were hummingly tight. Katie knew that they didn't have a prayer if the fire started to spread, but she had to do something. Essie joined them, and a moment later one of the roughies, blood streaming from a badly cut mouth, also came over to help.

A shrill cry cut through the noise. Katie looked up. One bright angel of flame had floated down quite close to Mei, who was still doggedly trying to cut the rope, although she was crying and her face was tight with fear. Katie pushed her away. She looked around, and, finding nothing else, ripped off her skirt and began to beat at the blaze with it. Somewhere behind her, she could hear Mei had begun to scream, over and over again, until her voice ran out. One bright tongue of flame began licking its way up the side of the canvas, it was hopeless, but Katie couldn't stop. She kept beating at the fire. This was all Sam had. She had to save it for him. Then she felt someone pull her away.

"Stop it, Katie!" Essie said. "It's too late!" Essie was right. The fire had gotten beyond them. A good part of the canvas was already burning, the whole thing was going to go up. But there was still one thing she could do. She broke away from Essie and, ignoring Essie's cry of protest, ran inside the burning tent.

Thick black smoke filled the top. It was becoming difficult to breathe, and Katie couldn't see a thing, but she didn't need to see. She knew the layout inside the tent. As quickly as she could, she made her way through the audience stalls, up onto the platform, and into the back. She opened the bottom drawer of Sam's table and removed the cashbox. Flames lit up the top momentarily, as a large strip of canvas burned free of the tent and fell inside with a crash, sending sparks and burning embers cascading down on her. Hastily, lungs straining, Katie ran to the back flap and made her way out into the night air.

2

The last half hour had been one of the worst of her life, and yet—despite her grief for Jeff, her worry for her friends, and the imminent danger of the fire—Aggie felt better than she had all day. It was all starting to make sense. Dreams, visions, all that fire and smoke… it had been a *warning*. It wasn't inside her head, not a metabolic imbalance or a brain tumor. She wasn't going crazy—it was something real. Perhaps if she had accepted that sooner, Jeff would still be alive… but there was no time now for recriminations. Later, if there was a later, she could worry about that. Right now, there had to be *something* she could do.

She knew two things: that someone or something evil was here, on the lot, on the lot, bent on revenge against all of them; and that she was somehow able to see little bits and pieces of the larger picture that nobody else was privy to. There must be some way. She had to use that to help them. Some way, she had to force herself to see something they could use, something that would help defeat the Satanic plan that was working itself out here. It was going to destroy them all unless they could stop it. But up until now the visions had seemed to come at random. How could she deliberately induce them? Was there any one thing, any one person, who seemed to set them off? Jeff, of course—but Jeff was gone. But she had seen visions at other times. Times when Jeff wasn't around.

The phone rang. It was weird to hear such a prosaic, everyday sound in the midst of all the chaos that was unfolding around them. She thought of ignoring it, but she was never very good at that. "Hello," she said wearily as she picked up the receiver.

"Mom, thank God. I've been trying to reach you all day. Listen, we've been having car trouble. I don't think we'll be able to come until tomorrow," Susan said.

"I'm glad you called, baby," Aggie said. The last thing in the world she wanted was for Susan to come down now. Not into this mess. "It's okay. Really. I feel much better," she said.

"Are you sure? You sound awfully tired."

"I am tired. Busy tired. But I'm feeling better and that's the truth. I'll call you tomorrow, I promise. Probably, I'll drive up to see you when we're through here. I'm gonna get some sleep now. See you later." She kissed into the phone and hung up.

She touched the phone and smiled. Funny, the phone was about the only thing left that still felt friendly. It was a world of chaos out there, and she had to prepare herself to go back out into it. Then the idea hit her, and she felt so stunningly stupid that she hit her forehead. The telephone. She could call the police and fire department. She could get some help. She picked up the receiver and dialed the operator. Nothing happened. The phone simply went dead. She pressed down on the switch-hook, got a dial tone, and tried again. Again the line went dead. This time it stayed dead. It sent an icy chill through her. Whatever power was against them, it seemed to have them all cut off, trapped in a magic circle of isolation away from the rest of the world. She should have known. Surely the flames and thick black smoke would be clearly visible from the town, if anyone had been allowed to see it. This was *their* problem, and she knew that they would have to solve it themselves if it was going to get solved. They were on their own.

Thank God Susan wasn't heading down into all this. That was *one* thing she wouldn't have to worry about, anyway. You never stopped worrying about your children, it seemed, no matter how old they got. Children…

Jennie! Jennie had set off the first of the visions. Maybe, just maybe, she could trigger them again. It was worth a try. Quickly, she threw a blouse on, and went out to find the child.

3

Jennie began to cry when the fight broke out. She wasn't strong enough to stop the struggle, but she did see something that she could do, something important, and she pushed her way through the crowd as best she could. She had no idea what was happening. Why didn't anyone *do* anything? Where was Patch? Sam was trying to break things up, but it just wasn't enough. Where was her father, or Maxie? She saw three toughs grab a solitary woman and start punching her in the face and head while she screamed. Nobody lifted a finger to help her. Jennie elbowed several people out of the way and squeezed through spaces so small it didn't seem that even she could fit through them. At times, her speed and the fact that she could duck into places where others couldn't go were the only things that saved her.

"What's the matter with all of you?" she shouted, but her little girl voice went unnoticed by the ugly, tortured faces, and she moved on, never losing sight of her destination.

She reached the old man's side quickly, surprised to note that it hadn't taken her very long to cut through the thick of the struggling mob. Without asking what he wanted, she took hold of the chair and wheeled it across the lot, doing her best to avoid the combatants who flailed and wrestled all around them. The old man protested, but she ignored him. She would not stand by and watch him beaten up or trampled underfoot by this mob, if there was anything she could do to save him. Girls being hit was bad enough, but this poor old man couldn't survive such treatment.

"Little girl! Little girl, wait, please," he said. By this time, struggling desperately, she had managed to push him between the tents that marked the transition from midway to back lot.

She turned to speak to him, and noticed that the G-top was burning. "Oh my God!" she said, over and over again, renewing her efforts despite the old man's protests. She pushed him toward the side gate. "I'm getting you out of here," she said.

"No, stop! Please child," he said again. This time she paused to listen. "There's something important. Something I have to do," the old man said.

"But it's too dangerous here," she said. Confused, she continued to wheel him toward the gate. "At least let me get you out of the way.

There's a fire going on, you know," she said with remarkable calm. She found a spot between two trailers, away from the blowing smoke, and turned his chair around so that he could face the lot. "Will this do?" she asked.

"Jennie," Aggie called her, before the old man could answer.

"Aunt Aggie, I'm safe! I'm over here!" she answered.

The fortune teller caught up to them. She had been running, and her breath came in short, wheezing pants, one hand pressed tightly to her chest, as if she were trying to hold her lungs inside. "I tried your trailer... and... when you weren't... there, I... got so... worried," Aggie gasped. She reached a hand out toward Jennie. Then she saw the old man, and her eyes got that funny look again. The same funny look she'd gotten that night Jennie showed her the kitten. In spite of the fire, it was scary. Her eyes glazed over and her body went slack. She seemed to be barely breathing at all.

"I have to stop you, Morgan," Aggie said in a droning voice. "I have to save him." Her hands pulled an invisible something from her side, and twisted open an invisible lid. Whatever it was, she sniffed it and nodded. "This will do," she said.

Jennie looked back at the old man. His eyes were wide, and his hands were shaking worse than ever. There were beads of sweat on his leathery forehead. "It's okay," Jennie said, although she wasn't at all sure that it was, but she could tell the old man hadn't even heard her. All his attention was fixed raptly on Aggie.

Aggie thrust her hand forward several times, as if she were sprinkling some kind of liquid around. Then she struck her hand against the bottom of her shoe, leaned over to touch her invisible match to the ground, and jumped back from the flare-up of the imagined blaze. "That's for you, Jake," she shouted triumphantly.

"You know!" the old man said in a hoarse whisper.

Then, just as quickly as the whole thing started, it was over. Aggie slumped and caught herself on the arm of his chair.

"You know," the old man said again.

"You tried to kill him," Aggie said.

"Yes," the old man said. "I was sure that it had worked, too. That was when Morgan threw me out of the window," he said, gesturing at his ruined body. "That's why I've had to spend the rest of my life like... this."

Jennie understood none of it. She looked back and forth between the old man and Aggie as if they were both crazy. She wanted to run, but she couldn't move.

"Morgan's back," Aggie said.

"He warned us that he would be. 'Fire renews me,' he said, and told us he'd be back one day, stronger than ever. Now he wants revenge."

Aggie nodded. "Yes, revenge. He wants revenge on all of us. On the carnival, for using the lot—desecrating his bones—but most of all he wants revenge on you. Both of you. Jake, too. You have to make him see that," she stared gravely at the old man. "It's the two of you who have to stop Morgan. You're the only ones who can."

4

Flames licked their way up the side of the canvas. They were surrounded by fire on two sides now. Essie watched the little Asian girl, who was still frantically sawing away at the ropes, her eyes squinted, watering so badly that Essie was sure that she would cut herself. Fear for the girl motivated her as fear for herself never would have, and she grabbed the child and pulled her to safety in the middle of the lot. The girl struggled against her, surprisingly strong for someone so small. Posters freed themselves from their bottom ropes, snapping to attention in the heat-created wind, and burned like flags. They flew snapping from their masts, casting off trailing streamers of flame and soot, finally falling on top of the already raging canvas. One barely missed them as the child struggled against Essie's grip. She could feel the searing heat against her side.

"Katie!" the girl screamed, as Essie finally managed to pull her clear of the fire.

"Katie's in there? Oh, God," Essie said, torn between keeping the kid clear of the fire and running to try to rescue her friend. The choice was quickly taken out of her hands. In a blossom of flame and sparks and blackened threads, puffing billows of the canvas collapsed, showering the area with smoke and dust that choked their lungs and left them coughing, gasping for air.

The Asian girl's eyes glazed over. For a moment she just stood there, frozen, staring at the burning rubble. Softly at first, then gaining in hysteria, the child began to mutter in some foreign language. Essie choked back her own grief, and turned her attention to the girl. At first, she thought that the child was speaking to her, but the girl never looked away from the spray of flame and ash. The spate of words continued for some moments, and then there came a cry that sounded to Essie like "The bombs… bombs!" Then the girl collapsed against Essie's side, sobbing, and she held her tightly, stroking her hair.

"Oh, you poor thing," she said.

"Mei! What's the matter? Is she hurt?" Essie looked up to see Katie standing over them. Her dress was torn, and she was covered with soot and mud. Her hair was plastered to her head and neck, a few strands glued across her face. She clutched the cashbox to her as if it were a baby, but she was alive.

"Oh, Katie, thank God!" Essie said. Katie pressed the box into Essie's lap, the metal so warm that it made the skin on her legs itch even through the material of her skirt. Then Katie took the child from Essie's arms. Gently, she stroked her hair and whispered to her softly.

"It's okay, Mei. It's okay. I'm all right. Everything's going to be okay." Katie put her hand under her chin and lifted her face. Then, tenderly, she brushed the hair back from her cheeks and forehead.

Around them, the fire was growing, and smoke hazed the air. Essie looked around for a quick head count, but people were clustered in tight little groups fighting the flames and each other, and it was hard to pick out the carnies amidst the smoke and confusion. She focused her attention on Katie and the child. "Who is she?" Essie asked.

"She's Sam's daughter," Katie said with conviction. The girl looked up at her and smiled.

5

The noise was almost deafening. Voices cascading over and around the crackling roar of the fire, the canvas snapping in the warm currents of air, feet crunching over the infield turf, and the incessant coughing, which worsened with time.

Sam beat at the burning tent with a blanket. He tried to keep his attention on the job at hand, but the lot was awash with desperate activity. He wondered why the people didn't leave the lot—especially as many of them seemed half-crazy with hysterical fright—until some kids ran by yelling that all the gates were locked. Behind the burning ten-in-one, a youth in a satin jacket with J.P. Downey High School embroidered across its back, stood at the gate boosting his friends over. This was lowest part of the fence, with spikes only twelve feet high and crossbars top and bottom. It was a difficult climb, but he gave them a boost with his hands and allowed them to stand on his shoulders while they pulled themselves, laboriously, over the top, dropping down to the sidewalk on the other side. When the last of them had made it outside one reached through the fence with his hands to make a step for him. The boy put his foot on the hand and slid his sneaker through the bars to place it on the other boy's shoulder. He pulled himself chest-high over the pointed spikes, but having to step through the bars onto his friend's shoulders made the angle more difficult. His foot slipped. Sam left the burning tent and rushed to help, but he was too late. The boy had already impaled himself on the wrought-iron spear points that tipped the fence.

"Run! Get the police!" Sam shouted to the kids outside the gate. If they heard him, they gave no indication. The two girls stood there, uselessly, crying and screaming, while the other boys tried to get up the fence to deal with the body. Sam left them to it and went back to help with the fire. Carnies worked side by side, the men, women, and even one or two of the marks, all trying to strip the canvas off the poles in an effort to contain the fire to one small area of the lot. Luckily, spaces between the tents and the nearest flammable objects acted as firebreaks. But even then, occasional pinpoint fires would break out when the burning bits of canvas would tear loose and fly about to land on awnings, booths, or plush toy animals. Sam was kept busy cutting and pulling down the canvas, his arms blackened by soot and striped with running rivers of sweat. He was exhausted, and finding it hard to breathe. Platforms, costumes, money, wigs, even food—all burned with an incredible collective stench. Fortunately they had gotten the living things, people and animals, even the fat lady, out of the ten-in-one before anyone was hurt. Yet, despite the heavy labor, the danger, the emotional drain, Sam was grateful for the distraction, because here, under the heavy black haze, he could not tell if the dragon was still waiting, still watching him with those terrible eyes.

A shout went up. Sam, aware of what was happening, made an effort to move those men near him back from the fire-line as the canvas crashed down into a tangled heap, showering sparks in every direction. Already, some of the men were pushing the edges into a closely packed pile, as far away from everything else as possible. There was nothing left for him to do here. Jeff, that girl, and the schoolboy, no doubt others—they were all beyond help now; they could wait for the authorities to take care of later. He hoped that Katie and Mei had gotten off the lot and safely out of the danger zone. He couldn't see them from where he stood, but he had to assume that they were safe. He couldn't stop now to look for them. The fate of too many people seemed to rest on his shoulders. There was something he had to do.

He had to get those gates open. Soon. Dandy had the only key, but somewhere along the line, Dandy had disappeared. Sam had expected to see him when the fire first broke out, keeping order and shouting out commands, but the patch was nowhere to be found. He had simply locked the gates and vanished. He, and that politician friend of his, both. Probably, they hadn't gone any farther than the office. Sam decided to go have a look.

He rushed to the office as quickly as his tired body would go, avoiding the remaining fights, his soot-blackened skin making him look more like a bear than ever. "Patch," he called from outside the door, softly at first, then louder. There was no answer. Sam had no idea where else the boss-man might have disappeared to, but on the theory that Dandy might have gone to sleep—the way he'd been acting lately, Dandy might even be drunk on his ass—Sam tried the door. It was unlocked. That was odd. Dandy often left large sums of money in his desk—he made it a habit to always lock the door. Sam decided it was probably a good idea to check it out. Even if he didn't find Patch, he might find the missing key.

There was a man seated behind the desk. But there was no mistaking this fellow for Jim Dandy. He was a fat man, somewhere in his sixties, and he sat slumped in the seat, staring off into space. Sam craned his neck to peer into the back, but the curtains were opened, and even from where he stood he could see that there was nobody in either the bed or the donniker. He walked over to the stranger.

"Hey, mister," he said, shaking him by the arm. The man fell over, his head hitting the desk with a heavy thump, like a dropped melon. He touched the man's face, but his skin was as cold as marble in spite of the intense heat of the night. There was no doubt about it. The man had been dead for some time. Christ, four dead bodies on the lot—maybe more! What the hell were the cops going to say? It made him shudder to think of it—but that was Patch's problem. He had a more immediate problem. The gates just couldn't wait any longer. He had to let the people out before someone else got hurt.

Sam didn't know where Dandy had hidden the key, but he knew where he kept the tools. A bright red box, long and low, stuffed away in the back of the cabinet under the bunk. He wasn't supposed to know, but he had seen Dandy put them away one night after helping him fix a flat. Patch would be more upset at Sam's going through his things than he would be about everything else that had happened. It was the one thing nobody was allowed to do, for any reason, but this was an emergency. With a sinking feeling, Sam was beginning to realize that it wouldn't matter much any more how angry the boss-man got. He found what he was looking for. It was way back behind a welter of shoe boxes and old rags, bits and pieces of junk that Sam couldn't identify, and money—ones and change— scattered loosely all over. The hidey-hole smelled of grease and mildew. There was no crow bar in the box, but there was a tire iron.

The gate was locked with a chain, looped between the bars and linked together with a formidable-looking padlock. The gate could be pulled open only a few inches. Sam inserted the tire iron in the opening and twisted, forcing the chain to loop around itself. With all his might, he continued to twist until it would go no further. He took a deep breath, planted both his hands firmly on the bar, and—putting all of his weight behind it—pushed. The chain had reached its limit. The tire iron would go no farther. He added his knee and tried again. A searing pain exploded in his knee. The tire iron sprang up, hitting him on the wrist. Through pain that blotted out almost all sensation, he heard a rattling chime as the tire iron slipped through the unbroken chains and fell uselessly to the ground.

They were still trapped.

6

A large piece of cloth burned free from the grab joint awning and circled lazily in the air, sending up bright tendrils of flame. It soared lazily, like a large bird of prey, rising and diving, then rising again until it finally came to rest on the red upholstery of the topmost seat on the Spider. Gregor spotted it almost right away. He rushed to the ride instantly. It wasn't fear for his ride that spurred him, but the knowledge that three feet away from that ride was a field of gasoline and propane tanks. If the trucks and trailers caught fire, the resultant explosions would wipe every living creature off the lot.

Gregor opened the ride out, extending the arms and bringing the burning seat into reach. There was nothing to hand, no water, no sand, no blankets. He hastily peeled off his cotton t-shirt. Holding it by the hem, he slapped it down hard on the burning mass of vinyl and stuffing. Pinpoints of melted plastic flew up and landed on his arms and shoes and pants and around him on the rock-hard ground and meager blades of grass. The carny wiped his arms, then slapped at the flames again. The fire died, but an eager line of red and black still ate away at the red vinyl seats. Gregor jumped into the car. There was only one way to deal with the seat before it became a raging inferno yet again. He jumped onto the seat itself and stamped at the last burning bits with the bottom of his sneakers.

The seat bucked and jostled under his weight as he stamped out a tongue of flame, only to see another one pop up an inch away. The smell of burning plastic and cotton stuffing was making his stomach churn, and his head had started to spin. He found it difficult to keep his balance, and as he grabbed for the side of the car he realized that the ride had started to spin, and he was ten feet up in the air. It was a ride that spun in several different ways, all at the same time. The central post spun the eight legs in a clockwise circle, and on the end of each leg a pod of chairs turned within another circle as each chair swirled around on its own—and all the while the legs moved up and down as they went around, tilting the turning chair back and forth, accelerating the motion. He was almost thrown from the chair as it topped its arc and started back down. Shakily, he stood up again. It was dangerous, but it was his ride. No one was waiting down there to turn it off, and with the fire and fight going on, it seemed unlikely that he would be able to attract anyone else's attention. There was only one thing to do. He would have to jump. It was more difficult than it sounded, for not only was the ride set up so that when the chair reached its closest approach to the ground it was also swinging its fastest, but he had to jump well clear of the path of the chairs, or another chair would be along to smack him in the head before he could possibly roll clear.

He braced himself to jump, knees on the seat, hands lightly resting on the back of the chair for balance, as the metal arm started its downward decent. Then, just as the chair was about to hit its lowest point, the whole group at the end of the arm swung around, leaving him on the inside, near the machinery, with no place clear to jump to. He waited through one more circle. The chair was moving more quickly than he had ever allowed the ride to go. The motion was beginning to make him dizzy. He found it difficult to tell exactly where he was in relation to the rest of the lot. It was difficult to decide when it was safe to jump. Still, he had no choice. Suddenly, he thought of his son. How much the boy used to love this ride. Tomorrow, he really would have to write that letter. When the arm started to lower this time, he closed his eyes and leapt as soon as the chair was clear of the metal workings, without waiting for its closest approach to the ground.

He seemed to fall forever. Then the ground slammed into his legs with the force of a truck barreling down the highway. There was a blinding stab of pain. Something hit him in the side of his head. The world went dark.

7

Jake could feel the muscles move underneath his skin, feel the kind of limitless the energy he hadn't experienced in years. For the first time in almost forty years, he was totally free of pain. No joints ached, there was no gas in his bowels or belly, his head and his teeth felt fine. He took a deep breath, enjoying smells with a sharpness and clarity they didn't even retain in his memory. He thought about the things Eli had told him, the things Eli had done. Fighting to help him—or so he said. But that was a lie. Fighting to make him *old* again, would be closer to the truth. Fighting to bring him closer to death. No! He wouldn't allow it. Perhaps Eli had thought he was doing the right thing all those years ago. Maybe he even owed Eli for that. But there was a limit to how much you could owe anyone. He had been given a new life. He didn't owe *that* to Eli.

"He's jealous," Morgan whispered to him. "You have been given a second life, and he's never even had one."

Jake nodded. Morgan took him to the window, and pointed off into the distance. Standing in the eye of the skull, he could see his brother down below. They were twins, yet even after only a moment of youth, Jake couldn't believe it. Had he ever been that old? Looking at Eli had always been like looking into a distorted mirror, frightening and somehow depressing, but now he found himself exhilarated. No longer would he merely mark time, afraid to do anything, waiting to die. No longer would he live his passions as a series of memories.

Morgan/Redd put an arm around Jake's shoulders and looked him in the eye. "You are happy, Jake, aren't you? Do you want to go back to the way you were?"

"Go back? Go back to what I was? An old man, ready to die, my pathetic excuse for a life run by a crotchety old woman who would put me through anything just to keep me breathing another five minutes? You won't send me back, Werner? Will you?" He took the hand that had once belonged to Walter Redd.

"There is much to do, Jake. Many of these people will be against us. I must have this place. I need to build my strength even more if we are to win, Jake. Only then can I promise you. Those who will fight on our side will be rewarded Jake, as you have been rewarded. As for the rest, their deaths will help me build my strength—my strength will be made out of their deaths. As I taught you long ago."

"There can be no forgiveness," Jake said, his jaw was set in a firm line.

"Go and deal with Eli, Jake. He's the only one who can hurt us," Morgan said.

"But he's my brother," Jake protested.

"Exactly," Morgan said. He led Jake to the fire exit, and nudged him on his way.

Jake walked out into the hot, humid air. There was a time when he almost required this kind of heat just to keep his old bones moving. Now it was oppressive, but he was delighted to find that with his new-found strength, even the heat was no more than a minor annoyance. He ran across the lot for the sheer joy of running, breathing easily, stretching his muscles. Even the smoke didn't bother him, much. He felt so strong! It was worth anything, any price. It was wonderful to be young, and strong, and free. Nobody was going to take this from him…

Fights were going on all over the lot; sprawling pitched battles with people using any weapon that came to hand, from broken bottles and burning sticks to actual tooth-and-nail combat. Jake was almost caught up in one of these vicious little skirmishes, as the brawl spread out around him too quickly to evade. He whirled, and like a threatened tiger, punched the man who accosted him, smashing him savagely once, twice, three more times, drinking in the sheer animal joy of stretching his muscles, and then grinning in triumph as the man stumbled and fell. Still, enjoyable as it was, this sort of thing was a waste of time, not to be afforded, and thereafter he kept to the edge of the lot to avoid another encounter. Here, too, there was a problem. With most of the available manpower involved in these mad skirmishes, few were left to deal with blazes that now burned out of control in many places. Often, he was forced out into the melee in order to get around the burning tents and booths. The going was slow and difficult. Even at one booth that was not yet burning, he found his way blocked by a woman who was busily stripping cloth and bits of paper from the wood. As he started to circle one booth, something slammed into him, knocking him down. It was two large, beefy men who were locked in unarmed combat wrestling on the ground, right by Jake's leg, moving in tight little circles, a kind of drunken waltz. One punched the other, who tripped over Jake and went down, his adversary diving after him almost instantly. Almost amused, Jake watched them go at it as he regained his feet. They rolled over, then over again, until they were dangerously close to the inferno. He could just make out the words "Bluebeard's Castle" on the sign before they blackened and disappeared. One man got up, lifting the other by his shirt, then delivered a powerful blow. The man reeled back, right into the burning facade of the haunted house. The wooden front shivered and collapsed, landing on both men and missing Jake only by inches. He felt a hot needle of pain in his leg as shards of burning charcoal sprayed down on him. He skipped hastily out of the way. Where the attraction's facade had been, several linked trucks burned as if they had been doused with gasoline. He glanced back and noticed that the wooden skull, too, was beginning to catch; fingers of flame danced along the death's-head's cheeks and over the creaky platform that fronted the ride. It gave him an eerie feeling, but he was not afraid for Morgan; Morgan knew what he was doing. After a moment, he moved on.

He skirted the fires, ran across the still-warm ashes that had once been the girly show, and off into a field filled with trucks and campers. The fire didn't seem to have gotten this far, yet. He spotted Eli off to the side of a van, where he was sheltered from most of the smoke and could still see what was happening. Jake knew that his brother was watching him approach, but Eli's eyes were calm and steady, and the tremor had gone from his hands. Near him, an old woman and a young girl stood calmly by.

"I knew you'd come," Eli said.

8

It was dark and more than a little hot, but Dandy didn't care. His friend Mr. Redd had been very helpful. Very helpful, indeed. He was smart, that politician. Dandy had been wrong about him, he had to admit it. The man was smart enough to think of locking the gates so that everyone would still be there when the police came, just in case there were any questions. Dandy would never have thought of that. And he was helpful, too, not hardly like a mark at all. "Listen Mr. Dandy. I have a lot of connections in this town. Why don't you just disappear for a while and let me take care of things, huh?" he had said. Well, hell, the fire was almost out. Dandy trusted his roughies to take care of that. Where better to hide than inside the dark ride? No one would be going on rides now, after all. And Redd was in with all the bigwigs in this town. If he took care of things, it would leave Dandy smelling like a rose. Besides, Mr. Redd had been kind enough to provide a little refreshment. No cheap guzzlers, these local politicians. They didn't stint themselves a goddamn thing. Two bottles of the finest single malt that had ever crossed an ocean. One down and one to go. Then, when it was over, Redd would give him the high sign, just like they'd agreed, and he'd be sitting pretty. Dandy had to admit that Redd was right about one thing: if he'd tried to handle it himself—well, Jeezus, three deaths *and* a fire, in one night…

What a day. Time to get out of the carnival business for sure. First that fat old man has to go and drop dead on him, and then… he'd never seen anyone go crazy like that college kid of Maxie's. College kids! He should have warned Maxie about them from the start. Nothing but trouble. And Essie… He thought about that lush body, and those hands. What talented hands she had! All these years he never pegged her for a whiner. He was disappointed, but he wasn't going to make an exception in her case. No woman was ever going to get a second chance to go off on him like that. Not even that one. Besides, she *was* getting a little long in the tooth. There were lots better out there. Lots tastier fish in the sea. Lots. That dancer of Sam's they called the Viking, for instance. She was sure some looker. Dandy didn't really think that Sam would mind, but even if he did…

He opened the second bottle and took a long, thirsty drink. Or, maybe it was time to start planning that new identity he'd been thinking about. He had always had a hankering to try his hand at some of those posh places. There was a man he knew in Oklahoma who ran a casino... crushed velvet and crystal chandeliers. Yes, sir, that was the life for him, all right. Dandy wondered how he would look in a red tuxedo.

Even drunk as he was, it was impossible to sneak up on the long-time carny. He heard the footsteps crunching on the sand and whirled around. "Well, Mr. Redd," Dandy said, holding out his hand.

Morgan avoided his grasp, clapping an arm around the carny's shoulders instead. "You know, son, there are things I can do for you," he said.

Dandy nodded. Oh, he knew, all right. From now on, it was going to be cash and Cadillacs; any woman he wanted and all the women he wanted. With someone like Redd on his side, he could go just as far and as fast as he wanted to. And to think that just a few days ago he thought his luck had run out.

"You have some friends out there. Some interfering friends," Redd explained. "I keep trying to help you, and they keep getting in my way. I've been watching one in particular: that big, dark man. When the cops get here, he's going to spill his guts. I won't be able to help you then."

"Sam?" Dandy said, surprised. "Sam would never..."

"Well, maybe not. Don't be too sure, though. He's jealous of you. I think he's always been jealous of your luck. Jealous of the way you run things. He knows that tall blonde's attracted to you. He's jealous of that, too. He'd just love a chance to get you out of the way so that he can take over. Look at what he's been doing all night. Managing things. Giving orders. Complaining to everyone that you aren't doing your job. Why take a chance on him spoiling everything for you? It's no skin off my nose, but if you're smart, you'll find some way to keep him busy until I get things squared away. Pick a fight with him. That should do it. That way we won't have to worry about it."

Two women were fighting. It was the first thing Dandy noticed when he emerged from the back of the dark ride. The Viking had Cinda down on the ground, and was banging her head repeatedly into the dirt. Dandy grabbed her by her shoulders and pulled her back.

"What the hell's goin' on here?" he asked.

"That bitch…" the Viking said, though she made no real effort to pull away from him. Redd was right about her. She did go for him. He could tell. That meant he was probably right about everything else, too.

Cinda pushed herself up on one elbow, rubbed her head with her free hand and opened the only eye that still seemed to work. The other eye, red and swollen, was already beginning to purple.

"Well, Cinda, what's your side?" Dandy asked.

"I don't know, Patch. She just jumped me," Cinda said.

"Okay, ladies. Enough of this," he said. He let his arm loosen, and it dropped to cover the Viking's breast, accidentally at first. But he let it stay there. He heard her draw a breath and felt her stiffen, then relax. She turned toward him, pressing her breast more fully into his hand, and smiled.

"It's quiet in the back," she said, in a honeyed voice.

"I got things I gotta do first, Darlin'," he answered. But took her around with him as he looked for Sam. She slid her hand through his belt and fondled his buttocks as they walked. Blind and deaf to fight, fire, and chaos, straining his slacks with anticipation, he walked through the ashes, calling out to Sam as he went. The Viking gripped his arm and gestured. She seemed excited, as if she were truly enjoying herself. He looked where she pointed.

For the first time, the chaos around him pierced his consciousness. "Holy Shit," he gasped. It looked like a saloon brawl from a cliched old Western movie, with people fighting in groups of anywhere from two to twenty, burning rides and booths in a circle around them, except that there was no denying that this was real. Some had makeshift weapons, but most used their natural ones of hands, feet, teeth, nails, and brute strength. He spotted one large man just as he landed a solid right cross to the jaw of a rather delicate looking woman. She went down. Almost immediately, an even smaller woman jumped on the man's back, applying teeth and nails to the tender areas of his face and neck. Dandy had no idea what the war was about or whose side anyone was one. A teenage boy stood behind the counter of the Penny Pitch, throwing plates and glassware at anyone who dared to come near him.

The shock was too much for him. Dandy found that he no longer cared about the lot or the people on it. He had no desire to find out what was going on. He wasn't even sure that Redd's proposal interested him any more. All he wanted was to get out of there. With a few hours, even a few minutes of head start, he could go right back to square one and start over.

Dandy started toward the gate, but a fight broke out in his path. He moved to avoid it. At least ten people were pummeling each other in a tangled mass. He saw them bump into the burning Ring Toss, saw it fall, saw sparks come puffing up like fireworks. They sprayed up in an arc, cascading down on the plywood skull that covered the front of the dark ride. The skull began to burn in several places. Redd had better get his ass out of there, if he was still inside. Then Dandy spotted Sam and Katie.

Dandy had been headed for the gates, but at the sight of Sam, a spark of anger began to smoulder inside him. Sam had always been jealous. Just like Redd had told him: he knew it now. That sonofabitch! Pretending to be Dandy's friend, and all the while the fucking louse was scheming behind his back.

With the Viking still trailing behind, Dandy moved cautiously toward them, doing his best to keep clear of both fighting and fire. He reached them safely, but before he could decide exactly what to do, torn between a now burning resentment, and at the same time an odd feeling of relief that they were okay, the Viking uttered a low growl in her throat and lunged for Katie, claws first.

Everything seemed to happen at once. Some little gook girl appeared out of nowhere and attacked the Viking, arms and feet flailing. Before Dandy could move, Sam reacted. He reached them almost instantly, but instead of protecting his employee, he seized the Viking roughly, lifted her off her feet, and threw her against the fence.

She was hurt! Dandy could see that the Viking's arm was smeared with blood, and her face was a mask of pain. Sam had hurt her. A sudden flood of hate washed through him. How could Sam treat *his* girl this way? It was jealousy. Sam *was* jealous of him. Sam still wanted the Viking. That was it. He resented the fact that she had gone with another man. Well, Dandy wasn't having any of that. Pick a fight? Picking this one was going to be a pleasure, and he wasn't doing it just for Redd, either. He lowered his head like a bull, raised his arms, and charged.

9

For a moment, Aggie thought she had slipped back into her dream. That face. It was a little bit older, a little bit more mature, but it was the same face. The face of the boy she'd seen lighting the fire, the face she'd seen confronting Morgan, the face of the boy who had fallen from the third story window. It was the face of the old man who sat ruined and shrunken in front of her, made young and vital and dangerous.

"I knew you'd come," Eli said, and the sound brought Aggie back to reality. So this was Jake. Jake, made young again! Her mind reeled at the staggering enormity of Morgan's power.

"Then you must know why I'm here," Jake said.

"If you can kill me, Jake, then go ahead. After all, it's not for me that I'm here. I'll be dead soon, no matter what you do. But think, Jake. That's a fine body he's given you, young and strong and handsome. I know that it must mean a lot to you… but is it worth more than the love of your family? Does it mean more to you than Joella and Darcy, and the kids?" Jake turned his back. He didn't want to hear this, the choice was already made, but his brother's voice continued to drone on as Jake watched the black smoke billow against the sky.

"That's right, Jake, watch the fire. Look at the flames and remember how it was that last night. Can you remember? I tried to take you away, but you refused to go with me."

"Shut up!" Jake shouted.

"The house was burning, Jake. Do you remember? You *must.*"

"Shut up, Eli!" Jake screamed again, but Eli's voice droned on.

"He picked me up and threw me out the window. Do you remember now, Jake?" Eli asked.

"Shut up, shut up!" Jake's eyes were cold, and his hands curled up in tight, ready fists. "Maybe you *didn't* try to kill me too. I don't know about that. But you killed *him*, that's what you did! He was my lover, only you couldn't stand that. He gave me strength and power, and you were afraid that dear little Eli wouldn't be in control any more. Well, look who's in control now, Eli. Look who's in control!"

"Morgan's in control, brother. That's who's in control. Certainly not *you*," Eli said.

Jake raised his fists and started forward. There was no time for Aggie to react, and, after all, what could she do? She didn't have the strength to fight off a young man in prime condition.

Jennie's reaction time was faster. She ducked down and tackled Jake by the back of his knees, making him fall backwards. It was the head start that Aggie needed. She grabbed the handles of Eli's wheelchair and started pushing it toward the main lot. "Run, Aunt Aggie!" Jennie yelled behind them.

Aggie pushed the chair. It was a difficult thing to push over the dirt and debris, but she went as fast as she could, hoping to find someone who could help her keep the old man alive. And he clung to life as he clung to the chair, with all his feeble strength, against the jostling she gave him. Without him, there wasn't a prayer that anyone could save them from this… whatever-it-was that Morgan had become. She didn't know why she was so certain of that, but in the last few minutes, she had come to have faith in her feelings.

Jake wasn't delayed for long. Before Aggie had gotten even as far as the midway, he'd caught up with them, grabbed at her arm, and literally thrown her to the ground. There was no time to get up. She rolled over and grabbed his foot. He kicked out, trying to shake her off, and missed her head only by inches. She held tight to his foot, hugging it with her arms, but it wasn't enough. He let go of the chair and turned his attention to her. He raised his arm and stooped toward her, obviously intending to swat her like a fly, but she held on to his shoe and rolled, making him lose his balance and fall. Then, suddenly, Jennie had the chair, pushing it across the lot much faster than Aggie could have.

Jake was on his feet first, but Aggie was right behind. He ignored her, chasing after the little girl who—in spite of the better time she was making—was still pushing the chair much too slowly to ever get away from him. Aggie found herself next to the duck pond, and reached under the counter. She knew where the gun would be if the agent had one. There was no gun, but there was something else that she could use. A sap. A homemade job, wire and lead weight wrapped around with electrical tape. She caught up to Jake as he was trying to wrestle Jennie away from the chair. The child was tenacious as a pug dog, holding on to the wheelchair handle so tightly that Jake was forced to pry open her fingers to loosen her grip. *Hold on, baby!*, she thought. Aggie rushed up behind Jake and smashed the sap frantically into his head. It was not a well-aimed blow, but it was enough. Jake fell to his knees, groaned, and dropped. He was on the ground and, for the moment at least, he wasn't moving.

Aggie took the handles of the chair and pressed on. Somewhere she found the strength to move the chair through the rubble that had once been the G-top and out onto the main lot. A loud crack sounded behind them. Only then did she pause to look over her shoulder, just as the plywood skull collapsed. Where the skull had been stood, now the burned-out hulks of several trailers hooked together, but a brick house of gothic proportions, huge and beautiful, completely untouched by the flames. She was beyond shock. The sight slowed her only a moment, for though Aggie had no idea how Jennie had managed to delay him, Jake was now getting to his feet, and Jennie—who stopped to hit him again—was catching up to her quickly.

"Over there," the child said. She took the chair out of Aggie's hands and pushed it over to the merry-go-round.

"This isn't safe," Aggie said.

"It's all we've got, Aunt Aggie," Jennie said. Between the two of them they lifted the chair and carried it into the center of the carousel, then Jennie pulled the lever. They watched as the horses started to spin between them and all comers. "At least he'll have to get over here before he can do anything. That'll buy us some time," the child said.

10

Dandy was all over Sam before Sam had a chance to realize what was happening. The big man's first instinct was to pull his punches, avoid hurting a friend, but it was quickly obvious that Patch was seriously trying to hurt him. He felt the whole force of the smaller man's body ram into him, and found himself laying on the ground. Beside him, the carousel spun madly, and the cloth of harness and stirrups on the merry-go-round horses was starting to burn. Sam caught a hint of movement out of the corner of his eye, and rolled in the opposite direction as Dandy jumped at him. He heard the women scream. A flash of silver in the firelight told him that Dandy had his knife out. He lunged for Sam again, missed, and fell.

While Dandy recovered, Sam rolled to his feet. The two men squared off. Dandy licked his lips nervously. Sam feinted left, then spun right quickly, tripping over the two-foot-high fence that circled the carousel. It was the fall that saved him, as Dandy lunged once again with the knife. But it was only a momentary respite. Dandy jumped the fence and stood gazing down at Sam, who rose slowly to his feet. They seemed to freeze like that as time ticked by.

Behind Dandy, like a distant dream, Sam could see Katie start toward him, see the Viking rush to stop her, see Katie hit the taller woman square in the stomach, see Mei rush to Katie's aid. Then Dandy came to life. He lunged with his knife, stabbing out before him like an adder's tooth. Sam kicked out. He missed the crotch he aimed for, but landed a solid blow to Dandy's thigh; Dandy staggered back and tripped over the low fence. Sam went after him, but Dandy was on his feet at once, vaulting back over the fence to meet him; he had managed to keep hold of his knife. They grappled for the knife. Sam grabbed Dandy's wrist and tried to make him drop the knife, but for a small man, Patch was very strong, well able to hold his own against the bigger man's flabby bulk. He broke free of Sam's grasp. They fell back against the carousel platform and bounced away, each in a different direction. Sam spun around, but Dandy had recovered first. Knife at the ready, he lunged. Sam barely had time to grab a passing bar and hop up onto the merry-go-round platform, which spun him neatly out of the way.

It was a brief pause. Dandy, too, had made it onto the platform, and now he was coming toward Sam with his knife thrust forward. Sam backed away, never taking his eyes off of his adversary. He backed up carefully, avoiding the burning horses which rose and fell in time to the tinny strains of John Phillip Sousa blaring down from the overhead speakers. He backed until he felt something hard and solid against the back of his legs. The bench. The damn bench was in his way. He had forgotten all about it. There was no time to turn and walk around it. Once his back was turned, Dandy would be on him in an instant. He felt for the edge of it with his hand, hoping to put it between him and the patch without giving any ground, but Dandy was steadily advancing.

It was then that he saw Jennie. She had a blackjack in her hand, and she crept up behind Dandy, her weapon raised and ready, but the force of the spinning ride was too much for her, and it was obvious that she was having trouble keeping her balance. Sam knew he should stop her. This was much too dangerous for a twelve-year-old girl. But she seemed to be the only chance he had.

Dandy must have heard her. He ducked just as she swung, but she still managed to hit him a glancing blow on the arm, and the knife went clattering away, across the platform and out onto the dirt.

Sam didn't waste a second. He lurched forward and smashed Dandy in the face with all the force he could muster. It was a clumsy blow, but Dandy—distracted by watching his knife sail away—didn't have time to avoid it, and it had immense power behind it. Blood exploded from Dandy's mouth and nose, and he reeled back against a silver carousel horse, clutching at its neck to keep himself from falling. Sam didn't give him time to recover. He crowded Dandy against the wooden horse, and pounded him again and again with a succession of short, clubbing blows, putting all his weight behind them. He pounded until Dandy's eyes rolled senselessly back in his head and his legs gave way.

Sam backed off a few feet and allowed Dandy to fall. Behind him, he felt the heat of a horse that was beginning to burn. Sam looked around for something to beat out the flames with, but nothing came to his eye. He had already used and lost his T-shirt on one of the tents. Not that there was much point in trying to save the ride with most of the carnival already destroyed. Still, he would get Dandy out of there, even if the s.o.b. had been doing his level best to kill him a minute before. He tried to pick up the unconscious body, and found that he barely had enough energy left to roll it off the burning platform into the center of the ride.

Staggering with exhaustion, Sam crossed the carousel platform and dropped down to his knees on the dusty earth. Katie was still fighting the Viking, but it was obvious that she no longer needed any help. The Viking lay prone on the ground, and Katie sat astride her, pulling the long blonde hair back and slapping the tall woman's face repeatedly. When she saw Sam fall, however, she got up and ran to his side. The Viking wasted not a moment. She got to her feet and headed for the back lot with a stride that showed that she was not badly injured. As for Dandy, Sam would go back to deal with him in a moment.

11

Jake watched the three of them head for the carousel. It amused him to see them, cowering there in the center as if he couldn't possibly get at them there. And then the fight broke out, and he backed off for just a moment. Better to wait. Better to get them alone if he could. Much better. Besides, Morgan was coming. He could see him now, walking toward them, calm and smiling. He wanted to watch the payoff. Well, Jake would give him a show worth looking at.

He watched the two carnival men going at it on the ride, and smiled. Yes, this was it. This was what Morgan wanted. Let them all take care of each other. Fewer to deal with later. He watched the girl sneak up behind the pitchman. Should he call out, warn him? No, much better to see what happens. A glancing blow. He watched the knife as it spun out of the man's grasp. It rolled across the platform and came to land at Jake's feet. Good. It was just what he needed. Just the right touch. It was meant. Smiling, he leaned over and picked it up. Morgan was only a few feet away, lounging up against the tank that even now held the charred body that had once been the bozo. Jake held up the knife, and Morgan smiled.

The fight was still going on, but Jake no longer felt like waiting. The time was right. He grabbed hold of the ride as it passed and lightly bounded up onto the platform. Eli saw him. The old man craned his head as much as he could to keep Jake in sight as the platform twirled around him. That was good. Eli was frightened. Good. The worse the better. And Eli thought Jake owed him something? Well, Jake did, but it was not the kind of thing that Eli had in mind.

Jake folded the knife and put it away. Later, but not just yet. He waited by the inner edge of the platform until his brother's face rolled around again, then stepped down into the center.

"Hello, Eli. I found you, but then, you never were very good at hide and seek," Jake said.

"Jake, you don't understand. Eli didn't go there that night to kill you. He went there to save you," Aggie said, moving slowly toward Jake.

"What the hell do you know about it," Jake said. He felt his eyes narrow as he turned to look at her. "And who the hell are you, anyway?

Never mind. You don't know anything. Shut up." He turned again toward his brother. "I've wanted to do this for a long time," Jake said.

"No, Jake!" Aggie said. "Eli didn't know you were there when he set that fire. It was *Morgan*, Jake. It was Morgan who wanted you to die in the flames with him. It was Morgan, who tried to keep you there to die with him."

"Stop!" Jake said. He put his hands over his ears, but it wouldn't keep the voice away. The old lady droned on.

"Don't you remember, Jake. You've *got* to remember. It was Morgan who tried to kill you. Eli saved your life. Eli rushed at Morgan and fought with him to give *you* time to get away. He bought your escape, even though it cost him the rest of his life! *Please* remember."

The words echoed like an earthquake through his skull. "It's not true!" he shouted. "Stop it! Stop lying to me!" he said. "Bitch." Images rushed at him. They didn't make sense. They only made him dizzy. He backhanded the old lady across the mouth, and watched in gratification as she staggered back and fell. Her mouth was bleeding. That lying mouth.

He pulled the knife from his pocket and opened the blade out slowly, watching Eli's eyes grow wide. The world spun around as he focused his attention down and down to a point on his brother's throat.

"Eli rushed at Morgan and fought with him, and *you* ran away. That was when Morgan threw him out the window," Aggie finished, raising herself up on one elbow, wiping the blood from the corner of her mouth.

He touched the blade to his brother's withered skin. Eli looked up at him through that ruined face. "It's true, you know," Eli said, sadly. Jake tried to ram the knife home, but his arm refused to move. Flaming horses rode around him in a circle, and with them came memories. Memories of another fire. Of being tapped, held fast, unable to move as the flames roared around him. Jake looked over at Morgan. His image was distorted in the heated air, but his maniacal laughter floated across the strains of "Semper Fidelis" as if it were part of the music. The march seemed to get louder and louder, until it filled his consciousness with sound. Then other images broke through. Memories of torture and torment, of humiliation and perversity, of small cruelties smilingly committed. Pictures of Eli. Eli facing up to Morgan. Of suddenly being able to move and running… running for his life down a long, smoke-filled hall, his lungs burning, gasping for air. Memories of freedom and fresh air combined with pictures of Eli, broken and twisted, lying on the grass. And Morgan, his body engulfed in flames, dancing in the window like a madman.

Jake pulled the knife back. "You did it for *me*," he said, softly.

12

Aggie felt relief rush through her as the knife disappeared. Jennie, light as a bubble, jumped up on the carousel platform and walked across. Jake just stood there, looking back and forth from Morgan to his brother and back again. It was time for Aggie to leave, they had business to take care of without her, but the damn thing was moving. How on Earth was she supposed to get on it? She grabbed a pole as it whizzed past, and felt it jolt out of her grasp almost immediately. But she had to do it. Most of the horses were burning, and some of the platform and awning. She tried again, but, as before, she made no progress.

Katie, laughing, leapt up on the platform and walked across to where Aggie was standing. "It's okay, Aunt Aggie. It's not that hard. Mei, you get her other arm," she said to the child who appeared by her side.

Aggie pointed to Morgan, and put a finger to her lips, but Katie seemed not to understand the need for quiet. She tried to get Aggie onto the moving platform, and Aggie tried to co-operate. She really tried to move when they told her to, but by the time she lifted her foot, the pole was already out of her hand. The girls were laughing, and for some reason this frightened her. She had seen enough to know that there was no telling what Morgan would do. He continued to watch them as if they were a movie he wasn't sure he liked. Besides, if she didn't get off soon, she would be stuck there forever, and the damn thing was going to burn down around her ears.

"I can't, Katie. I just can't," she said.

"It's okay, Aunt Aggie. I know someone who can help. Sam!" she shouted.

"Katie, please. You must be quiet. This isn't over yet," Aggie said. Katie looked at her strangely, but stopped shouting.

Essie approached the ride. "Have you seen Patch?" she called.

"He's over here," Katie shouted.

Aggie sighed. "Please, Katie. This isn't over yet," she repeated. She watched Essie leap onto the ride, wishing once again that she was that nimble, but nervous to have so many people under Morgan's eye. They all seemed to think the worst was over, but there was still something important that had to be done.

Sam was obviously tired. He was laying on the ground with his eyes closed, but he opened them when Katie called, and made the effort to get to his feet, and staggered toward the carousel. He grabbed onto a bar, just barely managing to make it to the platform before he whirled out of sight. When it came round again, he was standing on the inside edge, perilously close to a horse that was engulfed in flame. He stepped down into the center.

"Okay, Aggie," he said. "Now just relax, and I'll get you across." He said.

A sound caught their attention. Dandy moaned and got to his feet. Jake watched as Sam moved quickly to put himself between the patch and the women. Whatever Dandy wanted to do, he would have to go through Sam before he could get at them. But the women weren't his goal. He leaped suddenly at Jake and struck him, knocking him aside. In one quick motion, he picked the old man up out of the wheelchair, cradled him in his arms, and ran across the carousel platform.

"You want the old man scragged?" Dandy shouted at Morgan. "I'll take care of him for you."

Jake was only down for an instant. In one smooth motion, he was back up on his feet and bounding onto the carousel platform. Essie screamed and followed behind. Jake grabbed the back of Dandy's shirt and pulled him down. Dandy fell, Eli landing on top of him, and the carousel spun them out of Morgan's sight momentarily. Jake swore an oath. He would get them. He would get both of them. Hadn't they hurt his brother enough? When Morgan came into view again, Jake saw him raise his hand in a motion that Jake was all too familiar with. As Essie bent down to take care of the two men, Jake jumped, head first toward Morgan. He came up short and rolled, but he didn't reach Morgan in time. The fire in the canopy intensified, blazed up brightly enough to light the entire lot, and collapsed in an explosion of flying embers. Dandy, Essie, and Eli were underneath. The rest were trapped behind. Jake chopped off all emotion. There wasn't time. His grief for his brother's death could come later, if there was a later. Right now, he had something to do. He pulled the knife from his pocket and rushed at Morgan.

"And you, Brutus?" Morgan said. "Did you really think you could hurt me this way? Old man! You are an *old man*. What can you do to me?"

Morgan said, and Jake felt the youth run out of his body as if it were his very blood ebbing away. His knees wobbled as if they would give way under him. His hand shook, and the knife fell from his fingers, barely missing his foot as it landed blade down in the dirt.

Jake turned and looked back at the ride. "I'm sorry, Eli," he said. "I'm so sorry." The ready tears of age blurred his vision. He never knew what hit him. Before he realized it, two powerful hands had him firmly under his arms, and he was lifted off the ground. Jake fought as well as he could, but Morgan was much too strong for him. He found himself being thrust inside a cage, and, the next thing he knew, his head was being held under water. The Bozo tank. Morgan was trying to drown him in the Bozo tank. He struggled and fought, tugging at the hands that held him down, but his lungs were starting to burn, and his head felt as if it were trapped in a vise.

The platform canted to one side and stopped turning, but that didn't help much. The whole damn thing was burning. There was no way over it. They were trapped.

Poles collapsed, falling onto the burning mass of wood, and embers flew. Sam grabbed Mei and sheltered her from the burning chips with his body. She reached into her pocket and placed something in his hand. "Father, I'm sorry. I only wanted us to be together," she said. He could hear the tears in her voice. He opened his hand, and saw her little dragon resting on his palm.

"Oh, Mei, I want that, too," he said, and he leaned forward and kissed her lightly on the forehead. He looked up at Katie, and saw her smile, though he knew it was becoming difficult to breathe. Then he noticed something else. The clouds. The black clouds. Only they weren't clouds. They weren't smoke. They had definite form, and they walked majestically forward, looming over the lot. They were dragons.

Suddenly Jake was free. His head popped up to the surface, and sucked in life-giving air. Morgan still loomed above him, the upper half of his body inside the cage, but now his attention was elsewhere.

Jake looked where Morgan was staring. There was something there. Something large and black and menacing. At first, he couldn't make out what it was, but after a second, it resolved itself into some kind of animal. A dragon. Whatever it was, Morgan seemed badly frightened by the appearance. That bought Jake time. Like an ancient, wizened monkey, he summoned the strength to pull himself up to the perch.

Sam could barely see the dragon through the flames. They seemed to be floating over the lot. He watched them absorb the smoke and soot from the air, until they took on solid form. They pulled the clouds down from the sky until they were one, connected to cloud and smoke, and they floated up like a bridge between. Two dark gray dragons in the sky. Then they roared, and fire shot from their mouths. They roared again, and the rain began to fall.

It fell in torrents, as if a dam had burst above them, and they now stood under a waterfall. So heavy was the rain that they could actually see it, washed back and forth by the wind, as solid sheets of water. The fire died back. Hot metal hissed as the cold water hit it, pounding it again and again.

Jake rubbed his eyes. They were not dragons at all, but clouds. Dark, heavy storm clouds, so obscured by the smoke from the fire that he had thought at first that they were sitting on the ground. A blast of lightning split the sky, and Morgan flinched.

Jake saw his chance and took it. He jumped down from his perch, landing with his thighs around Morgan's head and thrusting him under the water. Pushing against the bars of the cage, bracing himself with all his strength, he held Morgan under the surface. Rain began to fall, rushing in heavy torrents that made the bars slippery, but Jake held on, even though Morgan bucked and thrashed. The movement turned the bozo's body, and the death's-head pressed against his leg, staring up at him with tortured, lifeless eyes. Morgan made a final push that almost unseated Jake, but the old man looked at the spot where his brother's body lay, and somehow found the strength he needed. Finally, Morgan went still, but Jake continued to hold him under, watching the lot around him as fires died to embers, hissed and went out, and all the while Jake held Morgan's head under, until there could be no doubt, until his own strength deserted him and he fell from his seat into the water.

The tiny tank was crowded with bodies. Jake knew he had only to lift his head a few inches to gulp in desperately needed air, but he didn't have the strength to do even that. He felt the hands that grabbed him by the collar, felt himself being lifted into the air, and then pulled roughly from the water. He rolled over the edge of the Bozo tank and tumbled down to the ground, rolling over on his back. His eyes opened.

"You okay?" Aggie asked. Jennie peered anxiously at him over Aggie's shoulder. He nodded, unable to do any more. "Well, rest for a minute. Then we'll take you home."

Home. He thought of Joella and Darcy. They must be worried half to death. He had been supposed to be there hours ago. What on Earth was he going to tell them? How would he ever explain?

"Home?" the Asian girl said, an edge of worry in her voice.

Sam came up with Katie on his arm, and clapped his free arm around her shoulders. "You are home," he said.

CPSIA information can be obtained
at www.ICGtesting.com
Printed in the USA
LVOW03s0821040318
568589LV00002B/328/P